THE GHOSTS OF
PEPPERNELL
MANOR

Books by Amy M. Reade

Secrets of Hallstead House

The Ghosts of Peppernell Manor

THE GHOSTS OF PEPPERNELL MANOR

AMY M. READE

LYRICAL PRESS
Kensington Publishing Corp.
www.kensingtonbooks.com

LYRICAL PRESS BOOKS are published by

Kensington Publishing Corp.
119 West 40th Street
New York, NY 10018

All Kensington titles, imprints, and distributed lines are available at special quantity discounts for bulk purchases for sales promotion, premiums, fund-raising, educational, or institutional use.

Special book excerpts or customized printings can also be created to fit specific needs. For details, write or phone the office of the Kensington Special Sales Manager: Kensington Publishing Corp., 119 West 40th Street, New York, NY 10018. Attn. Special Sales Department. Phone: 1-800-221-2647.

Lyrical and the L logo are trademarks of the Kensington Publishing Corp.

First Electronic Edition: April 2015
eISBN-13: 978-1-60183-301-3
eISBN-10: 1-60183-301-6

First Print Edition: April 2015
ISBN-13: 978-1-60183-302-0
ISBN-10: 1-60183-302-4

Printed in the United States of America

For Jeanne

Acknowledgments

There are so many people who deserve huge thanks for the publication of this book.

First, I would like to extend my appreciation to Martin Biro, my talented and all-around fabulous editor at Kensington whose ideas and encouragement have been invaluable to me. I consider myself a very lucky person to know Martin and to be one of "his authors."

Second, I would like to thank everyone who read my first novel, *Secrets of Hallstead House*. I appreciate each and every one of you!

Third, I wish to thank the visitors to my website, blog, and social media pages because you help make writing the thing I love to do each and every day.

Finally, of course, I would like to thank my family and friends for their unending support and encouragement and for being my personal cheerleading squad. You all mean the world to me, and I love you.

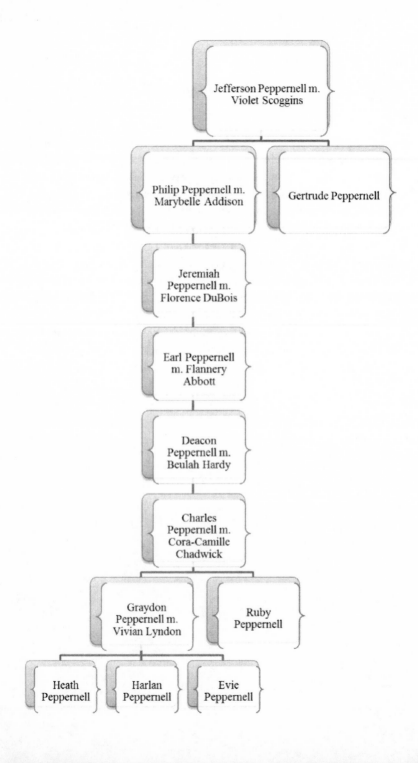

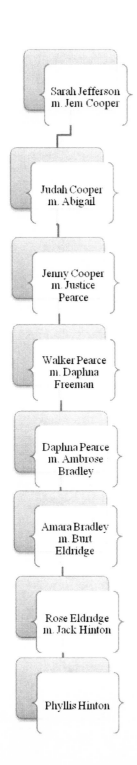

Sarah Jefferson
m. Jem Cooper

Judah Cooper
m. Abigail

Jenny Cooper
m. Justice
Pearce

Walker Pearce
m. Daphna
Freeman

Daphna Pearce
m. Ambrose
Bradley

Amara Bradley
m. Burt
Eldridge

Rose Eldridge
m. Jack Hinton

Phyllis Hinton

PROLOGUE

"Sarah, you'll have to stay here tonight to take care of Philip and Gertie during the party."

Sarah nodded, her dark eyes revealing nothing of the deep resentment she felt toward her mistress. She should have known. The children would have to stay upstairs while guests thronged the ballroom on the first floor. Though Mrs. Violet Peppernell paid Sarah a high compliment by trusting her with Philip and Gertie, Sarah nursed a smoldering anger at being unable to go home to see her daddy, who would be leaving tomorrow. Mrs. Peppernell knew that, but she didn't care about him. He was invisible to her.

Sarah fed Philip and Gertie upstairs in the nursery and then told them a long story before putting them to bed. They liked her stories. They were sweet children, but it wasn't the same as rocking in her mother's chair and spinning tales for her nieces and nephews.

While Philip and Gertie slept, Sarah stood staring out the window, wondering what was happening at home. She was going to miss her daddy. Tears stung her eyes and rolled slowly down her cheeks as she tried to imagine her life without him, but she wiped them away impatiently. Mama had told her to be strong. After all, she was fifteen, practically a grown woman. And these auctions were just a part of life.

It was just after one o'clock in the morning when Mrs. Peppernell came upstairs and Sarah was finally able to go home. She walked across the sweeping front lawn of Peppernell Manor guided by the light of the full moon, listening to the rustling of the oaks, then veered off into the small wood where she lived with her extended family and the other slaves in small, dingy cabins. It was silent in the woods except for the nighttime insects with their soothing chirps and clicks.

Sarah tiptoed around the small garden plot in front of her cabin and started up the wooden steps, being careful to avoid the creaky spots so no one would wake up. She was reaching for the door handle when a soft noise made her turn around. She tilted her head, listening hard.

She heard it again. It was a shuffling sound coming from the cabin next door. The family that had lived there had all gone away, Sarah didn't know where, so the cabin was supposed to be empty. Maybe there was an animal inside.

Quietly, she walked to the next cabin and peered in the front door. She didn't want to meet a fox or an angry raccoon.

But it was too dark to see anything.

She was afraid to step inside. She had second thoughts and started to back away toward her own cabin.

That's why she wasn't able to stop her daddy when he killed himself a split second later with a flash of light and the roar of a shotgun.

CHAPTER 1

It had been a long drive to South Carolina, but Lucy and I had made the best of it, giggling through nursery rhymes, eating fast food, making silly faces at each other in the rearview mirror, and playing I Spy on every highway between Chicago and Charleston.

We arrived one sultry afternoon in late August last year. I barely remembered the back roads from Charleston to Peppernell Manor, so it was like watching the scenery unfold over the miles for the first time. Spanish moss hung low to the ground from stately trees over a century old. Perfectly still water reflected the magnolias and camellias and the hazy sky in the Lowcountry lakes and waterways that we passed. Lacy clumps of wildflowers nodded languidly as we drove by. Lucy was interested in everything that whizzed past the windows of the car, commenting excitedly on all the new sights as we drove toward Peppernell Manor.

"Look at the cows! Moo!"

"Look at the pretty flowers!" she would pipe up from the backseat in her high-pitched little-girl voice. I loved driving with her because she helped me see all the things I missed with my adult eyes.

As we got closer to Peppernell Manor, I found myself sharing her excitement. I hadn't been there since college. My thoughts stretched back to the only other time I had visited South Carolina, when Evie took me to her home for a long weekend. We had gone sightseeing in Charleston, horseback riding, boating on the Ashley River, and on a tour of an old Confederate field hospital nearby. But despite all the fun we had, it wasn't the activities I remembered best about that trip—it was her house.

Manor, actually. Peppernell Manor had been in her family for generations and even though it had seen better days and was in need of some work, it was exquisite. As a lover of art I could appreciate its romance and graceful architecture, but as a history major I was more interested in the home's past as a plantation house.

It was to this plantation house that I was returning, this time with my daughter.

CHAPTER 2

I had been surprised to get Evie's phone call a month earlier at my office in Chicago with that offer that was too good to refuse.

"You remember Peppernell Manor," Evie had said.

"I remember it very well," I answered.

"It needs refurbishing badly. Gran doesn't know what to do with it. I told her that you're the best restoration specialist money can buy," she told me excitedly. I smiled into the phone.

"There's a lot of work that needs to be done. It needs attention from top to bottom. The whole family voted and the job is yours. If you want it," she added hastily.

I was thrilled. Of course I wanted it!

But I had some practical concerns. First, I wasn't sure I should leave my business for an extended period. Luckily, my assistants, a capable young architect and his interior-designer wife, assured me that they would manage the restoration firm during my absence with the same attention to detail and respect for the past that had made Warner Restorations a success.

Second, and more importantly, I knew I would have a hard time convincing my ex-husband to let Lucy come with me and there was no way I was leaving her behind to take a job in South Carolina.

"You must be nuts," he said flatly when I first broached the subject with him.

"Think about it, Brad. It would only be temporary, while I'm working on the restoration. And we could come back to Chicago a few times so you could see her for extended periods. Or you could even come down to South Carolina to see her and stay as long as you like. And I'll make sure she calls you every night."

Silence. I waited. Brad loves Lucy, but he loves himself more. I could almost hear him thinking about all the free time he could have without a toddler to care for on the weekends.

"You would take good care of her?"

"I won't even answer such a stupid question."

"Well, let me think about it."

"That's all I ask."

In the end, he decided his weekends with the new girlfriend were more important than his weekends with Lucy. I knew that's what would happen. Lucy and I left a few weeks later.

And after several long days on the road, we had finally arrived at our destination. I turned off the main road. Driving up to Peppernell Manor was not like going up any other driveway. I slowed the car to a crawl so we could enjoy the view. The sweeping allée, the rows of oaks that lined the long brick drive to the house, looked as old and graceful as it had during my first visit to this remarkable place. The branches of the trees arched over the drive to form a dappled tunnel through which visitors were given their first glimpse of the home beyond. Lucy squealed with delight when she saw those big old trees. She had never seen anything like that long drive with its arching branches back in Chicago. At the end of the allée the driveway formed a wide, sweeping circle in front of the house.

The manor house was a gem of Federalist architecture. It was a huge square structure with white clapboard siding that was set off by tall black shutters outside each of the many windows. A large veranda yawned between two enormous white pillars. The brick front steps separated at the top to sweep down to the ground from the left and the right. Below the veranda and stretching all around the manor were whitewashed brick archways through which one could glimpse large windows gazing into the basement. Despite the beauty of the old house, I could see where the paint was peeling and where the hinges had come loose from some of the shutters. The manor had a neglected air about it.

I parked my car along the side of the circle and got out to extract

Lucy from the back. As I helped the small, wriggling body out of the car seat, we both turned to see Evie running down the front staircase.

"Carleigh!" she shouted, a huge smile lighting up her face.

I put Lucy down and turned to give my friend a big hug. Though we had kept in close contact in the years since college, I hadn't seen her since graduation and I had missed her. We shared photos online and frequent e-mails and phone calls, but it wasn't the same as seeing each other in person.

Evie crouched down next to Lucy, wrinkling her linen sheath dress. "You must be Lucy. I recognize you from your mom's pictures!" she said brightly.

Lucy nodded, averting her eyes from Evie, and held my hand.

"Lucy, you remember me telling you about Evie. She's our good friend," I told her gently. "You can say hello."

"Hello," she said shyly, then turned her head to face my leg.

Evie smiled. "I'm very happy to meet you, Lucy. There are more friends to meet inside the house. Would you like to go in?"

Lucy nodded again, her face still pressed against my shorts.

I picked her up and took the hand Evie offered me and the three of us walked up the stairs and into the manor.

We stepped into the expansive and breathtaking entry hall. Its marble floor and soaring ceiling lent an elegant coolness to the space that belied the sweltering heat and humidity just outside the door. A scuffed but gracefully curving mahogany staircase swept upward to the second floor. At the opposite end of the entry hall I could glimpse through another door the slow-moving Ashley River as it meandered past the property. Though not visible from this particular bend in the river, the magnificent, historic city of Charleston lay downstream about fifteen miles and across the water.

I set Lucy down, but she stayed close, grasping my hand. Evie pointed to the room on our right.

"Carleigh, you remember Cora-Camille, my grandmother," Evie said in her sweet Southern drawl. "She's right in there and she can't wait to see you."

We walked through the wide doorway into a large drawing room with tall windows that invited the light in from outdoors. Cora-Camille Chadwick-Peppernell, Evie's warm and gracious grandmother, stood up from where she had been reading a book on an old-fashioned sofa. She walked over to me with her hands outstretched.

"Carleigh Warner. It's been such a long time! Evie keeps us up to date with stories about you and your beautiful little girl, but it's just not the same as having you here. Welcome back!" She looked at Lucy. "I am so happy to meet you, Lucy. Will you call me Cora-Camille?"

Lucy shook her head.

Cora-Camille laughed. "How about Miss Cora? Do you like that better?"

"Yes," the child answered, her blond curls bobbing up and down.

"Then Miss Cora it is."

She held out her hand to Lucy, who took it after a quick look at me for approval. They walked over to the sofa where Cora-Camille had been sitting and she motioned Evie and me to sit down in the two chairs facing her.

"The others are all out right now, except for Ruby," Cora-Camille said with a smile. "They're all thrilled that you're here to do the restoration."

She looked fondly at Lucy. "I can't tell you how wonderful it is to have a child in this house again," she said wistfully. She turned to my daughter to talk of little-girl things, like dolls and stuffed animals and dress-up clothes. Evie got a work-related text and left the room, apologizing for having to reply right away.

While Cora-Camille and Lucy chatted, I had an opportunity to observe Evie's lovely grandmother. She had stood straight and tall the last time I was here, years ago, and though time had been kind to her, I could see the evidence of her aging. Her back was slightly less straight than it used to be, and her shoulders hunched forward just a bit. Her face was crisscrossed with wrinkles, the signs of a life well led. Her hair was a little thinner than I remembered it, but still a soft, glorious white. She and Lucy were both giggling and I knew they would be fast friends.

Evie returned and grinned at Cora-Camille and Lucy. "This is so good for Gran," she said softly. I nodded.

Cora-Camille turned to me. "Did you meet Ruby when you visited us before?"

"Not that I recall," I replied. I knew Ruby was Evie's aunt, Cora-Camille's daughter. Evie had spoken of Ruby in the past, but only briefly. I knew Ruby suffered from anxiety issues.

"Ruby has been so excited to meet you and Lucy," Cora-Camille told me. "She's been in the kitchen for hours, baking something special for you for dinner tonight."

Lucy bounced up and down. "What is it?" she cried.

Cora-Camille laughed again. "It's a surprise. You have to eat your dinner and then you'll find out."

"Is dinner now?"

"In a little while," I answered. "We have to get our things out of the car first and unpack."

She seemed eager to help with the unpacking, so the two of us and Evie walked back outdoors and took two suitcases from the trunk of the car. Though Lucy's bag had wheels, she struggled with it. I suggested that she take her stuffed bunny, Cottontail, into the house so I could take her bag. She agreed readily and ran ahead of me into the house, excited to introduce Cottontail to Miss Cora. Evie and I carried the bags upstairs, returning to the car several times for more luggage.

Once the car was unpacked, I moved it to a four-stall garage that had been erected on the left side of the driving circle since my last visit. Though it was relatively new, the garage had an antique look to it, with distressed white wooden clapboard siding and a loft, presumably for storage. The structure matched the manor well.

I went back into the house in search of Lucy. I could hear her talking excitedly in the back of the house, so I wandered back toward the kitchen. There I found Lucy, Cora-Camille, Evie, and another woman I assumed to be Ruby.

Lucy turned to me, pointing to a gorgeous cake on the counter. "Mama! Ruby made cake!"

Ruby smiled shyly at me, her eyes downcast. She was of medium height and appeared to be in her sixties. The sides of her shoulder-length brown-gray hair were pinned to the top of her head with a barrette. She was dressed in a simple light pink shirtwaist.

"The cake is red on the inside!" Lucy said, grinning.

"How did you know red is Lucy's favorite color?" I asked Ruby with a wink.

"I love to make red velvet," she answered in a quiet voice.

"It looks delicious," I told her. Then, turning to Lucy, I suggested, "Why don't we go upstairs and see where you and I are going to sleep?"

"Okay."

Evie led the way upstairs to one of the two guest bedrooms on the second floor. We had placed all the luggage on the floor just inside the door, so it was a bit of a mess. But the room was spacious and inviting, with plenty of storage for us to put away all of our clothes and other belongings. Lucy immediately went to the window to see what she could identify outside. She turned to me and yelled, "There's water down there!"

Evie joined her at the window, explaining that the water was part of the Ashley River and was very important to the Peppernell Manor farm.

"Are there animals on the farm?"

"Yes. We have some cows and horses, and of course chickens, and some sheep. Would you like to see them?"

Lucy jumped up and down, clapping. "Yes! Yes!"

Evie smiled at her. "Once you and Mama are done unpacking, we'll go for a drive and you can see some of the animals, okay?"

"Okay!" Lucy was beaming.

It took over an hour to hang up and put away all the clothes Lucy and I had brought. When we were done, we went downstairs in search of Evie. We found her in the kitchen talking to Ruby and she offered to take us to see the stables and pens. Lucy couldn't wait to see the animals. We all climbed into my car, but I let Evie drive. She swung out of the garage and down the long allée to the main road. She took a right turn and went a half mile or so, then pulled off the road onto a bumpy dirt track. We drove slowly for a couple minutes, then stopped next to an old stone stable. On the far side of the stable were a pen and another, larger, stone building.

"Want to see the horses first, Lucy?" asked Evie, her eyes twinkling.

"Yes!" came the answer from the backseat.

The three of us went into the stable. I was struck by the coolness of the building, despite the heat outside. It smelled of horses and leather. Horses could be heard whinnying and chewing and stomping, and Lucy could hardly contain her excitement. She ran along the stone floor, making neighing noises and peering in each stall, shrieking and clapping with delight at every horse. She pulled Evie along with her, demanding to know all their names.

"Can I ride one?"

"Sure," exclaimed Evie.

"No," I said firmly.

Evie glanced at me sheepishly. "Spoke too soon. Sorry."

"That's okay. I just think she's too little."

"But I want to ride one!" cried Lucy.

"You're too small to ride a horse. Maybe when you're bigger."

That's when the wailing started.

Evie grimaced. "I started all this. I'm really sorry."

I smiled at her. "It's no big deal. She's just exhausted. Lucy, would you like to see the other animals before we go back to Evie's house?"

Lucy nodded, red-eyed and sniffling.

Evie led us to the next stable. The tour of the second stable was quick because Lucy was getting so tired. We saw ducks, sheep, cows, pigs, and chickens, but by the end of the tour Lucy was barely able to drag her feet. I picked her up and we headed for the car.

Back at the manor, she took a short nap in our room while I caught up with Evie in the drawing room downstairs. Though I had wanted to wander through the rest of the rooms in the house, Evie convinced me to chat for a while before dinner, promising that we could tour the home after dinner.

"So how have things been—really—without Brad?" she began.

I grimaced. "Good riddance to him and that stripper girlfriend of his. Her name is Jilly, but I call her Jiggly. Not to Brad's face, of course.

"Can you believe he said I wasn't spontaneous enough? I guess if 'spontaneous' means leaving your family behind for someone you barely know, then he was right.

"When he first left, I was heartbroken. And furious with him and Jiggly. I felt like a failure. I was always exhausted, but I couldn't sleep at night. I cried a lot. It took me a long time to realize that the anger and hate were hurting me and Lucy much more than them. I had to let it all go for my own sanity. So I've moved on; I've stopped being so angry and now all I feel is relief. Not that I would ever want to go through it again, but it made me finally face the fact that he wasn't the one for me."

She put her hand on mine. "I'm so sorry for everything you had to go through. How'd he meet Jiggly, anyway?" I smiled at her use of my name for Jilly.

"At a bachelor party for his brother."

"You know, I never liked Brad, even in college," she revealed in a conspiratorial tone.

"Why not?" I asked in surprise.

"He was a control freak. He always had to be part of everything you did. We could never do anything alone, just us girls."

"I never noticed."

"Love is blind, Carleigh."

"I guess. But if it weren't for him, I wouldn't have Lucy. So I'm at least grateful to him for her."

"That's true," she conceded, then changed the subject.

"Are you dating? You look fabulous. I've always been jealous of that long red hair of yours," she sighed.

I laughed at her. "I'm through with men for a while. I'm just concentrating on Lucy and my work. Speaking of men, how's Boone?" Evie and Boone, a banker, had been together for years, but neither was ready to get married. Both of them always joked that they were already married to their jobs.

"Oh, he's the same," she answered breezily. "Works all the time, travels a lot. The bank sent him to Singapore this time. That's why I came back here for a while. It's lonely in Atlanta without him. All I need is a computer and I can work from anywhere."

"I'm glad you can be here while I'm here," I told her. "It'll be fun. And besides, I'm sure you'll want to see the house as the work progresses."

"I'm excited to see how it goes," she agreed. "Mother and Daddy were hoping they'd be home by tonight to see you and Lucy, but they're visiting friends and they won't be here until tomorrow."

"It'll be nice to see them," I said.

Lucy appeared in the doorway to the drawing room just then, rubbing her eyes and dragging Cottontail.

"I'm hungry," she announced.

Evie stood up. "Dinner should be ready by now. I'll go check."

She left and Lucy climbed up into my lap. I nuzzled my face in her soft curls. We sat quietly like that until Evie poked her head in the room a few moments later to announce that dinner was ready.

The dining room was toward the back of the house, next to the drawing room. It was a long rectangular room with drab, fraying antique wallpaper and a threadbare rug that must once have been beautiful. Heavy cherry furniture gleamed in the sunlight still streaming through the windows. *This screams old money,* I thought. I assumed this space was one that I would be working on very soon.

Cora-Camille confirmed that the moment she sat down for dinner. "Carleigh, I'm not sure how much you remember of this house, but it's probably gotten even worse since you were here last. This dining room, for instance, is downright ugly. This old place has such a rich history; I hate to see it in decline. I didn't even realize how bad it had gotten until I saw a book of beautiful old photographs of the manor taken when photography was new, and then it hit me. You see, I tend to concentrate more on the farm than the house. And I just couldn't decide what to do with it until Evie reminded me that restoring old buildings is your specialty. I can't wait to see it the way it was always meant to be."

"It will be beautiful when it's done," I assured her. "After dinner I'd like to take a look around and get an idea of what I need to do."

"Wonderful. I can go with you, or Evie can."

"I'll go, Gran," Evie offered.

"Then I'll play with Lucy," Cora-Camille replied happily.

A woman came into the dining room just then and placed dinner plates in front of Lucy and me.

"Phyllis, I'd like you to meet Carleigh and Lucy Warner," Cora-Camille stated.

"Nice to know you, Phyllis," I said, smiling.

"My pleasure," she replied in a soft, cultured tone.

Phyllis was a thin woman, probably in her fifties, with flawless mocha skin and large, expressive black eyes. She had close-cropped salt-and-pepper hair. Her hands moved gracefully as she served the food.

"I don't know what we'd do without Phyllis. She is the best house manager we could ask for," Cora-Camille said. "And she's a great cook, too." Phyllis smiled at her in reply, then went back into the kitchen.

"Phyllis wasn't here when you visited, but you might remember her mom," Evie told me. "Phyllis lived here a long time ago when her mother was the house manager, then she left for college and worked in Charleston for years. When her mom passed away, we were lucky to have Phyllis come back to take her place to help manage the property. Her degree is in hospitality."

Ruby, who had been sitting silently all through dinner, nodded. "Phyllis is nice. I do the baking, but she does the rest of the cooking." She lapsed back into silence.

"And Ruby's baking is delicious, too," Cora-Camille acknowledged with a smile.

When dinner was over, Lucy called Brad and told him all about the manor. Then she and Ruby and Cora-Camille went into the drawing room. Lucy had brought three dolls downstairs and the six of them were planning a tea party.

Evie and I walked slowly through the rooms downstairs. I had already had a look at the drawing room earlier in the day. It needed painting, of course, and the plaster ceiling medallions and cornices needed attention. They appeared to be peeling, but I would have to examine them more closely from the top of a ladder or scaffold. The hardwood floors were scuffed and worn, so those might need to be completely replaced, or at the very least sanded and refinished. The withdrawing room, which was a small room accessed only through the drawing room, needed work, too. The walls, entirely paneled, were in need of refinishing. Many decades ago, the withdrawing room was a private space where gentlemen would gather after a dinner party to smoke, play cards, and imbibe fine spirits while the ladies stayed in the drawing room. Years of cigar and pipe smoke were visible on the withdrawing room walls.

On the other side of the entry hall were a ballroom and a small sitting room, with the kitchen toward the back of the house. Though the ballroom and sitting room had obviously been magnificent at one time, age and climate conditions had taken their toll. It was hard to identify the true colors of the wallpaper in the ballroom because it had become so dingy and gray. And in the sitting room, the tattered wall coverings even appeared to harbor some mildew. The room smelled musty and unused. Evie confirmed this. "We only use these rooms about once a year," she said sadly.

"Give me some time, and people will want to use these rooms again," I told her, smiling.

Luckily, I found that I had little work to do in the kitchen. Since kitchens were not my specialty, I was glad to learn that the large, open space had recently been updated to make life easier for Phyllis and Ruby. Evie said I might be called upon to add a few cosmetic enhancements in the kitchen, but that was all.

After we had completed our circuit through the rooms downstairs and I had taken notes on my highest priorities, we went back into the drawing room where Lucy was obviously enjoying being the center of attention.

"Time for bed, sweetie," I told her.

"I want to play more."

"Not tonight. You've had a long day," I told her.

She sighed. "Time for bed, sweeties," she told her dolls.

Cora-Camille smiled at her. "We'll play again tomorrow, okay?"

Lucy yawned and nodded.

I realized how tired I was as I was putting Lucy to bed. I returned downstairs, bid everyone good night, and went to sleep early.

Lucy and I woke at the same time the next morning to the sight of sunshine streaming through the tall windows and the sounds of songbirds chirping loudly outside. At our home in Chicago we rarely heard birds singing, so their presence outside the windows was quite a treat for both of us.

We went downstairs and greeted Phyllis in the kitchen. We sat at a long table and had a hearty breakfast of grits, eggs, and fruit. I hadn't eaten grits in years and this was Lucy's first experience eating them. They were delicious.

Evie came in while we were eating and suggested that we take a look at the outbuildings of Peppernell Manor before going into Charleston to visit some of the textile and paint shops that I would be using for the restoration. I eagerly agreed and she and I set out with Lucy in tow.

We went outdoors where the moist, sticky heat, even this early in the day, was oppressive. We strolled slowly down the driveway to a turnoff that led toward the outbuildings, also called dependencies. We walked through a wide grove of thickly planted trees that separated the buildings from the manor. I remembered that I had loved exploring the dependencies on my previous visit. As I recalled, there had been a barn, a carriage house, a kitchen, and a privy. The barn was still in use, though a much larger and more modern barn stood down the road.

We hadn't gone far into the grove of trees before we saw four very small, very old, decrepit buildings. I couldn't remember having seen them before.

"What are those?" I asked Evie.

"Slave cabins."

I was struck by her words. Although I knew Peppernell Manor had been home to slaves before the Civil War, the sight of those cabins made the slaves' existence somehow more tangible to me.

"They're not in great shape," I noted.

Evie nodded. "They probably should have been torn down years ago just for the sake of safety, but they're part of Peppernell Manor's history. I would hate to see them disappear."

We walked along in the silence of the trees for a moment, lost in our own thoughts. Lucy remained quiet, seeming to sense our pensiveness.

When we emerged on the far side of the wood, green leafy fields stretched out before us under the morning sun. In the distance, several men and women walked slowly among the field rows, hauling large baskets and picking late summer vegetables. Two tractors stood between the rows, ready to haul away the harvest.

"How many people work on the farm?"

"It depends on the time of year. Right now we have about fifteen men and women working. They're all migrant workers from Florida; they move around the South all year long to plant and harvest different types of crops."

We continued walking along the edge of the wood until we came to a large stone building.

"You remember the old barn," Evie said. "We keep some farm equipment in there and Gran's office is in there—she runs the farm—but mostly the barn is still there just because it's part of the property's past."

I walked into the barn through the enormous open double doors. Sure enough, there was a hayloft above me, complete with pitchfork. Antique saddles and harnesses hung from iron hooks on the walls. The barn was dilapidated; I could see from the large cracks and crevices that the foundation would need work. I peeked into a room that had been built onto the side of the barn. Though it was a newer addition, it had a vintage look to it that matched the rest of the building. A desk, filing cabinets, and an old table that held a large basket of fresh produce were the only furnishings. Cora-Camille's office, I supposed.

We left the barn and continued our walk between the fields and the woods. Soon we came to another stone building, this one round and somewhat smaller than the barn. I remembered this as the carriage house. A wide pathway, probably a century and a half old, led from the front of the carriage house into the woods.

"Lucy, the people at Peppernell Manor used to keep their carriages in this building," Evie stated. "Do you know what a carriage is?"

"Yes. My doll has one," Lucy answered proudly. "But we had to leave it in Chicago."

"The horses would be led from the barn to this building and attached to the carriages and then the carriages would go through the woods to the long drive in front of the house. The woods aren't very wide here."

"Is the carriage house used for anything now?" I asked.

"My brother Heath lives here. Did you ever meet him? When he's not working in Charleston he helps Gran run the farm, even though she likes people to think she still does it all herself." Evie laughed.

I vaguely recalled having met one of Evie's brothers on my previous visit to Peppernell Manor. She had two brothers, twins, and she was the baby of the family.

"You'll see Heath and Harlan at some point. They're both really busy," Evie noted.

We followed the old carriage pathway through the woods, which were quite narrow at this point, and emerged a short distance from the main house. The woods curved around the back of the manor toward the banks of the Ashley River. At the edge of the woods stood a small building. Lucy pointed to it.

"How come there's a moon on the door?"

Evie smiled at her. "That's where the people in Peppernell Manor used to go when they had to use the bathroom. It's called a privy."

Lucy's eyes widened. I could practically see the wheels in her mind turning. I hastened to add, "Lucy, people don't use this privy anymore. Remember we used the bathroom in the house last night?"

"Good." She frowned while Evie and I laughed.

We circled around and came to the back of the manor. A small two-story building stood next to the house, connected to it by a short, narrow hallway that was open on the side facing the river.

"That part of the house used to be the kitchen. People would cook the meals in there and then carry the food through that open hallway to the dining room. That was before there was a kitchen in the house," Evie explained.

Lucy nodded, probably not terribly interested in what Evie was saying.

"Are you going to want me to work on the dependencies, too?" I asked Evie as we walked back toward the manor.

"You can confirm it with Gran, but I think she'll want you to work on the barn. The carriage house was remodeled when Heath moved in and the kitchen dependency was remodeled when Phyllis moved in, so you probably won't have to touch those."

"Phyllis lives on the property?" I asked with some surprise.

"Yes. She's a direct descendant of one of the slave families that worked this plantation. She was offered the kitchen dependency when she started working here, but she didn't want it at first. Eventually she decided that it would be nice to live close to her job, plus she likes that it keeps her connected in some way with her family's past."

I nodded absentmindedly as Lucy pulled me along.

We skirted a small marshy pond not far from the kitchen dependency. I eyed it nervously. "I hear that every fresh body of water in South Carolina has at least one a-l-l-i-g-a-t-o-r," I said, spelling the word so I wouldn't upset Lucy.

Evie laughed. "That's nothing but a legend," she informed me.

We walked into the entry hall of the manor through the riverside entrance. I was struck again by the beauty of my surroundings and couldn't wait to get started on the restoration work. Evie said she would drive me into Charleston to show me where I would likely be getting some of the materials I would need to start the job. Cora-Camille would be only too happy to watch Lucy.

"That would be great. I'd also like to visit a nursery school in Charleston to get Lucy enrolled before the school year starts," I told Evie. "I did some research online before we left Chicago and I found one that sounds perfect for her."

"Fine. I'll be ready to leave in about thirty minutes."

A short time later as Evie and I drove down the main road, across the river, and into Charleston traffic, we discussed what should be done first in the manor house.

"I know it's still August," Evie mused, "but I know Gran would like the common rooms done before Christmas. Maybe you should start work on those first."

"I can start anywhere she wants," I replied. "If she wants certain rooms done by Christmas, I'm going to have to get to work as soon as possible. Does the family entertain a lot during the holidays?"

"All the time," Evie answered, rolling her eyes.

"Maybe I should start in the entry hall, then move to the drawing room and dining room. They seem to be the rooms downstairs that get the most use. The entry hall is what people see first when they come into the house and the other rooms are the most likely to be used during the holidays, I would guess."

"Yes, plus the ballroom. Mother and Daddy host a big open house every December in the ballroom. It gets decorated all fancy and everybody loves it."

"That sounds amazing!"

"I'm sure you and Lucy will be on the guest list this year," Evie replied with a wink. "Mother, especially, will be anxious to show off your work to everyone who comes to the house."

"Will I be expected to set up the decorations?" I asked dubiously.

"No, Phyllis does all that every year. She's a wonder when it comes to fancy decorating." I breathed a sigh of relief. Thank goodness for Phyllis.

It had taken under twenty minutes to get from Peppernell Manor to the heart of Charleston. *Not too bad,* I thought. I began to concentrate on the beautiful, centuries-old architecture we were passing. The history contained within all those walls fascinated me and I could feel the aura of Charleston's rich past all around.

We stopped first at a textile store where Evie introduced me to the owner, a specialist in locating and reproducing antique wall, window, and floor coverings. Evie explained that I would be using the owner's services in the months to come, and I had a feeling that I would be spending lots of time in this particular store. We went 'round to other shops, too, where similar conversations took place. It was nice to be able to meet local vendors and know that they were as interested as I in accurate historical restorations.

After we had stopped at several shops, I asked Evie to drive me to the nursery school I had found online. I hadn't made an appointment to visit, but the staff was very gracious. After I had met several of the teachers and looked around the premises, I was convinced that Lucy would love it there. I enrolled her on the spot in a program that allowed her to stay until midafternoon so I could work at the manor. I was excited to get home to tell her about it.

When we arrived back at Peppernell Manor, it was close to lunch-time and Lucy had met two newcomers. I recognized them immedi-ately as Evie's parents, Graydon and Vivian Peppernell, and I embraced both of them enthusiastically.

Graydon, a tall, stocky man with a mane of silver hair, held me away from him, his hands on my shoulders. "Carleigh," he began in his thick Southern drawl, "we are thrilled to have you here with us. And your little girl is just a peach." He was beaming. Apparently Lucy had charmed him.

Vivian, a petite woman with frosted blond hair and a tailored look about her, smiled at me. "I guess Evie has had you into Charleston al-ready to visit some of the restoration shops around town. What did you think?"

"I thought they were very professional and their work is beautiful. They'll be great to work with," I replied. "I hope when I'm done that you're thrilled with your home."

She smiled again. "I'm sure we will be. Of course, if you need my help, you're always welcome to whatever I have in my gallery." I thanked her warmly. Evie had told me that Vivian ran a renowned an-tique gallery in Charleston. Though we hadn't visited her store ear-lier, I felt sure I would be spending quite a bit of time in there, too. I remembered from my previous visit that Vivian was an art lover. She had worked at an art gallery at that time, so she must have decided that antiques were more to her liking.

We all ate lunch together in the dining room, making it a more formal affair than breakfast had been. Lucy did remarkably well, only having to be reminded twice to use utensils. After lunch I took her upstairs for her nap; then I descended by myself into the base-ment to have a look at what projects might lie in wait for me down there.

The cavernous basement was fascinating. I knew from my re-search about antebellum plantations that basements had several uses. The first thing I noticed when I walked down the old wooden stair-case to the basement, after the expansive brick floor in an intricate herringbone pattern, was the huge fireplace in the center of the space. This, I had learned, would have been used to heat the basement in winter and to keep food warm before serving. In addition, food was actually cooked in the cellar before the kitchen dependency had been built. There were a variety of small rooms down there, each with its own historical use. One room had a thick wooden door with a large rusted lock that appeared to be unused now. I suspected, based on research I had done, that room had once been used to house spices, wine, and other valuables. There was another room containing rows of wooden shelves that I assumed had been used as a storeroom for roots, vegetables, and other foods requiring cool storage. As I wandered around, my footsteps echoing on the bricks, I also found an old plantation office, other storage spaces, and work rooms that had probably been used by house slaves. There were more modern items in those rooms now, but I could imagine what it had looked like in the mid-nineteenth century.

I wrote as I walked, noting the spots in the basement that would probably need repair; there were many such areas that were cracked and peeling. When I was done in the basement, I went back up to my room to wake Lucy from her nap. Refreshed, she was now ready to hear my news about her new school. As I suspected, she greeted the announcement with a mixture of excitement and apprehension. She asked me lots of questions about where I would be during the school day and whether she would eat lunch there. She knew her little friends from Chicago were starting school soon and that she would be able to share stories with them when she saw them again. She also seemed a little frightened of going to school in a new place. Understandable, but maybe if I started while she was young I could instill in her a lifelong acceptance of change and a penchant for new experiences. No husband of hers was ever going to accuse *her* of being boring and staid when she grew up.

I explained to her that I would drop her off every morning and go back to the manor to do my work, then I would pick her up later in the day so we could spend time together at Peppernell Manor. She happily agreed and we went downstairs in search of other playmates.

We found Ruby in the kitchen. She was baking several different kinds of quick bread; she had banana, cherry, and blueberry breads all in the works. She asked Lucy if she'd like to help deliver the breads to the farm workers, and of course Lucy was thrilled to join her. The two of them wrapped the breads while we chatted and then Ruby donned a large straw hat. Together she and Lucy walked out the front of the house with the warm loaves in a wicker basket, talking amiably. Evie had informed me that Ruby baked so much that the people who lived in Peppernell Manor couldn't possibly eat it all, so

Ruby often gave the goodies away to the people who worked for them on the farm.

I spent the afternoon assessing the rooms upstairs to develop a restoration plan. Across the front of the manor was the huge master bedroom. Its antebellum use had been as a public space for parties, dancing, and musical concerts, but now it functioned as Graydon and Vivian's bedroom, complete with an en suite bathroom, sitting room, and Graydon's spacious office. An internationally known writer of spy thrillers whose books had been made into several popular movies, Graydon needed a large private space in which to work.

Behind the master suite on the right side of the house were two rooms: Ruby's bedroom and a guest room that was currently in use as Evie's bedroom. They were large and sunny but, like the master suite and most of the rooms downstairs, they needed work on the walls, floor, and ceiling. The room I shared with Lucy, behind Graydon and Vivian's room on the left side of the house, was in similar shape. Cora-Camille's room stretched across the back of the house facing the river. It, too, needed some attention.

When Lucy and I sat down for dinner that evening we were joined by Evie, her parents, Ruby, Cora-Camille, and a very tall, good-looking man with brown eyes just like Evie's and a Roman nose like Graydon's. Evie placed her hand on his arm and introduced him with a broad smile as her brother Harlan. Harlan was the epitome of Southern gentility as he stood, took my hand and bowed over it, then did the same with Lucy, who stared at him with wide eyes.

"I've been looking forward to meeting you, Carleigh. I've heard a lot about your work," Harlan began. "What are your plans for completing the restoration?"

"If it's all right with Cora-Camille, I think I'll get started in the entry hall because that space is the first one people see when they come indoors. Evie mentioned that it would be nice to have the public spaces done by Christmas, so after the hall is complete I'll move on to the drawing room, then the dining room, then finally the ballroom and small sitting room. After the holidays I can start the rooms upstairs and the basement."

Harlan leaned back in his chair and nodded. "I think that's a good plan." Then looking around the table at the others gathered there he said, "I've been talking to some friends of mine in Charleston about this restoration."

A palpable silence descended upon the room as everyone stopped eating, Vivian with her fork halfway to her mouth. *What just happened?* I wondered.

"Yes?" asked Cora-Camille.

"You know, Gran, it's going to cost a fortune. I'm pretty sure I can get enough investors together to pay for all the work that needs to be done, and then they could manage the property for you going forward. It would make your life much easier."

Vivian spoke first. "Harlan, I think that's just wonderful! That would be a huge help!"

Then Cora-Camille spoke.

"I don't know, Harlan dear. I have sufficient funds to pay for the restoration without getting any additional money from outsiders. And my life really isn't that difficult."

"I know you have plenty of money, Gran, but I'd like to see you be able to keep it and do what you want with it. With investor involvement, you'd be able to do just that."

"But this restoration *is* what I want to do with my money. I want to see this manor restored to its original grandeur before I die."

"Gran, don't talk like that," scolded Evie.

Cora-Camille patted her hand. "I'm not going to live forever, honey."

"I'm not telling you what to do, Gran. I just think it's a good idea if you give it some thought," Harlan said gently.

"I will, Harlan. I'll give it some thought," Cora-Camille promised.

"Good. Now, where's Phyllis? I'd love some coffee," Harlan said.

Phyllis came in shortly bearing a tray loaded with cups and saucers. She left and then returned a moment later with cream and sugar. A coffee urn stood waiting on the sideboard.

"Phyllis, there is a large stain on my napkin, and I noticed that there are spots on several other napkins, too. Can you please make sure that these napkins are cleaned properly the next time?" Vivian asked acidly.

Phyllis looked at her with big dark eyes and replied quietly, "Yes, Mrs. Peppernell." Everyone else remained silent, though Graydon shot his wife an angry look, shaking his head.

Talk for the remainder of the meal was of the weather and the farm. Everyone seemed to agree that the heat and humidity wouldn't break until sometime in September.

Later that evening after Lucy had spoken to Brad and fallen asleep and the downstairs was empty of other people, Evie and I each sat with a glass of wine in the drawing room. I asked Evie about Harlan's investor proposal.

Evie sighed. "Harlan wants to bring in a group of investors who will pay for the restoration. But they aren't doing it just to be nice, of course. They want something in return. And Harlan's idea is to open up Peppernell Manor to paying visitors. Tourists." She spoke the word as if it left a bad taste in her mouth.

"How would that work? Could strangers just come in and roam around? Where would your family live?"

"He wants the downstairs to be public. The family would continue living here and the upstairs would still be private, of course, but our access to the downstairs rooms would be limited. We certainly wouldn't want to be down there enjoying a glass of sweet tea with people walking through the drawing room."

"And Cora-Camille is against the idea?"

"I think she wants the manor to remain in the family. She doesn't want a bunch of strangers to have a financial interest in her home."

"Why is Harlan trying to persuade her to go with the investors?"

"Because this manor will probably belong to him and Heath and me someday. If it's a big tourist destination, it will be worth even more money than it's worth now."

"What do you think?"

Evie shrugged. "It's Gran's house. She should do with it what she wants. The whole investor idea has some positives, though. For one thing, if the manor was managed by an investment consortium, no one would ever have to worry about spending the money for its upkeep. Second, lots of people would be able to go through the manor and see what life used to be like for the people who lived on plantations back in the nineteenth century."

"What do the others think?"

"Heath thinks that Gran should go with her heart. And Daddy doesn't really weigh in because it's his mother's house. Mother loves Harlan's idea, though. She thinks Peppernell Manor would make a great tourist destination."

We sat in silence for a little while, enjoying the last of our wine, before bidding each other good night.

The next morning I went to a home store to get some of the supplies I would need to start the ceiling restoration in the entry hall. I was going to work from the top down. I had contacted a Charleston plasterer before leaving Chicago, so he met me at the manor during the afternoon to begin supervising the repairs. We didn't get too far the first day, but we got the materials organized and formulated a plan to tackle the cracks and bows in the ceiling. The ceiling border contained beautiful decorative detailing of leaves and vines, and it would take a good deal of time to just repair the small cracks in the details.

Thankfully, Cora-Camille and Ruby entertained Lucy while I worked. It would only be a few more days until she started nursery school, but it was a big help to have built-in babysitters at the manor whom I could trust with my daughter.

Dinner that evening was noisy, almost festive. Besides the people who had been there the previous evening, we were joined by Heath, Harlan's twin brother. Like Harlan, Heath was very tall, well over six feet. He was handsome in a scholarly way, with lanky limbs and tortoise-shell glasses. He and Harlan clearly enjoyed each other's company and liked to tease one another. Watching them and Evie, it was evident that they loved to dote on her and that she loved the attention.

After I put Lucy to bed Evie, the twins, and I retired to the drawing room to talk. Heath sat down and said to me, "I think I remember you from the first time you visited here. You and Evie were always going somewhere, never content to just stay home. And always talking about your boyfriends!" I blushed. It didn't sound like he remembered me fondly and I was embarrassed. Luckily he changed the subject; he seemed very interested in the specifics of the work I was doing on the entry hall ceiling. I explained my plans, then asked him about his work.

"I practice law in Charleston," he said with a sigh, "but my heart belongs here on the farm. If I could sell my practice and farm full-time, I'd be a happy man."

Evie smiled. "Why don't you just do it?"

"Because I wouldn't make any money. It's hard to make ends meet as a farmer. And I'd hate to leave my clients high and dry."

"Harlan, what do you do?" I asked.

"I'm a real estate developer. My office is also in Charleston. Right next door to Heath's, in fact. We work together on real estate projects occasionally."

"What have you seen of Charleston this trip, Carleigh?" asked Heath.

"I haven't really seen too much of it yet," I admitted. "I've seen the insides of some shops that specialize in restorations and textiles and things like that, but I haven't done any sightseeing. I'll take Lucy one of these days and spend some time looking around the city. It's beautiful."

"I'm sure Evie can give you some good sightseeing ideas. She knows every nook and cranny of Charleston."

"Maybe I'll even go with you," Evie suggested.

"Great!"

Talk then turned to Lucy, her age, her interests, and how she was adjusting to life on a plantation in South Carolina. No one asked about Brad, and for that I was thankful. We were all having such a nice evening together; I would have hated to spoil it by having to discuss the divorce.

Eventually the small party broke up and Evie and I went upstairs, Heath went back to his carriage house, and Harlan left for his home in Charleston.

I was immersed in my work for the next several days. Lucy played with Cora-Camille and Ruby, spending time indoors with tea parties and doll dances, and outdoors walking around and picking flowers. Her clear, sweet voice was never far away, and I knew I would miss her terribly when she went to nursery school.

I was right. That first day of nursery school was a hard one for me, much harder than it was for Lucy. She smiled and waved as I stood in the doorway of her classroom, tears streaming down my face. I spent the rest of that miserable day wandering around downtown Charleston, looking into shops, ordering lunch only to find myself too depressed to eat, and counting the minutes until I could pick her up. When I finally got her back at the end of her school day, I cried again. She chattered excitedly all the way back to Peppernell Manor. She talked about the artwork she did, about her teachers, and about her new friends, none of whose names she could remember. She asked what I thought Ruby and Miss Cora had been doing while she was at school. I told her that Ruby was probably baking and that Miss Cora was probably waiting anxiously for Lucy to get home. She seemed thrilled. She enjoyed repeating her stories to Cora-Camille and Ruby, then again at dinner, and finally again to Brad that night on the phone.

As the next few days passed, it became easier for me to drop off Lucy and work while she was in school. During those days, I worked diligently with the plasterer on the ceilings in the entry hall and drawing room. He was an older man with a great talent and I learned some valuable skills from him. We had decided that it made sense to start work on the ceilings in the drawing room, withdrawing room, and dining room before moving forward with the restoration of the walls and floor in the entry hall.

But as much as I was learning and enjoying my work, the best part of my day was always when I picked up Lucy and brought her home.

CHAPTER 3

I was working alone in the drawing room on a quiet, drizzly day when there was a knock at the front door. I was on a scaffold so I hoped there was someone else around who could answer it. But no one appeared, and as I was stepping down from the scaffold, the door swung open and Harlan stepped in, beckoning to someone behind him.

I was surprised to see not one, but several people walk into the entry hall. Besides Harlan, there were four men and one woman. Harlan saw me at the bottom of the scaffold and stepped into the drawing room, inviting the others to join him. My hands were covered with a powdery film from the plaster; I tried to wipe them off onto my cut-off jeans as I glanced down at my flip-flop-clad feet, sharply aware of how I looked compared to all these polished professionals in suits and expensive shoes. I wiped a few strands of hair out of my eyes and made a feeble attempt to straighten my ponytail. Harlan smiled and turned to the somber-looking group behind him.

"I'd like you all to meet Carleigh Warner, the genius restorer behind all the work being done at Peppernell Manor." Embarrassed by his praise, I smiled and received several thin smiles in return, but nobody attempted to shake my powdery hand.

"Carleigh, this is the group of investors I was talking about the other night. I thought it would be helpful for them to see the manor in person before we move forward with discussions about setting up a funding schedule for the restoration."

I looked around at the group. "If you have any questions, I'll be happy to answer them," I said.

Nobody spoke.

"If we have questions after the tour, we know where to find you," Harlan declared.

I got back to work. I didn't know Cora-Camille had changed her mind about the investment group. Then again, maybe she hadn't. She hadn't seemed enthusiastic about their participation in the restoration and funding. She was spending the afternoon in the new barn down the road; maybe Harlan had chosen this time for the tour because he knew Cora-Camille wouldn't be around.

I could hear Harlan discussing the history of the old home and its dependencies as the group made its way slowly around the first floor. Then they all trooped down to the basement and came up again several minutes later. They were a little more animated now, asking questions of Harlan and engaging each other in conversation and speculation. Harlan brought several of them back into the drawing room, where they proceeded to ask me several questions about the length of time it would take to complete the restoration work, some of the techniques I would be using, and the estimated costs of certain aspects of the project. I answered their questions as best I could, then Harlan saw the group to the front door. He came back into the drawing room alone. "I'm not sure how that went," he began. "They didn't seem too happy, did they?"

"They didn't look happy to me, but maybe investors are always sour," I told him with a grin.

"Maybe you're right. I'll talk to them tomorrow. Say, are you busy for dinner tonight? I thought you might enjoy a meal at one of Charleston's fine eateries."

"Uh, I don't know," I stammered, suddenly in a panic. *Is this man asking me out on a date?*

Harlan spoke again. "Evie can come if you'd like. We could make a little party of it."

I sighed inwardly with relief. *Not a date, just a dinner with friends.* "Okay, that would be fine. I have to make sure someone can help Lucy with her dinner, though."

"There'll be someone here to look after her, and you'll be back before her bedtime. Shall we meet in Charleston at around six?"

"Sure. Where in Charleston?"

"I had a place on Broad Street in mind. An old, old restaurant with excellent food. I'll write down the address for you. Sound good?"

"Okay."

No sooner had he written down the address for me than Cora-Camille walked in the front door.

"Who were all those people?" she asked Harlan. So she didn't know about his tour after all.

He appeared uncomfortable as he shifted position, flicking a glance in my direction. "I thought I'd bring out a few of the people who are interested in possibly helping to fund the restoration. They just wanted to see the place."

Cora-Camille frowned. "Darlin', I've been thinking about it and I just don't believe that it's a good idea to bring investors into this project. I have more than enough money to pay for the restoration. If we invite your investor friends, they'll want to see a return on their money, and my home will end up being used by people looking to get rich."

"But Gran, just think of all the good we could do if this house were used to teach people about the antebellum South."

That's when Cora-Camille dropped her bombshell.

"That may happen anyway, Harlan. I'm thinking about changing my will and leaving the management of Peppernell Manor to the state of South Carolina. That way people will be visiting this home for many years to come, but the proceeds will go to the state. Not a bunch of people looking to make a quick buck."

Harlan's eyes widened. "I didn't know that, Gran. I hope you'll forgive me for bringing those people through here."

"That's all right, dear. I know you were just trying to help."

I interjected. "Cora-Camille, maybe we should sit down and talk about this. If you're thinking Peppernell Manor may be opened up to the public, that will change how I go about my work. We'll need handicap access—"

"Let's worry about that when the time comes," she interrupted. "For now I just want you to restore my home." She smiled.

Harlan gave her a hug and she went into the kitchen, his eyes following her. He turned to me and said, "See you tonight."

"Sure. I'll be there at six." With that, Harlan let himself out the front door. I ran lightly upstairs and knocked on Evie's door. She opened it a moment later and I asked her if she had time to go into Charleston for dinner with Harlan and me. Unfortunately, she had a conference call with colleagues on the West Coast, so she would be busy at six o'clock. She smiled broadly at me. "You have a date with Harlan? That's great!"

"No," I hastened to clarify. "It's just a friendly meal. That's why we invited you, too."

"Oh. Well, I'm sorry I can't go."

Now that Evie couldn't go to dinner, I didn't want to go anymore. But I had already told Harlan I would meet him at the restaurant, so I didn't have a choice. A few hours later I put on a crisp, white, silk tank top and a pair of capris and left the manor, promising Lucy I would be back before her bedtime.

When I got to the restaurant, I was dismayed to see Harlan waiting for me outside wearing a three-piece suit. I was obviously not dressed appropriately for dinner. He looked me up and down and suggested that we go to another restaurant down the block, one that was a little less formal. I apologized to him, explaining that I hadn't realized we were going to a fancy restaurant.

During dinner Harlan and I talked a little about the restoration, but Harlan mostly regaled me with stories about his job. He seemed to love his work, but I privately thought that all the meetings about money . . . and the stress over money . . . and the searching for new sources of money . . . sounded dreadful. Eventually the conversation got around to the investors he had brought to the manor earlier that afternoon.

"I'm going to have to talk to the folks who went through the house this afternoon," he said. "Gran's announcement certainly came as a surprise to me. The plans of the group may have to wait."

Sounds like they'll be waiting forever, I thought to myself. He must have read my thoughts.

"I think Gran will come around. Family is the most important thing to her, and eventually she'll realize that investor funding is the best course for the family after she passes."

"How do you figure?" I asked.

"She's always talking about what will happen after she dies. You've even heard her. The best way to assure that the family continues to get an appreciable income will be to accept an infusion of cash so we can modify the property to become a travel destination for folks who want to know more about the South before the War of Northern Aggression."

"I guess you have your work cut out for you, then."

He smiled wryly. "I sure do."

After dinner, he walked me to my car and bid me good night, taking my hand and bowing over it as he had when we met. Even though Harlan had suggested that I invite Evie to this "little party," I felt through the entire meal like I was on a date—but all I wanted from Harlan was friendship. I was so relieved that he didn't try to kiss me that I actually felt weak-kneed when I got in the car. I was happy to get home to my very wound-up daughter who had spent most of the evening riding Graydon's back as though he were a horse.

CHAPTER 4

The next day I was working on the ceiling in the withdrawing room. I was alone; the plasterer had decided that I could be trusted to perform repairs to the plaster ceilings without his constant presence, so he had gone back to Charleston until later in the day. I was focused on my work when I thought I heard a sound behind me. I turned quickly and saw Phyllis standing in the doorway to the withdrawing room. She held a broom and a dustpan in her hands and was staring at me with her dark eyes. I suddenly felt uncomfortable. I wondered how long she had been standing there.

"Hi, Phyllis. What's up?"

"Nothing. I'm just watching," she replied.

"Okay. Just let me know if you need me to move or something," I told her, still puzzled as to why she was just standing there.

She turned to leave the room, shaking her head. I heard her say, half to herself, "Sarah isn't going to like this at all."

I had no idea who Sarah was. I didn't really have time to figure it out, either, since I had to finish what I was doing and get into Charleston to pick up Lucy.

Dinner that night was an uncomfortable affair. Vivian had apparently been apprised by Harlan of the possible change in Cora-Camille's will, and she insisted upon talking about it at the table.

"Cora-Camille, I hear you're thinking of letting the state of South Carolina manage this home and property."

Silence. Harlan shot his mother a warning look.

Cora-Camille, unruffled, continued eating. Finally she spoke in her clear Southern drawl. "Yes, Vivian, I am. I've been thinking that Peppernell Manor could do the most good for the most people if it were managed by the state and used as a cultural center."

"But why? What will happen to the people who live here after, God forgive me, you're gone?"

"Vivian, please," Graydon growled.

"I would make sure that the family is allowed to live here," Cora-Camille assured her. "I wouldn't leave you all homeless."

"But how could we continue to live here with people coming in and out all the time?"

"It would be no different from the living arrangements if this home were taken over by the investors that you and Harlan keep trying to push on me," Cora-Camille noted, a small crack appearing in her calm veneer.

"Well!" Vivian exclaimed, apparently highly insulted. "I think we'd have more control over the situation if this beautiful old treasure weren't managed by the state."

"I don't." Cora-Camille shot her a look that indicated that the conversation was over. Harlan hadn't said anything during the exchange. I wondered what he was thinking.

I was frantic to change the subject and stop the tension that was rising between the two women. I suddenly remembered my brief conversation with Phyllis.

"Phyllis came to watch me work in the withdrawing room today," I began. "Who is Sarah?"

All eyes turned to me in surprise. Vivian put her napkin down slowly, sighing with disgust. She turned to Graydon.

"Graydon, we cannot have a domestic who goes around talking of such things. I am going to have to sit her down. The way she goes on is foolish."

Graydon looked at his wife gravely. "Vivian, she's entitled to say whatever she wants. Who cares if she wants to talk about Sarah?"

"I do."

"Well, let her be. She's not hurting you."

"She's embarrassing me and the rest of this family."

Graydon shook his head and went back to eating. I gave Evie a bewildered look.

"Sarah was Phyllis's great-great-great-great-great-grandmother or something like that," Evie explained. "She was a slave who lived on this property. She worked in the manor and had her first baby when she was fifteen. Phyllis feels very close to Sarah and talks about her all the time as if she still lived here."

"Phyllis talks to a ghost?" I couldn't believe what I was hearing.

"Yes. Believe me, everyone has that same reaction at first. But you'll get used to it—we all have."

I shrugged. "If you say so. So why wouldn't Sarah like what I'm doing?" It felt strange to be wondering about a ghost's opinion.

"Talking about ghosts is disgraceful," Vivian grumbled.

"Vivian," Graydon warned.

She shot him a dark look.

"I don't know," Evie responded to my question. "Sarah's opinions aren't always easy to figure out."

I wasn't sure what to say next, so I turned to Lucy to help her with her dinner. I hoped to talk more about Sarah with Evie later that night, but she got a call from Boone and spent the evening in her room. I didn't mind too much, since I was very tired; I fell asleep just after Lucy did.

I had been asleep for a couple hours when the house phone rang just after eleven o'clock. There was no phone extension in my bedroom, but I had seen one out in the hall on a small table. With everyone in the house carrying a cell phone, this was the first time I'd heard the phone ring. I heard Graydon's deep voice answer the phone, then I heard a soft knock at my door.

"Carleigh," Graydon whispered. "Are you awake?"

Fuzzy-headed from sleep, I shuffled to the door and opened it. Graydon handed me the phone with a smile. "Got a new boyfriend?" he teased.

I frowned. Why would anyone be calling me this late, and not on my cell? Why wake the entire household?

"Hello?"

A gravelly voice answered in a thick Southern accent. "You better get outta there, Carleigh. You're gonna find yourself in grave danger."

"Who is this?" I demanded angrily. When there was no reply I slammed the phone down. Graydon, who hadn't even gotten back to his room, turned around.

"What's the matter, Carleigh?"

I was trembling. I was afraid my knees wouldn't hold me up. I told him wildly, "I don't know who that was. He just said I'd be in grave danger if I stayed here."

Graydon had obviously seen his fair share of hysterical women and knew just what to do. "Carleigh, take it easy, honey. It was just some joker playing a stupid prank. Come here." He held me in a big bear hug for a few minutes, smoothing my hair, then spoke again. "You are perfectly safe in this house. No one is going to hurt you here. I can sleep outside your bedroom if you'd like."

I took several slow, deep breaths. His words made sense. Of course some jerk was just playing games, acting stupid. I would have loved for him to sleep outside my bedroom, but I was too embarrassed to admit it.

"Thanks anyway, Graydon. We'll be okay. I can't let some prank get to me." I forced a laugh.

"That's a good girl. Now go back to sleep." He took the phone off the hook before going back to his own room. I returned to my room, brought Lucy into bed with me, and wrapped my arms around her. She remained asleep, but I lay awake for the rest of the night.

Who could it have been? The only men I'd met were Graydon, Heath, Harlan, and employees of the stores I'd visited. There was Brad, of course, but he wouldn't waste his time with silly tricks— would he? No, it had to be someone I'd met since arriving in South Carolina. My mind turned the possibilities over and over, but no one had any reason to want me to go away.

The next day dawned hot and humid again. I got an early-morning text from Lucy's school stating that there had been a pipe leak in two of their classrooms overnight and the nursery school would be closed that day. I was actually happy to get the text, since there was no way I'd be able to focus on my work after that late-night phone call and it was about time that I took a day off anyway. I told Lucy I would take her into Charleston for a girls' day out and some touristy sightseeing. I hoped spending a few hours away from the manor would help me stop worrying about the phone call.

She and I and Cottontail set out early and headed straight for a park. We found White Point Garden, a small park right on the waterfront where we could explore together. There was a beautiful white gazebo there, as well as statues, lots of strong, ancient trees, Civil War sculptures, and a fountain. I had a hard time keeping Lucy dry and on solid ground once she got a look at the fountain. After spending some time at the park, I took Lucy's stroller out of the car and I pushed her up Meeting Street at a leisurely pace, stopping when either one of us wanted to. We wandered in and out of shops and boutiques and even found a bookstore where we could curl up on a couch and read together. We thoroughly enjoyed our time sightseeing. As it got close to lunchtime, I was pushing her in the stroller down Broad Street when I was surprised to see Heath walking toward us. He was slowly leafing through a document and didn't see us until he was quite nearby.

"Interesting reading, Heath?"

He looked up, startled. "Oh. Hi, Carleigh. Hi, Lucy. What are you two doing in town today?"

I explained about the leak at the nursery school and told him how we had spent our morning as Lucy complained about how hungry she was.

"I'm heading right over to that deli to grab lunch," he said, pointing across the street. "Why don't you join me?"

"I'm hungry now!" Lucy wailed.

I laughed. "Okay. We'll come with you. If this child doesn't eat soon, she might waste away."

Heath grinned and the three of us made our way to the deli. Once we had ordered and found seats out on the sidewalk under a bright umbrella, our conversation turned to the places that Heath thought we should visit on our "day off." Knowing I was interested in history and architecture, he suggested that we first visit Rainbow Row, a string of over a dozen colorful historic homes built on East Bay Street. He also insisted that we visit St. Michael's Episcopal Church, not far from Rainbow Row, on the corner of Market and Meeting Streets. Built in the mid-1700s, Heath told me, it was the oldest church in Charleston and a National Historic Landmark. I listened as he discussed Charleston's history and some of the buildings that I simply had to see while I stayed at Peppernell Manor. He was very knowledgeable and I wished he could spend the afternoon with us acting as our own personal tour guide.

As lunch came to a close and we sipped the last of our sweet tea, a woman walked by our table. She was very tall with jet-black hair that cascaded down her back. A striking white sheath dress and red high-heeled shoes showed off her olive skin and fabulous figure.

Heath looked up at her and almost choked on his tea. The woman slowed down, staring at us, then smiled coyly at Heath, tossed her head, and walked on.

"Friend of yours?" I asked Heath.

"No," he answered, the tone in his voice brooking no follow-up questions. He gathered up his papers. "I hate to cut this short, but I do have to get back to the office. Court at two o'clock," he explained.

"No problem. See you later, and thanks for the history lesson and suggestions," I told him.

Lucy walked for a short distance after lunch, but it wasn't long before she started to get tired. I put her in the stroller and soon she was sound asleep. I was glad it was naptime, since I wanted to get a nice leisurely look at Rainbow Row and St. Michael's. Lucy might have had other ideas if she had been awake.

I walked to St. Michael's, where I was awed by the beauty and grace of the oldest church in Charleston, with its towering white spire, bright red doors, breathtaking stained glass, and ancient cemetery containing the graves of many historic figures from South Carolina, including two signers of the United States Constitution.

Then I wandered over to Rainbow Row, which I found easily. The street was like something out of a painting; indeed, I had seen many renderings of Rainbow Row in art gallery windows in Charleston. House after pastel house were delightful to see. I enjoyed the architecture and landscaping and the quaint atmosphere aided by antique lampposts, as well as the house markers that told some of the homes' histories, such as the original owners and the year of construction. Eventually Lucy started to stir in her stroller, so I snapped a few more photos with my phone and we set off for an ice cream shop I had noticed nearby. Once we had eaten our fill of strawberry ice cream, Lucy and I went to one more playground before heading back to Peppernell Manor. It was a great day, and I was almost sorry to get a text that evening that the nursery school would be open the following day.

That night I told Evie about the prank phone call.

"You're kidding," she responded, mouth agape.

"I wouldn't joke about that."

"Who do you think it was?"

I sighed. "If I only knew, I wouldn't worry so much about it."

She seemed to brighten. "I'll bet Daddy's right. I'm sure it was just someone with nothing better to do than make prank calls."

"But how did the person choose me? And how did they know I could be reached at your house?"

"People can get phone numbers anywhere these days. And there are lots of people who know you're staying here. It could have been someone from one of the stores you've visited, or someone from Lucy's school, or someone from back in Chicago. Anyone can fake a Southern accent. I don't think you have anything to worry about."

I hoped Evie was right.

I got right back to work the next morning. Having only to finish the plaster ceilings in the ballroom and sitting room on the first floor, I was excited to get past that phase of the work and begin the next phase, which would be the walls. The plasterer said I was doing a great job, and I was thrilled to be learning a new skill.

The two ceilings took several days of painstakingly intricate work, but I was very pleased with the result when it was finally done. The smooth white surface adorned with Greek key borders was beautiful, and the members of the family agreed.

"Carleigh, that ceiling is a work of art," Cora-Camille gushed.

"It certainly is. In all my years here I've never seen the ceilings on the first floor look better," Vivian agreed.

Graydon folded his arms over his chest. "Carleigh, honey, I'd say you've outdone yourself," he boomed in that thick Southern drawl of his.

Evie beamed. "I told you she'd do a great job, didn't I?"

But I couldn't rest on my laurels for long. I needed to get started on the walls. The morning after I finished the ceilings, I dropped Lucy off at school and returned to Peppernell Manor to clean up all the materials I had been using and to disassemble the scaffold. I was done a little while before I had to pick Lucy up at school, so I decided to drive into Charleston to visit one of the paint stores I would be using. Ruby asked me if she could ride along, since she had to visit a baking supply store near my destination.

"Sure," I told her. "I'd love the company."

I tried to make small talk with Ruby in the car on the way into Charleston. She told me about a couple of new cake recipes that she wanted to try and asked me about the colors for the rooms downstairs in the manor.

"What color is the dining room going to be?"

"Cora-Camille said that the dining room used to be wallpapered,"

I answered. "So we'll try to find something that looks like the original paper, if we can find a sample of it, and go from there. If we can't find something similar, we'll use wallpaper that would have been popular during the mid-1800s."

"What about the drawing room?"

"That's going to be a coral color. Big rooms like that in plantation homes used to be painted bright, cheery colors. There's some evidence that the drawing room used to be coral. Your mom and I are going to come up with a custom coral color."

"That sounds pretty. What about the ballroom?"

"I don't know yet what we're doing with the ballroom. Cora-Camille decided she wants me to do the drawing room and dining room first. Then the entry hall, then the ballroom. I'm hoping to get those rooms done before Christmas because of the big party that Graydon and Vivian throw every year for the holiday."

"That party is fun. The ballroom always looks beautiful."

I smiled. "That's what I've heard. It sounds wonderful."

"Sarah was never invited to parties in the ballroom."

Sarah again. I didn't really know how to respond. Did Ruby believe in ghosts, too? "She wasn't?"

"No. She was a house slave. House slaves were not allowed at parties, except to serve people."

"Hmmm."

"You haven't met Sarah yet. She's Phyllis's great-great-great-great-great-grandmother," Ruby noted, counting five "greats" on her fingers.

"She sounds interesting," I commented. I didn't know what else to say. After all, she was talking about a dead woman.

"She is."

By that time we were at the baking supply store, so I let Ruby out and told her where I would be, just a few doors down the block. I watched Ruby as she, clad as usual in a pastel shirtwaist and a huge straw hat, entered the store with a big smile. I then drove to the paint store and parked outside.

I had to wait a short time for the owner to finish up with another customer. When it was my turn, I talked to her about paint colors and finishes, and we spoke at length about the paint color for the drawing room. We were engrossed in a number of books, flipping back and forth between books and pages and paint swatches, when Ruby came in.

"Hi, Ruby," I greeted her. "I'm going to be a few more minutes. Do you want to have a seat and wait for me?" I looked at my watch. "Oh, wait. I have to run over and pick up Lucy from nursery school." I turned to the shop owner. "Can we continue this in about fifteen minutes?"

"Of course," she answered. I grabbed my car keys from the counter and started out the door, but Ruby touched my arm.

"I can go get Lucy," she told me shyly. "I know right where her nursery school is."

Ruby's past struggles with anxiety sprang to mind, but then I thought of all the times she had been gentle and good to Lucy since we arrived at Peppernell Manor. I didn't want her to think I didn't trust her. I must have hesitated a moment too long, because she hastened to assure me, "I'm on the list of people who are allowed to pick her up, right? I'll hold her hand and bring her back here." She looked at me with pleading eyes and a hopeful smile.

"All right," I decided. "I'll be done soon, so you don't even have to bring her back here. Just wait right outside the school and I'll pick you up."

"Okay." She strode out the door, a woman with a purpose.

But I never should have let Ruby pick up my daughter.

CHAPTER 5

I left the paint store about ten minutes later, laden with paint swatches and books that I was borrowing from the shop owner. When I swung into a parking spot in front of the school, Lucy and Ruby were nowhere to be seen. I walked into the school, assuming that Lucy had insisted upon using the bathroom before going back to Peppernell Manor. She loved the nursery school bathrooms, with amenities sized just right for little girls and boys. But when I pushed open the bathroom door, all I heard was my voice echoing in the tiled room.

I hailed a teacher in one of the classrooms. "Have you seen Lucy?" I asked her. She sent me to the director, who was in the office.

"Ruby Peppernell picked up Lucy today," she replied in answer to my question, scanning the day's sign-out sheet. "She had identification and she is one of the people authorized to pick up Lucy. Aren't they out front?"

"No," I replied, swallowing hard. My voice and knees started to get a bit shaky. Why had I ever put Ruby's name on that list? Why had I allowed her to get Lucy?

"Don't worry. We'll find them in a jiffy," she assured me gently. She talked quietly to another teacher on our way out the door, and that teacher joined us, walking around the corner of the building when we got outside.

I was becoming frantic.

I started yelling, "Lucy! Ruby! Lucy!" The teachers soon joined in my shouts. But there was no response.

I needed to do more, faster. I said to the teachers, "You keep looking. I'm going to take the car and start driving up and down the streets nearby. They can't have gotten very far."

The teachers agreed and I sprinted to my car. I gunned the engine and pulled out of my spot with squealing tires. I drove quickly up the block, then turned and slowed down to search both sides of the street for my missing daughter and Ruby. Tears were blurring my vision and I had to keep wiping my eyes with my T-shirt. I was yelling for Lucy and Ruby out the open window, but hearing nothing. Passersby looked at me as if I was crazy, but I kept shouting.

I swung the car into a parking lot to turn around when from a half-block away I saw a woman wearing a large straw hat walking through a wrought-iron gate. I raced forward in the car only to see the woman disappearing into a house. I was trying to decide whether I should knock on the door to the home when I saw another woman walking up ahead. She too was wearing a large straw hat. I drove forward and sobbed with relief when I saw that it was indeed Ruby. She was holding Lucy's hand. Both had ice cream cones. I screeched to a halt.

"Lucy!" I screamed. My daughter turned around. She waved. "Hi, Mama!"

I choked on my tears as I dropped to my knees and hugged Lucy fiercely. She was bewildered.

"Mama, why are you crying?" she asked, clearly alarmed.

"I couldn't find you," I sniffled.

Ruby looked on, her face becoming red. "It was my fault, Miss Carleigh. I thought we might have time to get ice cream before you came to pick us up."

I looked at her angrily. "I told you to wait for me outside the school!" The tears started again. "Didn't you realize how terrified I would be?" I screeched at her.

Then Ruby started to cry. People were watching. I didn't care. "Get in the car," I ordered her. I strapped Lucy into the back and returned to the nursery school. While Ruby and Lucy waited in the car, I went and explained to the teachers, who were still outside looking and yelling, that I had found them and that we were going back to

Peppernell Manor. I also asked them to remove Ruby's name from the list of people authorized to pick up Lucy.

Ruby cried all the way back to Peppernell Manor. I didn't speak to her. I didn't try to make her feel better. I wanted her to experience some of the pain I had just felt. It didn't take long for Lucy to start crying, too. She was obviously upset by the tension in the car, and I waited until we were in our room in Peppernell Manor to explain why I was angry at Ruby.

"I told Ruby to wait for me outside your school. She was not allowed to take you for ice cream," I explained. "I do not want you to go alone with Ruby anymore."

"But I love Ruby!" Lucy wailed.

"You can still play with Ruby, but you have to stay in the house with her. You can't go anywhere with Ruby unless I am with you. Do you understand?"

She nodded mutely.

I left her in our room to rest while I went in search of Ruby. I had calmed down considerably and I wanted to talk to her about her mistake.

I found her in the kitchen, furiously kneading bread dough. "Ruby, can I talk to you for a minute?" I asked softly.

She shook her head.

"Please listen to me, Ruby," I urged. "I've had a chance to calm down and I want to talk to you."

She sighed. "Okay." She stopped kneading for a moment.

"Do you understand why I was so upset?" I asked her.

"Yes. I shouldn't have taken Lucy out for ice cream. But I thought she would love it."

"I don't mind if Lucy has ice cream. That's not the issue. I was upset because I couldn't find her. Or you. I asked you to wait outside the nursery school for me and you didn't. I didn't know where you had gone and I was very worried."

She hung her head. "I'm sorry," she whispered.

"I know you are," I told her gently. "I know you'll never do it again."

"I won't," she assured me.

"Friends again?" I asked with a smile.

"Yes," she answered, her eyes downcast. I left the kitchen as she got back to her bread-making. I wasn't ready to get back to work, so I asked Evie to keep an eye on Lucy, then I wandered outside. The shadows were lengthening as the sun sank lower in the sky. I let my feet take me where they wanted; they led me to the quiet of the woods and the old slave cabins. I pushed open a creaky door and stepped gingerly into the first cabin. It smelled musty, like wet earth and mildew. The walls were made of horizontal wooden slats; thin ribbons of light peered through the cracks between the boards. A few pieces of paper fluttered from the walls. The room was divided in half by a brick fireplace. Small heaps of leaves and other detritus littered the corners and from one of the piles there came a small rustling sound. I had apparently disturbed a mouse's peace. A few lopsided hooks hung on the walls and one hook hung on each side of the fireplace. *Probably for hanging cooking utensils,* I thought.

A knock sounded softly behind me. I turned to see Phyllis step into the cabin. I was surprised to see her.

"Hi, Phyllis," I greeted her.

"I saw you come out here," she answered. "Sarah does not like this place to be disturbed."

"I'm sorry. I didn't know that. I just wanted a look inside. I was thinking about how I would love to restore these cabins."

She stared at me, mouth agape. "How could you even think about restoring these homes?" she asked angrily.

I blinked in surprise. "I thought you'd like to see them as they would have been in the mid-nineteenth century."

"Do you know the heartbreak that took place in these homes?"

"Well, I've read a lot about it. It was horrible. That's part of the reason they should be restored, don't you see? So people can understand what life used to be like for the slaves on these Southern plantations. So people can see how different life was for the slaves than for the master and the mistress who lived in the great house."

Phyllis shook her head. "You want other people to see where the slaves lived? You want people coming through here to *learn?*" she jeered. "It would just be white people making money off the backs of the slaves . . . again," she added in disgust. "Do you know what stories Sarah could tell you about the things that happened in these little cabins? They'd curl that pretty red hair of yours."

"I've been wondering how Sarah speaks to you," I said.

She gazed at me for a moment before answering.

"The same way you do. With her mouth. But only when I'm alone."

"Oh. Will you tell me some of Sarah's stories?" I asked.

Phyllis walked to the door and sat down in the doorway, hugging her knees. She closed her eyes. "Sarah told me this once. Her daddy knew that he was going to be sold off to a plantation many miles away from here. He was scared. Sarah's mama cried and cried. The sale was going to take place the next day. He wasn't going to be able to see his family anymore. He would rather have died than be separated from Sarah's mama and their babies, but see, that's what was going to happen. So that's what he did. He died. He shot himself right in that cabin," she said in a faraway voice, pointing to the cabin next door. "That's what he did."

We were both silent for many moments. Then I asked Phyllis, "Why do you stay here?"

She looked at me almost pityingly. "You wouldn't understand."

"Try me."

"I stay here because this is where I can take care of my family's memories. That's all they left behind. Memories and stories. If I'm not here to take care of them, what's going to happen to them? They'll fall silent, just like those slave owners always wanted. I can't let that happen. So I stay. Sarah tells me the stories and I tell them to others."

"Does Sarah ever tell any happy stories?"

"Sure she does. Some nights the slaves would fiddle and dance right here in the dark in front of their houses. If they couldn't be heard up at the great house, it was okay. No one stopped them. They had songs that belonged only to them, and they would teach the kids the songs and the fiddle. Those things got passed down from one family to the next.

"But mostly Sarah's stories aren't happy. She was a house slave, so that meant she had to work up in the great house, doing laundry and cooking and cleaning and watching the kids as if they were her own. And she was at the mistress's beck and call all the time. Then when she went to her own home at night, she would have all those same things to do for her own family. The same with the men and boys who worked in the fields. They would work all day from before dawn until after dark and then they'd have to go home and do all their own chores before they could go to bed.

"Did you know that slaves were beaten more often for being tired than for doing a poor job at their work? They just worked and worked until they were ready to drop. When they did sleep, it was on a dirty pile of rags or straw."

"I don't know what to say, Phyllis. I don't think there are adequate words. I'm so sorry that Sarah had to go through those things."

Phyllis had a troubled look in her eyes. "So am I."

She seemed to shake off her melancholy then, perhaps deciding that she had confided too much in me, a virtual stranger. She rose to leave. "I don't know what you have planned for these slave cabins, but I won't stand by and watch them turned into a tourist trap like the rest of Peppernell Manor. They are part of history. My history." She turned and I watched her make her way slowly back to the manor.

I knew I wanted to restore these old cabins. Now I had a mandate, unwittingly given to me by Phyllis. And Sarah. Make the cabins real, make them true to their original inhabitants and their lives and hardships. Make a different kind of memory for Phyllis and Sarah.

I peeked in the other cabins before returning to the manor. They were much the same as the first one. Cracks in the walls, hillocks of leaves in the corners, a palpable sense of decay and sorrow. The second cabin had dark stains on the floor. I wondered with a shudder if those stains were from the blood of Sarah's father.

Back indoors, I went right upstairs to check on Lucy. As I was walking past Vivian's room I could hear her talking to Harlan. The door was slightly ajar, but I was sure they hadn't heard my footsteps in the carpeted hallway. Though I felt like a naughty schoolgirl, I stood listening to their conversation for a moment.

"I think your idea is very wise, Harlan."

"Which one?"

"The one to tear down those ugly old slave cabins and make that area the gift shop. They're nothing but an eyesore on this lovely property and we don't need a constant reminder of this home's past."

"The problem is going to be Gran, Mother. She just doesn't understand that this will be the best thing for the family after she's gone."

"Maybe your father and I can have a talk with her. She'll listen to him. Of course, he doesn't understand why this is the best thing for the family, either. I'll need to sit down and have a talk with him first."

I walked quietly to my room and slipped inside. If Phyllis didn't want me to restore those old cabins, I was positive that she would be furious if she knew of the plans that Harlan and Vivian had for her ancestors' homes. This would be devastating to her. And I couldn't imagine Cora-Camille liking the idea one bit, either. Somehow I had to get them both to see that restoring the old cabins could be done respectfully and responsibly.

Lucy wanted to go outside for a walk, so we strolled around the house, smelling the jasmine and roses and chasing butterflies. I hadn't forgotten the prank phone call and I was careful to stay close to the house as long as Lucy was with me. We had fun playing outside until dinner was served. It was a rather quiet meal. Harlan was there, but he didn't say much and left soon after he was finished eating. Vivian obviously had something on her mind and ate in silence. Ruby stole frequent glances at me and smiled shyly at Lucy, but said nothing. She still seemed shaken, as I was, over the events of the afternoon. I felt a bit guilty that she apparently hadn't yet recovered from my outburst and lecture, but on the other hand, I was glad to see that she hadn't brushed it off as unimportant.

Cora-Camille left the dinner table early, saying she didn't feel well. Her joints had been aching for a couple days, she said, and she thought she might be coming down with the flu. Evie went with her and then returned a bit later, explaining that Cora-Camille had refused pain relievers and instead taken some chamomile tea and gone to bed.

"Poor dear," she clucked. "I worry when Gran doesn't feel well. She's not getting any younger and the way she works so hard in the farm office would be enough to make anyone sick."

"I think she's fine," replied Vivian. "She's got a lot on her mind with the farm and the restoration and it's not uncommon for people to have physical ailments when their minds are not calm."

Graydon nodded in agreement. "Gran's fine, Evie. Don't worry. If you want to fret about someone, fret about me. I have been reworking the same chapter for over a week now and I'm ready to bang my head against a wall."

Evie laughed. "Daddy, when have you ever let one chapter get you down? Do what you always say—get outside for some fresh air and let it go for now."

Graydon looked at her fondly. "You're absolutely right, Evie. Why don't you ladies all join me for a walk tonight? All of you. What do you say, Viv?"

"That sounds nice. Carleigh, will you bring Lucy along?"

"Sure. That'll be fun. A little fresh air before bedtime."

"I want to go outside!" Lucy yelled. Nobody had asked Ruby if she wanted to go, so I did.

"You coming, Ruby?"

"I think I'll stay in and make sure Mother doesn't need anything."

After dinner Lucy called Brad. Thankfully she didn't tell him that Ruby had taken her without my permission. She only told him that she went out for ice cream. When she hung up we all trooped outside and Graydon led the way across the vast lawn in front of the manor. He walked hand-in-hand with Vivian; Evie, Lucy, Cottontail, and I followed them. We walked along the quiet main road and listened to nothing but the crickets. Only one car slowed down to pass us while we walked.

We walked for a short distance, then Evie's parents decided to go back inside. Lucy stopped for the millionth time to pick Queen Anne's lace from the side of the road and I urged Graydon and Vivian to go inside without waiting for us. Lucy and Evie and I took our time going back in the gathering twilight.

"Your parents seem very happy tonight," I remarked to Evie.

She smiled, seeming to know what I was getting at. "You mean happier than they were a couple nights ago? They fight all the time because Mother can drive Daddy up the wall with her airs, but he loves her. She's the only one who can calm him down when he gets in a mood. She has this thing about social classes mingling, but he thinks it's all silly. Daddy likes everyone. Mother's gotten worse about it since she bought that antique gallery."

We were making our way slowly up the long drive back to the house when Lucy suddenly remembered that she left Cottontail by the side of the road while she was picking flowers. She was getting droopy from being tired, so Evie took her indoors while I went back to the road to look for the lost bunny.

I searched in and among several clumps of Queen Anne's lace where Lucy had stopped to pick specimens for her bouquet, but the growing darkness made it hard for me to see. Finally I spotted Cottontail lying limply by the side of the dusty road, waiting patiently for me to pick him up. I had turned around and started back toward the driveway when I heard a car behind me on the road. It came closer, its bright headlights cutting through the darkness. The headlights swept over me and I sidled closer to the edge of the road.

The driver had seen me.

CHAPTER 6

The car crept a little closer to the side of the road where I was standing and with a sudden violent burst of speed, it started hurtling toward me at a breakneck pace. I screamed and jumped back into the weeds on the side of the road, twisting my ankle and falling hard onto the ground. I looked over my shoulder as the car passed. About fifty feet away, it screeched to a stop and began to back up. It performed a lightning-quick K-turn and gunned toward me again. I dived farther into the weeds near the road as it veered in my direction, barely noticing the pain searing through my lower arm and elbow. It went just a little way down the road and I saw its brake lights come on again. I was terrified that it would turn around and head for me a third time. Heart thudding, I dashed across the road and hid behind the huge stone pillar that stood sentry at the entrance to the Peppernell Manor driveway. The car had turned around again. Like a hunter stalking its prey, the car slowly cruised past the entrance to Peppernell Manor, searching. I stayed hidden until it finally drove off, then I ran up the drive and into the manor as fast as I could. I crashed through the front door and slammed it behind me, thankful that Lucy wasn't there to witness my terror. Evie came out of the drawing room, an alarmed look on her face.

"Carleigh! What's the matter?"

"A car just tried to run me down," I gasped. "Where's Lucy?"

"I told her to run upstairs and get her pajamas on. What did the car look like?"

"I couldn't see it. It was too dark and I was so scared that I wasn't thinking about that. I just wanted to get back in the house." I buried my face in my hands.

"It was probably just some kids out joyriding, looking to give someone a good scare. Let me get some bandages for your arm and knee." She went out to the kitchen and returned a moment later with ointment and bandages for my cuts and scrapes. I also had a large bruise developing on my shoulder.

"Between this and that phone call, I'm terrified. If anything happened to me, what would happen to Lucy?"

"Take it easy, honey. Nothing is going to happen to you. Or Lucy. I have a feeling that the two incidents have nothing to do with each other."

I was still trembling. "I hope you're right. I need to go up and tell Lucy good night." I still held Cottontail by his big forepaw.

"You just sit down for a few minutes and compose yourself. I'll tell Lucy that you're still looking for the bunny and I'll make sure she's ready for bed."

I smiled gratefully at Evie and went to the drawing room. I sat in one of the comfortable armchairs with my eyes closed and breathed deeply for several minutes before I felt steady enough to go upstairs to tuck Lucy in for the night. *What if something did happen to me? What if I really am in danger? How am I going to protect Lucy?* I didn't have any answers.

What I needed was to see my little girl, feel her arms around my neck and her sloppy kisses on my cheek. I went upstairs to find Evie just tucking the covers around her. She smiled at me when I walked in.

"Look what Mama found!" she cried.

Lucy clapped her chubby pink hands and held them out to receive Cottontail. She hugged him tightly and then thanked me, grinning from ear to ear. I sat down on the bed next to her while Evie stole quietly out the door.

"Where was he?" Lucy asked.

"Right in one of the clumps of flowers," I answered. "I think he likes the smell of them!"

She laughed and reached out to hug me. I hugged her back and only reluctantly let her go when she said in her muffled little voice, "Mama, you're crushing me!" I laughed and lay down next to her on the bed.

"How about a story before you go to sleep?"

"Yes!"

I reached for her favorite book of stories on the nightstand and we read until her eyes closed and she was sound asleep. Luckily she had not noticed the bandages on my limbs. I watched her sleeping for a while, listening to her easy breathing. *Should I take her back to Chicago?* I wondered. I had made a commitment to restore Peppernell Manor, but if it wasn't safe to be here, perhaps it would be best if we went home.

But what if the phone call and the incident on the main road had both been meaningless pranks? The person on the phone had known my name, but as Evie had said, that could have been an employee of any of the vendors I had used in Charleston or any number of other people. There were quite a few folks who knew my name and that I was staying at Peppernell Manor. And maybe the car earlier really had been driven by a teenager looking for trouble. I sighed. I needed to sleep on it.

I went downstairs, where I found Evie in the drawing room, waiting for me with a glass of wine. I smiled gratefully.

"How did you know that's just what I wanted right now?"

"Because if I were you, I'd want a drink, too."

We chatted for a while in the low light of the drawing room, being careful to talk only of inconsequential things. Evie seemed to know that I didn't really want to talk about my troubles.

We stayed up talking until it was very late, just like old times. When I finally dropped into bed, I fell into a deep sleep quickly.

The next morning I felt better both physically and mentally. Something about the brightness and energy of a new day always gave me hope and courage. I had felt that so many times during my divorce. I took Lucy into Charleston for school with a renewed sense of strength and without the fears of the previous night. As scared as I had been at the time, my rational mind told me that I had nothing to worry about. And as for the phone call, it probably *had* been one of the employees of the stores where I was spending so much time. Maybe that person just didn't appreciate outsiders or, as I had heard incomers to Charleston described, people "from off." For the most part, everyone I had met in South Carolina had been welcoming and delightful, but there were always going to be a few bad apples. I dropped Lucy off with a promise to see her later that afternoon.

When I got back to Peppernell Manor, I got to work on the walls of the drawing room. Cora-Camille and I had come up with a coral-hued paint through extensive research and painstaking color-matching from several old bits of paint that we found still clinging to the walls of the drawing room underneath layers of dirt and grime and other paint colors. After consultation with the paint shop owner in Charleston, a beautifully colored paint had been developed specially for use in the Peppernell Manor drawing room. Cora-Camille named it Peppernell Sunrise. She was surprised by how bright it turned out to be, but she seemed excited to see it on the walls. Though I had the paint, the walls had to be prepped first. The old layers of paint and wallpaper had to be scraped off as thoroughly as possible, then several cracks in the plaster had to be repaired, then the walls had to be sanded to a uniform finish. This would take several days of hard work, but I was anxious to get it done so I could do the fun part—the painting.

I worked steadily through the day until it was time to pick up Lucy. We ran a few errands on our way home and didn't get there until it was almost time for dinner. Phyllis made a wonderful meal, but unfortunately Lucy and Evie and I were the only ones who were there to enjoy it. Graydon and Vivian were having dinner out with friends, Heath and Harlan were absent, and Cora-Camille was again not feeling well. She was still suffering from joint pain and she was nauseous. Ruby stayed upstairs with Cora-Camille and Phyllis took dinner to her on a tray. For the three of us in the dining room, dinner was lighthearted and fun, a little different from the usual formality. Lucy giggled her way through the meal as she seldom had since leaving Chicago. Evie suggested we go for a walk after dinner, and Lucy was eager to go. I agreed, telling Evie that we would go as long as we stayed on the property and didn't venture onto the main road.

Now that we were in the waning days of September, it had gotten just a bit cooler as darkness arrived and it felt good to walk around outdoors with the breeze from the river on our faces. We wandered through the woods and past the carriage house, where Heath was working outside, digging in the garden that grew profusely next to the front door. In the light from the antique coach lamp he sat on his knees in the dirt, trowel in hand and a big scraggly shrub next to him on the ground.

"Hi," he grunted.

"What on earth are you doing out here in the dark playing in the mud?" Evie asked.

"I rescued this bush yesterday from a house in Charleston. The owners just dug it up and put it by the curb. I'm going to try to bring it back to life."

Lucy put her nose into the bush. "That smells good!"

"It's called gardenia," Heath told her. "It's kind of sick right now, but I hope it will be healthy again soon."

"Me too," Lucy replied, looking very serious.

Heath invited us all inside for lemonade and we followed him into the carriage house. It had, indeed, been refurbished and updated into an apartment fit for a single man. It was full of comfortable furniture, all in browns and grays, with buffalo checks and masculine stripes.

A short time later Heath thanked us for stopping by and invited us to visit anytime. Lucy nodded sleepily, responding that we would.

I bathed Lucy quickly and got her into bed before she fell asleep on her feet. Then I went down to the dining room to sit and talk with Evie for a while. The drawing room was in a shambles from my work. Ruby came down while we were in there.

"Ruby, how's Gran feeling?" Evie asked.

"She can't sleep and she's thirsty," Ruby replied. "I'm going to take a pitcher of water up to her so she can keep it next to her bed."

Evie looked concerned. When Ruby returned upstairs, she shook her head and said, "I'm so worried. She's old to be battling the flu. She hates being sick because then she can't get over to her office on the farm and do her work. Being able to get out and stay busy keeps her feeling young.

"It's been that way ever since Granddad passed away. She started working over there when he first died, and that's what kept her from falling apart. But as time passed, she really started to love the work and now a day without work is like a day without sunshine."

"When did he die?" I asked.

"Just before I went off to college, so it's been about eight years now. Granddad Charles was the best," she added with a wistful smile. "As much as I miss him, Gran must miss him even more." We talked for a bit longer, then I went upstairs to bed.

Over the next several days I made steady progress on the walls in the drawing room. Once the plaster repairs were made and had dried, it was time to paint. The trim around the windows had been removed and taken to a shop in Charleston for resanding and I planned to paint the trim after the walls were complete. It took three days and three coats of the coral paint to finish the walls. During that time, Cora-Camille seemed to be getting worse. She finally agreed to let Graydon take her to the doctor, who diagnosed her with flu and bronchopneumonia. He suggested putting her in the hospital, but she flatly refused. So Cora-Camille stayed in bed and dutifully took her antibiotics. Since she couldn't come downstairs to see the progress I was making in the drawing room, I took pictures on my cell phone each day and showed them to her in the evenings. She was shocked when she first saw how bright the color was on the wall, but it grew on her quickly and I heard her telling Graydon and Vivian how much she loved it. By the time the paint had dried on the third coat, the trim had been delivered and I was ready to start painting it. I set up two sawhorses in the garage and painted in there. The trim was mostly white, but I added coral to the accent molding to make it stand out. When the trim was back where it belonged around the windows and doorways, I took a picture of it and went upstairs to show Cora-Camille. She looked at it listlessly, then smiled at me. "It's beautiful," she said, wincing. "I'll bet it didn't even look that nice when the manor was first built."

"Mama's right," Graydon agreed, coming into the room behind me. "I never would have thought that anything that color could look good on a wall, but you've proven me wrong."

I smiled at him. "Bright colors were more popular than you'd think in the mid-1800s. Cora-Camille and I have talked about possibly making the ballroom a rich shade of peacock-blue."

Graydon looked skeptical. "You sure about that, Mother?"

Cora-Camille made a noise that sounded a bit like a laugh. "You just leave it to me and Carleigh, Graydon. You'll see."

I left the two of them alone with a concerned glance behind me. Cora-Camille seemed to be getting worse.

That night at dinner talk centered around what I would be tackling next. "When do you think you'll be done with the dining room, Carleigh?" Vivian asked.

"I don't really know. I need to repair walls before I can prep and paint or wallpaper them, then I have to do the floors. But I promise the manor will look beautiful for the Christmas party."

"Speaking of parties, I'd like to have one al fresco someday soon," Vivian said. She turned to Graydon. "What do you think about hosting a Lowcountry boil in Carleigh's honor sometime?"

"I think that's a great idea," Graydon agreed.

"What's a Lowcountry boil?" I asked.

Evie answered. "You'll love it. It's an outdoor party where we set up a bunch of picnic tables. We spread newspaper down the tables and then cook up a *huge* pot of red potatoes, corn on the cob, onions, sausage, and shrimp and lots of seasonings, then drain it all and dump it right down the center of the tables and everyone helps themselves. It's lots of fun."

"It sounds great!" I answered enthusiastically.

The rest of the meal was a loud, happy discussion of the guest list and other party plans. Even Ruby, who had been eating dinner each evening with Cora-Camille in her bedroom, seemed excited about it, and she promised to impress with several different types of dessert.

Immediately after dinner was the normal time for Lucy to place her call to Brad. When we had finished eating, we went up to our room and I gave her my phone. By now she knew which speed-dial button to push to get her dad on the other end of the line. I listened inconspicuously to Lucy's end of the conversation, as usual.

"Hi, Daddy."

"Yes. My teacher says I'm very smart." I smiled.

"It's hot here. Sometimes Heath gives me lemonade."

"He's tall. He lives in the small house."

"Really?" Her eyes grew wide.

"That would be fun!"

"I'll show you my school!"

And that's how I knew Brad was planning a visit.

CHAPTER 7

I got on the phone and asked for the specifics so I could make suggestions for his hotel arrangements. He wanted to stay in Charleston. I gave him the names of a couple of boutique hotels I had heard of, then we discussed when he would arrive and how long he would stay. I wasn't about to make his reservations for him, so he said he would research the hotels and make a decision. He was planning to arrive on a Saturday and leave the following Friday. Brad was a day trader so he could work from anywhere. He planned to work each day while Lucy was in school. Lucy clapped her hands and did a little dance, excited that he was coming to visit her.

After she was tucked into bed, I joined Evie downstairs as usual to chat and I told her about Brad's impending visit.

She groaned. "I know Lucy must be looking forward to seeing him, but I wish for your sake that he didn't have to come here," she whined. "This place is like a haven for you and Lucy, and it will be all uncomfortable and weird when he's here."

"I don't think it will be too bad," I soothed. "He doesn't have any reason to come to the manor since he's staying in Charleston. He plans to pick up Lucy from school every day while he's here. I'll probably go to his hotel and pick her up every night and bring her back here. We agreed that she'll sleep here, since this is what she's accustomed to now and I don't want to interrupt her routine."

Evie seemed relieved. "Good. Let him stay in Charleston."

I smiled at her. "You really don't like him, do you?"

"No."

The next morning after I dropped Lucy off at school I returned to Peppernell Manor and got started on the walls of the dining room. It had previously been wallpapered; it had been common in the antebellum South to use elaborate paper on the walls of certain rooms. In the old pictures of the manor's dining room the wall covering was blurry, so we couldn't tell exactly how it had looked. Cora-Camille and I had decided that I should design something myself. I had spent some time in the specialty wallpaper store collaborating with the owner to design an elegant, colorful wallpaper depicting a mural of people walking and playing in a large park. There were flowers and trees, boats, couples and families in their Sunday best, small brick buildings in the background, and several gazebos offering shade to those who strolled through the landscape. Cora-Camille had seen the design on my phone. She was thrilled with the paper and couldn't wait to see it on the walls. The paper wasn't quite ready yet, the store owner had informed me, so I had several days to repair and prep the plaster walls. As I had done in the drawing room, I took down the trim, including a chair rail and the window and door surrounds, and took them to the shop in Charleston that had done such a good job with the drawing room trim.

Phyllis came in one day while I was working. She shook her head.

"What's the matter, Phyllis?"

"Sarah thinks you shouldn't be doing this. She knows what this house used to look like and she says you're doing it wrong."

"We know the house isn't going to look exactly the way it used to. What Cora-Camille wants to do is make the manor look *similar* to how it looked all those years ago. We're being true to the design ideas of the time, although it can never be an exact replica of how it used to be."

"Sarah doesn't want to see it when it's done."

"I'm sorry she feels that way. I'd like to hear her opinions."

Phyllis turned and walked away.

The next person to come into the room was Heath. "I stopped by for some lunch, but I guess eating in the dining room isn't going to be an option," he said with a smile.

"The dining room is out of service for a while," I replied. "Hopefully I can get it done within the next week or so. How does eating in the kitchen sound?"

"I'll eat anywhere as long as there's decent food. All I have in the carriage house are graham crackers and lemonade," he said with a laugh. "Want to come and see what's out there to eat?" His intense brown eyes locked on mine for just a second; I suddenly felt self-conscious and looked away.

But I was hungry and it was getting later in the afternoon, so I joined him in the kitchen, where we found chicken salad sandwiches, fruit salad, and some of Ruby's cherry pistachio bread. We sat at the long kitchen table talking after we finished lunch.

"Don't you have work in Charleston today?"

"I do, but I went in early this morning and I'll go back later this afternoon. I wanted to go over some of the farm books since Gran hasn't been able to do it herself. How's your work coming along?"

"Really well. Have you seen the drawing room?"

"No, I came in through the back. Does it look different?"

"Come on. I'll show you."

He followed me into the drawing room and looked around at the walls, letting out a low whistle.

"Wow. This sure looks different," he marveled.

"Do you like it?"

He pursed his lips. "I'm not sure. It's pretty bright."

I smiled at him, expecting that reaction. "Cora-Camille loves it."

"I know. She tells me every time I visit her," he answered, grinning. "You sure did beautiful work in here, even if it is a little too bright for me. What are you going to do in the dining room to top this?"

"Just wait till you see the wallpaper that's been designed."

He chuckled and then left, saying he had to get back to work. I, too, returned to work on the dining room walls until it was time to pick up Lucy. Much to my surprise, I found myself thinking about Heath as I worked.

That night at dinner Harlan joined us again. I hadn't seen him in several days. He and Vivian had clearly not given up hope that Cora-Camille could be talked into inviting investors to help fund the restoration project and turn Peppernell Manor into a tourist destination. They talked about it while we ate, since Cora-Camille was finally feeling well enough to join us, though she ate little. The antibiotics had taken a while to start working, but maybe she was finally on the road to recovery.

"Gran, have you had time to give any more thought to the funding ideas I've proposed?"

"Yes," Cora-Camille answered, sighing and passing a hand over her eyes. "Harlan, I know you want to help me pay for the restoration, but I've told you that I have plenty of money and I don't need or want the help. I simply do not want this home turned into a for-profit business."

"But Cora-Camille," put in Vivian, "don't you agree that it would be a help to get outside funding for such a big project?"

"I would agree if I didn't have the money myself," Cora-Camille told her in a weary voice. "But I do have the money. And this is how I want to spend it. As you all know, I have been thinking seriously about leaving the stewardship of this property to the state when I'm gone, and I think it would do more good if the state could manage it the way it manages other antebellum plantations."

Vivian sighed and shot Harlan a frustrated look, then she tried another tack. "Graydon, what do you think of Cora-Camille's idea?"

Graydon looked surprised to be asked. He put his fork down and slowly wiped his mouth with his napkin. I felt sorry for him. Vivian was essentially asking him to choose sides, either his wife or his mother. Being a true Southern gentleman, he was caught between a rock and a hard place, but he nonetheless cleared his throat and made his choice.

"I think Mother should do what she thinks is best. This is, after all, her home. We just live here. If she wants the state to administer the property, that's her prerogative."

Vivian looked at him through narrowed eyes. I felt sorry for Graydon, since I was quite sure he would be on the receiving end of a harangue later that night. She had evidently expected him to take her side, not his mother's. Harlan looked surprised, too.

"But don't you think it would be hard to continue living here if South Carolina were operating the property?" he asked his father.

"It doesn't really matter what I think, son, because it is not my choice to make. It's Mother's choice."

"But—" Harlan began.

"Not now, Harlan, dear," advised Vivian.

After dinner Cora-Camille retired early, saying again that she didn't feel well. Ruby went with her. Ruby's devotion to her mother was sweet and a little sad at the same time. She must be very worried when Cora-Camille felt unwell.

I went upstairs with Lucy to give her a bath and read for a while, and everyone else at the kitchen table disappeared to their various activities and destinations.

It was later on that night, when the house was quiet, that I heard the argument between Vivian and Graydon. I felt uncomfortable listening to them, but I really couldn't help it. Vivian's voice was raised in anger and I was in the room directly behind theirs.

"How *dare* you insult me like that in front of the family?" Vivian raged.

Graydon's low reply was difficult to hear.

"I don't care if she's your mother. You have to agree that it's silly of her to be thinking of handing the management of this place to the state. This family would stand to make a sight more money if it were placed in the hands of private investors."

Again, I couldn't hear the reply. I hoped Cora-Camille and Ruby and Evie couldn't hear Vivian's tirade.

She was quieter after that. I could still hear arguing, but I couldn't make out what was being said. Graydon had probably convinced her to keep her voice down.

The next morning I was downstairs eating breakfast in the kitchen when I heard a scream echoing from upstairs. I asked Phyllis to look after Lucy for a moment while I dashed in the direction of the sound. Evie had poked her head out of her bedroom door and Vivian and Graydon were coming out of their bedroom, too. Obviously none of them had been the source of the scream. It had to have come from Ruby or Cora-Camille.

Evie ran to Cora-Camille's room and pounded loudly on the door. Ruby yanked it open and howled, "It's Mother!"

Graydon raced past all of us into Cora-Camille's bedroom. Evie went in right behind him, and Vivian stayed in the doorway with me. Ruby had slumped to the floor next to the door and was sobbing.

Graydon approached us and said grimly, "Vivian, please call an ambulance. I can't find Mother's pulse. She's cold." Vivian let out a little cry and turned and fled to the hall phone, where she was quickly connected with a 9-1-1 dispatcher. She returned, saying the ambulance would arrive soon.

Ruby's keening was almost unbearable. Evie had knelt down next to Cora-Camille's bed and was stroking her veined hand, tears streaming down her face. Graydon had sunk into a chair near the bed, his head in his hands. Vivian stood next to him, her hand on his broad back.

The family needed to be alone. I went back downstairs, whispered to Phyllis what had happened, and hustled Lucy off to school. Of course she wanted to know who was screaming and why, and I told her that Ruby had banged her knee and gotten a bruise. I would have to think of something to tell Lucy later.

When I returned to Peppernell Manor, the ambulance was there and Cora-Camille's body, covered entirely by a white sheet, was being taken out on a stretcher. Ruby walked alongside her mother. Graydon followed slowly, his head hung low. Evie, her eyes puffy and red, held her father's hand and accompanied him. The two of them got into Graydon's car and drove behind the ambulance as it left the property.

I went inside and found Vivian sitting in the drawing room. She was wiping her eyes. When she saw me she patted the couch, inviting me to sit next to her.

"Carleigh, I'm sorry you'll have to explain all this to Lucy," she sniffled. "She'll be so sad." I nodded, wondering again what I would tell Lucy after school when she went in search of Miss Cora, her favorite playmate.

"I'm sorry I'm intruding on this family time," I apologized. "If you'd like me to go back to Chicago for a while, I can certainly do that."

She shook her head. "No, Cora-Camille would want you here. Poor old dear, she wanted to see the restoration before she passed." Her shoulders shook gently as she started crying again.

I didn't know what to do. My instinct told me to put my arm around her shoulders, but I didn't really know Vivian well enough to do that. Instead, I folded my hands in my lap and waited patiently for her to compose herself.

"Vivian, why don't you go outside for a walk? That might make you feel better."

She sighed. "Maybe you're right. I'll go out for a bit."

"Where's Ruby?" I asked.

"I think she's upstairs in her room."

I went upstairs and tapped on Ruby's bedroom door. After a moment she opened it and immediately turned and went over to a chair in front of the window. She looked disheveled and exhausted from crying.

"I'm so very sorry about your mom, Ruby."

She bent her head and began to cry again, soundlessly this time. "I miss her already," she gasped through her sobs.

I went over to Ruby and knelt on the floor next to where she sat, taking her hands in mine. "I'm sure you miss her terribly. You spent more time with her than anyone else. You and she had a very special relationship."

"What am I going to do without her?" she wailed.

Tears began rolling down my own cheeks as I watched Ruby, her thin body wracked with sobs. *How will she ever recover from this?* I wondered.

I held her hands in mine for several minutes until she had stopped crying again. I told her I would return, that I was going to the kitchen to get her something to eat. She shook her head, but I knew she needed strength and that food would help.

I found Phyllis sitting at the kitchen table, wiping her eyes on her apron. Cora-Camille had been her boss, so I wondered if she was worrying about her job as well as mourning her gracious employer. She looked up as I came into the room and stood up to get me whatever I needed. But I told her to stay seated, instead pouring Ruby a glass of sweet tea from a pitcher in the refrigerator and reaching for a muffin from a plate on the table. I told Phyllis I was going up to Ruby's room, but that I would be back downstairs again soon.

I found Ruby lying on her bed, facing away from the door. She appeared to have cried herself to sleep, so I left the tea and muffin on her nightstand and tiptoed out. Sleep was the best thing for her.

When I went back downstairs, Phyllis was still at the table. I motioned to a chair. "Mind if I sit down?"

"Not at all." Phyllis stared straight ahead for several moments. "I sure am going to miss Cora-Camille. She was such a nice lady."

I nodded. "I didn't know her well, but I will miss her very much, too. And I know Lucy will be very sad."

"Poor baby," Phyllis replied.

"What happens next?"

"I don't know. I guess Graydon and Vivian will make the funeral arrangements and then we move on somehow. I don't even know if they'll want me to continue working here."

I wanted to offer her some encouragement, but I wasn't sure, either. It sometimes appeared that Vivian was not fond of Phyllis and I didn't know if she would try to talk Graydon into letting Phyllis go. I actually wasn't sure they would want me to stay, either.

We sat in silence for several minutes, then my cell phone rang. It was Evie.

"Daddy and I are coming home," she informed me, sounding hoarse and exhausted. "How's everyone?"

"Your mother went out for a walk, Phyllis and I are talking here in the kitchen, and Ruby finally fell asleep."

"I'm worried about Ruby," Evie confided.

"Me too."

She sighed. "I called and had to leave messages for both Heath and Harlan. Heath is in court and Harlan wasn't answering his phone. They are going to be devastated."

I hung up and helped myself to a glass of tea, then went into the dining room to take stock of what I might be able to accomplish in the next few days, with a funeral approaching and the house in upheaval. Even though I had received a text that the wallpaper had arrived at the store earlier than expected, I didn't feel up to hanging wallpaper. That could be a stressful job under the best of circumstances. Cora-Camille had so looked forward to seeing that special wallpaper hung. Hanging it would be both emotionally and logistically difficult. I decided to spend some time out in the garage painting the trim that would hang around the dining room door and windows. It was tedious work, but would keep me busy and my feelings at bay for a while. Besides, I still needed to talk to Graydon about whether he even wanted me to stay and continue the restoration.

Evie and Graydon returned a short while later and trudged into the house, Evie gripping her father's hand. I didn't stop them. They looked worn out. I had seen Vivian returning from her walk earlier, and I hoped that she would let Graydon be alone before she started talking to him about the house or Phyllis or anything else that seemed trivial right now.

After lunch I went upstairs to see Evie. She opened her door to me and held out her arms. I gave her a big hug while she cried softly on my shoulder.

"I can't believe she's gone. I wish we had taken her complaints more seriously," she lamented. "They were probably the early signs of heart failure and we missed them. And she had a history of heart trouble! We should have been more attentive."

I didn't know what to say. It was natural for Evie to blame herself. I felt terrible for her, though.

"Is there anything I can do?"

"Not right now. What are you going to tell Lucy?"

"I don't know. I suppose I'll tell her that Cora-Camille has gone to heaven and we won't be able to see her for a very long time. I'm not sure what else to tell her."

Evie was silent.

"I have to go pick her up from school. Do you want to ride into Charleston with me?"

Evie knew I was trying to give her an excuse to get out of the house for a while, and she smiled at me gratefully. "I'd better not. If Heath or Harlan returns my call, I want to be here to talk to them. If I'm in the car, I'll fall apart and I don't want to scare Lucy."

"Okay. I won't be long."

I felt a sharp pang of sadness when I picked up Lucy, who was smiling as usual when she climbed into her car seat. She chattered all the way back to Peppernell Manor about all the fun she had at school.

Her first act after getting home from school each afternoon was to go in search of Cora-Camille, so I knew I would have to talk to her before we reached the manor. I parked the car and turned around in my seat to look at her.

"Lucy, when you go inside today Miss Cora is not going to be there." I paused and swallowed hard. "She has gone to heaven."

"Heaven?"

"Yes. She has gone to live in heaven, and we will see her again some-day. But not for a long time. It is very sad, and we will all miss her."

She cocked her head and looked at me intently. "Where's heaven?"

"It's a place we can't see."

"Can we visit?"

"No, I'm afraid not."

"Will she be home for dinner?"

"No."

"Will Ruby?"

"Maybe."

"Is Ruby sad?"

"Yes. Very sad."

"I want to find Ruby."

"Okay, we'll try. But she may be asleep right now."

"I'll be quiet."

I smiled at her and took her hand and let her lead me into the house and up the staircase to Ruby's room. She knocked softly on Ruby's door. A muffled voice answered. "Who's there?"

"Lucy."

"Come in."

Lucy and I pushed the door open slowly and found Ruby sitting up on her bed. Her hair and clothes were unkempt and she looked like she had been sleeping. As if sensing exactly what Ruby needed, Lucy walked over to her and gave her a big hug that lasted a very long time. Ruby stroked Lucy's soft blond curls and closed her eyes. I think having Lucy with her was helpful.

I left them and waited for Lucy in my room. Evie came in to see me.

"Did you talk to your brothers?"

"Yes. They took it just like I thought they would. They'll be over in a little while."

"I think I'll take Lucy out for dinner tonight. I don't want to intrude while the whole family is here."

"That's probably a good idea. Not that you aren't welcome to be here, but you'd be uncomfortable. Especially if Heath or Harlan gets emotional."

I nodded. Lucy came in to get Cottontail to take to Ruby. Evie smiled at her retreating back. "I think it will help having Lucy around. How can anyone act sad when that adorable little girl is smiling?"

A short time later Lucy and I walked out the front door to head into Charleston for dinner. She was excited. It was a rare treat to have dinner at a real restaurant. As we walked toward my car, Heath drove up in front of the house. He got out and looked away, saying as he did so, "Evening, Carleigh and Lucy."

I looked after him sadly. He had been close to Cora-Camille. This was going to be hard on him.

Lucy and I managed to spend several hours away from the house. When we returned, I hustled her upstairs for a bath and a story before bed. She got into bed with little fuss, almost as if she sensed the air of sadness in the manor. I went downstairs and found Evie in the drawing room with a glass of wine. I poured one for myself.

"How did everything go at dinner?" I asked.

"It was awful, just like I expected. No one said anything and Ruby cried the whole time and wouldn't eat. I am so worried about her. She'll be lost without Gran. Daddy feels a responsibility for Ruby, but he doesn't exactly know what to do around her. And when she cries . . ." She trailed off.

"Can I do anything to help?"

"Not right this minute. I guess we'll need help when it comes time for the funeral and having guests here. Good thing the drawing room walls are done, since there will be a lot of people through here over the next few days."

Evie was right. Once word got around that Cora-Camille Chadwick-Peppernell had passed away, the visitors started coming in droves. All the ladies brought casseroles, and there was enough food to feed all of Charleston. I wasn't sure what to do with myself during that time. I didn't know whether I should start any new projects or whether Graydon would want to halt the restoration. Luckily, he approached me a couple days after Cora-Camille's death.

"Carleigh," he said, "I want you to know that even though Mother has passed, we'd like you to continue your work here. She wanted the restoration completed, so we want to honor her memory by continuing the work she wanted done."

I was relieved. It would have been so sad to leave Peppernell Manor behind with only a portion of the restoration completed.

Lucy and I were staying.

Cora-Camille had chosen to be cremated, so there was a memorial service several days after her passing. Since the service took place on a weekday, Lucy was at school and I didn't have to worry about finding a babysitter for her or explaining what a funeral was.

It was a somber affair, the church filled to overflowing with friends and neighbors and farm employees who had come to say good-bye to Cora-Camille. The family was overwhelmed by the outpouring of grief and love at the funeral.

When I picked up Lucy from school that afternoon, it occurred to me that Brad would be visiting the next day. I had almost forgotten about him. I reminded Lucy that he was coming, and she was very excited to see him.

We were walking into the house when Evie came running down the staircase. Her eyes were wide and worried.

"Carleigh! Thank goodness you're home. I have to talk to you," she said in a rush.

I turned to Lucy. "Why don't you go see if Phyllis is in the kitchen? Maybe she can fix you a snack."

"Okay."

She trotted off and I turned to Evie. "What's going on?"

She took my hand and led me into the drawing room. "You're not going to believe this. The coroner called here today to talk to Daddy and he said that Gran had thallium in her system when she died."

I looked at her for a moment. She obviously expected me to know what thallium was.

"I've never heard of that. Is it bad?"

"I'd never heard of it either, until today. It's a substance that is poisonous if it's in a high enough dose. And the coroner said it was." Her voice had risen; she was wringing her hands furiously.

I gasped. "Is that what she died from?"

"No. The coroner said she actually died of heart failure. But he said that the thallium would have killed her very soon." She started to cry. I held her hand for a moment before continuing, letting her compose herself.

"How did it get into her body?"

"I don't know. Daddy and Mother are at the coroner's office right now trying to get more information."

"I don't know anything about thallium, but if it's a kind of poison, it seems to me it had to get in through something she ate or drank."

"But she ate and drank the same things that the rest of us were eating and drinking, and none of us are sick. Oh my gosh, that must be why she's been so sick." She looked stricken.

"Don't jump to conclusions just yet. We don't know what caused her illness or what caused her heart to fail. Why don't we wait and see what your mom and dad find out from the coroner?"

She agreed and went upstairs again while I went looking for Lucy.

She was laughing with Phyllis in the kitchen. It was amazing that she, without even knowing it, had the power to make people smile even in the midst of their sadness.

She and I were playing a game in the drawing room when Graydon and Vivian came home. Graydon went straight upstairs without a word and Vivian stood in the drawing room doorway, wiping her eyes with the corner of a hankie.

"Carleigh, I'm sure Evie is going to want to talk to you. We found out some rather unsettling information at our appointment this afternoon."

Vivian's words sent a chill up my spine. Looking at her, I inclined my head slightly toward Lucy to indicate that I couldn't discuss anything with my little girl around. Vivian nodded, saying, "I'm sure you and Evie can talk later on this evening."

Dinner was quiet. Both Heath and Harlan were there, but they didn't say much. Evie chatted quietly with Lucy. Ruby still did not feel like eating and declined to join us, despite Evie's pleas. Neither Graydon nor Vivian ate much, and I found myself becoming anxious to talk to Evie about her parents' meeting with the coroner earlier in the day.

After dinner Lucy and I packed a backpack with a few books and games that she had chosen to take with her to see Brad. She was going to take the backpack to school with her in the morning. After a bath and a book, she fell asleep quickly and I went downstairs where I knew I would find Evie in the drawing room. She greeted me with:

"You won't believe what Mother and Daddy found out."

"What?"

"The coroner said that Gran was being poisoned." Her tears started to fall again and she swallowed hard. "I can't believe it! They weighed her ashes and found thallium in an amount higher than what should have been there."

"What does thallium do?"

"It does all the things that were happening to her—joint pain, intestinal problems, pain in her feet. The coroner said that just one dose could have done all that, and that eventually her hair would have fallen out." Her tears came faster then. "She had such beautiful white hair!"

She spread her hands wide and said imploringly, "How could we not have known something was seriously wrong with her? I'll never forgive myself!" She was inconsolable now.

I stared at her, not knowing what to say. I put my arm around her shoulders.

"The coroner said . . . he'd have to . . . call the . . . police to—to begin an investigation into her poisoning . . . even though it didn't cause her death," she said between gasps of air. My arm tightened around her body as it wracked with cries.

The police?! My first thought was of Lucy. Thank goodness Brad was visiting and would keep her occupied in Charleston for almost a week, at least after school every day. I would have to decide whether to let Lucy spend nights with him, too, while he was here so she could be kept away from Peppernell Manor entirely.

"What are the police going to do?"

Evie was calming down a bit. "I don't know. I guess they'll come in and ask everyone questions."

"When?"

"We don't know," she answered with a shrug.

"What does thallium look like?"

"I have no idea."

"Where would someone get it?"

"I don't know. The coroner told Daddy and Mother that there aren't a lot of uses for it."

"Why would anyone do that to her? She was such a sweet lady."

"I wish I knew." Her breathing quickened. "It had to have been someone from the manor. What if someone from her own family did it?" Her eyes filled with tears again as her voice rose. "But we always ate the same food together in the dining room. How could she be the only one who got sick?" She raised fists to her eyes and wiped away her tears forcefully.

I spoke quietly. "We don't know how she got that thallium into her system. Maybe it came from some other source. Has anyone told Ruby?"

"Not yet. She will not take it well when she finds out. I suppose Daddy will tell her. I'd hate for her to find out from the police. Poor Ruby."

We sat in silence for a while, each lost in our own thoughts, and eventually I went upstairs. I knew Evie needed to talk and share my company, but my chief concern was for Lucy, who was alone in our room. I was beginning to feel spooked. I walked faster and faster up the stairs as I thought of her alone up there, then jogged down the hallway and burst into the room to find her sound asleep, blissfully unaware of all the grown-up problems swirling around her. I carried her into my bed, where I slept that night with my arms wrapped tightly around her.

When I dropped her off at school the next morning with a promise to see her that night at Brad's bed and breakfast, I felt a sense of relief that was almost like a physical weight had been lifted from my shoulders. She would be safe at school. And I dropped her off just in time, for when I returned to Peppernell Manor, the police were there in force.

They wanted to talk to me first. I was the outsider, they said, the newcomer to the household. Why was I there? How long had I been there? How long was I planning to stay? Who wrote out my paychecks? What was my relationship with the rest of the family? Where was my daughter? And so on. I gave them permission to search my room, and of course they found nothing of interest.

They questioned everyone in the manor and got permission from Graydon to search the basement and first floor of the house, as well as Cora-Camille's bedroom and the master bedroom and office. Phyllis gave them permission to search her apartment, and Ruby allowed them to search her room, too. When the police left that afternoon, they took several items with them from the kitchen.

I walked out to the kitchen and found Phyllis at the table with her head in her hands.

"They think I did it. I know it," she said flatly.

"Why do you say that?"

"Because they only took things from the kitchen. And I'm the one in charge of cooking and serving the meals."

"Did they take anything from your apartment?"

"Yes. Stuff from my own kitchen."

"Did they say anything to you before they left?"

"No." She sighed. "I better start looking for a new job. Graydon had told me that he'll keep me on, but this changes everything."

"It only changes everything if you're guilty of poisoning Cora-Camille, and I don't think anyone believes that you did it."

But what if she had done it?

She looked at me sullenly. "Vivian will be glad to get rid of me."

"Why?"

"Because she hates me. She doesn't want a black woman in her house."

"Oh, I don't think she hates you."

Phyllis cocked an eyebrow at me. "Have you ever seen the way she looks at me?"

"No, I guess I never paid attention."

"Have you ever heard the way she talks to me? Or about me? Have you ever heard her refer to me as a domestic?"

"Yes," I admitted. "I have heard her call you that. But Graydon stuck up for you."

"That's another reason she wants to be rid of me. Because Graydon is kind to me. I think she feels threatened."

"Well, let's just wait and see what the police have to say."

She nodded absently.

I needed to get back to work. My progress had suffered since Cora-Camille's death because I had spent so much time helping the family deal with the funeral arrangements and visitors. And now with this added danger enveloping the house in its pall, I knew I needed to keep my hands and my mind busy to avoid being overwhelmed with worry. I considered going back to Chicago even though the family wanted me to continue working on the restoration, but the police told everyone to stay local, so leaving wasn't an option. I called Brad and told him that I would come into Charleston to see Lucy and drop off her overnight things, if he wanted to keep her for a couple of days. I didn't mention the police or the poisoning. I just let him think I was offering out of the goodness of my heart.

CHAPTER 8

I got back to work on the trim for the dining room window and door surrounds. I worked steadily for hours with complete focus, hardly noticing the time slipping by and the shadows lengthening outside the garage. After finishing for the day, I hurried inside and showered, then joined the family for a quick dinner that turned out to be rather uncomfortable. The silence was thick and palpable. No doubt the family harbored unspoken suspicions and doubts in connection with Cora-Camille's death that loomed large over the table.

After dinner I grabbed Lucy's overnight bag and drove into Charleston to drop it off and to say good night to her.

When I arrived at Brad's bed and breakfast they were in the parlor playing one of the board games Lucy had taken. Brad looked slightly annoyed when he saw me, his lips in a thin line, but Lucy was thrilled. She threw herself into my arms and gave me a big hug. I hated to let her go, but she was excited to stay overnight at the hotel. She told me she and Brad had gone to a pizzeria for dinner, and that she ate all her food. Then they went for a walk and she got a cupcake from a bakery near the restaurant. She was chatty and animated, and I knew it wouldn't be long before she suddenly became exhausted and weepy. Part of me wanted to stay to help her calm down, but part of me maliciously wanted Brad to have to deal with it. It was clear from his expression and the way he kept clearing his throat that he wanted me to leave, so I kissed Lucy and told her good night. I told her I would see her the following afternoon since I had to run into Charleston to pick up the dining room wallpaper.

When I got back to the manor, I found Evie in the drawing room, curled up on the couch and sipping a glass of wine. There was a glass on a side table for me.

"What's up?" I asked.

"Who do you think poisoned Gran?" she asked abruptly.

I was startled. "I don't know. Maybe it was accidental."

"I'm suspecting everyone and I can't help myself," she said quietly. "How can I trust anyone around here?" She bit one of her fingernails.

"I think you need to let the police do their job. They'll find out who did it. And it's entirely possible that the poisoning was accidental. So let's not jump to conclusions; let's assume everyone is innocent until proven guilty."

She shook her head. "I just can't help it. I hate myself for distrusting my whole family."

I tried to soothe her. "Evie, we have no idea what happened. Let's take a deep breath and step back until we know all the facts."

"You're just trying to make me feel better."

"That's right," I said, smiling. "You'd do the same thing for me, wouldn't you?"

"Yes," she replied grudgingly.

"What can we do to keep you busy?"

She sighed. "I'm just thinking. Daddy asked me to go through Gran's clothes and things and decide what should be given to her friends, what should be donated to charity, and what we may want to keep. It's going to be an awful job."

"If you do it in the evenings, I can help," I offered.

"Would you?"

"Sure. As long as Lucy is staying in Charleston with Brad, my evenings are free. Besides, it'll help keep my mind off missing her."

"We can get started tomorrow night. I'm too tired to do anything about it now."

With that, we both went upstairs. I missed seeing Lucy's small body sleeping in the bed near mine, and it was hard to fall asleep. I eventually did, though, and woke up still tired. I worked on the drawing room floor during the day. I had decided to try to sand and reseal the old pine plank floors, so I moved the all the furniture to one side of the room and started the sanding job on the side of the floor that was bare. It was a hot, dirty job that took most of the day, but toward dinnertime I took a quick shower and drove into Charleston to pick up the wallpaper for the dining room. In Charleston I stopped to see Lucy at a park where Brad had taken her before dinner. She acted like she hadn't seen me in a year, holding my hand and showering me with hugs and noisy kisses, and my mood lifted considerably once I saw her. I hated to leave her overnight with Brad again, but she was safer in Charleston and I had promised to help Evie start sorting through Cora-Camille's belongings.

Brad pulled me aside while I was in the park with them.

"I don't think you need to come into Charleston tomorrow to see Lucy."

"Why not?"

"Because you've had her all to yourself since the end of August and it's only fair that I get some time alone with her."

My thoughts raced while I tried to think of a compelling reason that I had to see Lucy while she was staying with Brad in Charleston, but I couldn't think of one and I had to agree that it did only seem fair that he see her alone for the next five days or so. I reluctantly agreed and gave Lucy an extra hug before I left, assuring her that I would see her in a few days and promising that she would have lots of fun with her daddy while I was gone.

After dinner that evening, Evie and I got to work. We went into Cora-Camille's room, which hadn't been aired out since she passed away. It smelled musty and stale. Evie threw open the windows to let in the soft evening breeze and the outdoor sounds of rustling palmetto leaves and nighttime bugs.

Cora-Camille had quite a wardrobe. Evie and I spent at least two hours just sorting through the clothes in her bureau. We didn't even get to the closet. By the end of the evening we had filled several boxes with clothes for friends and various charities. We agreed to quit for the night and work again the following evening on the clothes in Cora-Camille's closet.

The next day I was finally able to start hanging the dining room wallpaper. It was a bittersweet job, since I felt Cora-Camille's absence keenly. She had so looked forward to seeing the dining room completely restored.

It was painstaking work, and I was ready to take a break when Heath came into the dining room around lunchtime.

"Ready for a rest?"

"Sure."

"Phyllis made ham salad. Ruby made bread. Sounds like a sandwich to me. Want one?"

I accompanied him to the kitchen and we made lunch. As we sat down at the table, Heath asked, "So how's it going in the dining room?"

I grinned. "Great. What do you think of the wallpaper so far?"

He grimaced. "It's not my taste. It's hard to believe that kind of thing was actually popular at one time."

"There's something very elegant about it. The wallpaper almost tells a story. Or you make up your own. I'll bet you could find a new detail every day on the wall."

He nodded. "Well, I know Gran was excited about it, so I'm sure it's exactly what she wanted. I wish she could see it."

"I wish she could, too."

"Did the police talk to you?"

"Yes. They had a lot of questions for me because I'm new to this area and I'm an outsider living in the manor. I guess it seems kind of suspicious."

"They talked to me, too, and they searched the carriage house. They didn't take anything with them when they left, though."

"I'm sure if they didn't find anything, then they'll leave you alone after this."

"I can't believe that anyone around here would poison her! Everyone loved her!" he burst out suddenly. Then he paused for a moment. "Do you suppose it was an accident?"

"I don't know. I hope so. But we just don't know enough yet."

He put his head in his hands. "That has to be the answer. It must have gotten in her body unintentionally. I can't stand the thought of someone poisoning her."

"I think everyone feels the same way."

"Are you nervous about having Lucy here?"

"A little, but she's spending the week in Charleston with her father. She was going to come back here to sleep every night, but I decided it would be smart to have her stay there while Brad is visiting. He's happy, she's happy, and I'm not worried. It's a win-win-win, except that I miss her."

"She's awful cute."

I smiled. "Thanks. She looks just like my mother."

"She's fun to have around. I saw Dad playing with her a few days ago. She made him smile even though he was missing Gran."

"She has that effect on people. I think all children have that ability to make adults smile, especially when they're overwhelmed with their own problems. Kids are somehow able to remove grown-up problems for a while."

"My wife hated kids. I always wanted them, but she put her foot down."

I was shocked. I didn't know Heath had been married.

"You had a wife?"

"Yes. We divorced several years ago."

"I'm sorry to hear that."

"Don't be. She's absolutely nuts."

"How so?"

"For one thing, like I said, she hated kids. But I didn't know that until after we were married. She let me go on thinking we would have children, and then she announced that she had always despised kids and wanted nothing to do with them. And while that was enough for me to want to divorce her, she also stole stuff and threw things around when she was mad."

"She stole things?" I asked incredulously.

"Yup. She'd steal anything from pens to makeup to artwork. I told you, she's nuts. She works in Charleston at a boutique that sells expensive clothes, and I swear I don't know how she ever got that job. That place must lose inventory every week."

"And she threw things, too?"

"Yeah." He chuckled. "One time she threw a plate at me because I was late getting home for dinner. Another time she threw a mug at me because I didn't want to go out with a bunch of other couples. She was awful."

He pointed to a small scar next to his eye. "This is a souvenir from the plate-throwing event."

"I can't believe that," I marveled. And I thought Brad was bad.

"I'm sure you're wondering why I married her. Everyone does," he continued. I remained silent. Of course I wondered, but it was really none of my business.

"We got married when we were too young. Well, *I* was too young. I don't know about her.

"You've seen her," he went on.

"What?!"

"Remember that day we were sitting outside for lunch at that restaurant in Charleston? You and Lucy were in town for the day."

"I remember."

"And while we sat there a woman walked by and seemed to pay a little too much attention to our table?"

I thought back to that day. There *had* been a woman, a beautiful woman, with a white dress and long black hair.

"The one with the long black hair?"

"That's the one. Her name is Odeile."

"She's very pretty."

"She may be pretty on the outside, but she's downright ugly on the inside."

I wondered why Evie had never mentioned Odeile. I didn't know what else to say to Heath so we sat in awkward silence for a moment.

"I need to get back to work," I finally told him.

"See you later?"

"Sure."

I returned to the dining room and worked for a long time on the wallpaper. It was tedious work, matching seams perfectly so that the scene portrayed on the wall flowed without interruption or blemish. I was very pleased with the outcome so far. Cora-Camille would have been thrilled, I knew.

CHAPTER 9

After dinner that evening Evie and I got to work cleaning out Cora-Camille's spacious closet, which had probably been a small sitting room at one time. Cora-Camille had an astonishing wardrobe, but there were also lots of clothes that had belonged to her late husband, Charles. Evie explained that her grandmother had never been able to bring herself to sort through or get rid of Charles's clothing.

"Why don't you start sorting out Gran's stuff while I work on Granddad's?" Evie suggested.

We talked companionably while we worked until I noticed that Evie had fallen silent. She was staring at one of Charles's suits that she held on her lap.

"Why so quiet?" I asked her.

"I just found this in Granddad's pocket," she answered, holding out a business card. I took it from her and read it aloud.

"PM Investments. What's that?"

"I don't know. I never heard of it. But that's Harlan's Charleston phone number on there."

"So what? He's a real estate developer. He probably has thousands of business cards."

"But there's something weird about this one."

"What?"

"Harlan lived in Atlanta when Granddad passed away. I remember because he drove up from Atlanta to say good-bye to Granddad the night before he died."

"So what's the big deal?"

She looked exasperated. "Don't you get it? The only business card I'd expect to find in Granddad's pocket is one from *before* his death. One with Harlan's Atlanta information. This one was printed *after* he died, with Harlan's Charleston information."

I was beginning to understand. "So you're saying that somehow this card got into Charles's coat pocket after he died?"

"Yes."

"How is that possible?"

"I have no idea."

"Well, I wouldn't worry about it. I'm sure there's a perfectly sound explanation. Why don't we get back to work sorting these clothes? If we're not done by the time Brad goes back to Chicago, I'll have Lucy every night again and it'll take much longer to finish the job."

We worked again sorting the clothes, but Evie was pensive, not saying much. When we went to our rooms late that night, we had boxed up almost all the clothes from the closet. Evie had decided to keep some of Cora-Camille's clothing for sentimental reasons, but most of it was going to charities and friends. Ruby had already gone through her mother's things and chosen the belongings she cherished most. Similarly, Graydon had told Evie that there were some of Charles's clothes that he wanted to keep and things that he knew Heath and Harlan wanted to have as a remembrance of their grandfather. Those items were boxed separately and left in Cora-Camille's closet for the time being.

The next morning Evie came down to breakfast early, just as I was finishing my oatmeal.

"I've decided to call Harlan and ask him flat out why this business card was in Granddad's coat pocket."

"Good. I'm sure that you'll feel better after he's explained the whole thing."

"Will you talk to him with me?"

I squirmed uncomfortably. I had no desire to be a part of that conversation. "Why do you want me to be there?"

Evie shrugged. "I don't know. I'd just feel better if you were there with me, that's all."

"What about Heath?"

"I don't want to have to tell Heath about the business card until we find out for sure that there's a logical reason for it being in Granddad's suit."

I sighed. "Okay, if I must."

She smiled. "Thanks, Carleigh. It means a lot to me."

She helped herself to a cup of coffee and said over her shoulder, "I'll give him a call sometime today. I've got a lot of work to do this morning." She took her coffee and went upstairs. I was glad to see that she was staying busy.

After Evie left I took a break from wallpapering in the dining room to begin work on the second half of the drawing room floor. Once again, the job was hot and dirty and time-consuming, but the results were magnificent. After an entire day of hard work, I was able to sit back on my heels and bask in the floor's shine. I strung tape across the drawing room door so nobody would walk in there, then ran upstairs for a shower before dinner.

When I had showered and changed, I went downstairs to find Evie and Harlan at the dining room table. Evie told me that Ruby and Heath would both be joining us, but that Graydon and Vivian had gone out to dinner with a group of friends.

When the five of us were seated around the table, talk centered upon the weather and how happy Lucy would be to see us at the end of her week with Brad. Ruby described a dessert she wanted to try making, which was great because she hadn't baked anything sweet since Cora-Camille had passed away. Besides being happy for her and pleased that she was getting back into her old hobby, I was thrilled that we would be having dessert again!

After dinner, Ruby went upstairs and Heath disappeared to the carriage house, waving to me as he walked out the door. I watched his long back retreating, thinking *I really like him,* then joined Evie and Harlan in the kitchen.

Once we were seated in the chairs flanking the long table, Evie cleared her throat.

"Um, Harlan, I'm glad you came over for dinner tonight because I wanted to ask you about something."

He smiled at her. "What is it?"

She intertwined her fingers several times and cleared her throat again before speaking. It seemed strange to see Evie act nervously.

"It's just that I found a business card with your phone number on it."

"Okay. So what?" Harlan asked.

"It was in one of Granddad's suits."

He shifted in his chair. "How did you find it?"

"Carleigh and I were going through the things in Gran's closet last night and there were lots of clothes that belonged to Granddad in there. I reached into one of the pockets to make sure there was nothing in it and I found the card."

He nodded slowly, turning a shade paler and saying nothing.

"Harlan? Say something. I don't understand how that card got in there if you didn't have that phone number until after Granddad died."

Harlan sat forward in his chair, his elbows on the table, his head resting in his hands. He looked up at Evie. "I didn't mean for anything to happen," he whispered.

"What are you talking about?" Evie had an uneasy edge to her voice.

"I wore that suit the night Gran died. I snuck into her bedroom wearing it."

"Why?" asked Evie shrilly.

"I wanted her to think I was Granddad. I wanted to tell her that I—Granddad—still loved her and I was waiting for her on the other side."

"And?"

"And nothing. I happened to have one of those cards in my hand and I shoved it in the pocket. I forgot about it. The thing is, my idea backfired. I think I scared her. I didn't mean to . . . I only wanted to comfort her."

"You think you scared her?" Evie asked incredulously. "You *think* you scared her? Her heart gave out! She's dead now!"

"Evie, please don't say it like that."

"Why not? That's what happened! She was literally scared to death!"

"But you make it sound like it was my fault."

"It *was* your fault!" Evie was yelling now.

"Please Evie, be quiet! Don't be so upset. Please don't tell anyone what I did. I never meant to scare her!"

"What is PM Investments? That's not the name of your firm."

"It stands for Peppernell Manor Investments. It's the company I set up to help get the funding to restore this house," he said quietly.

"Just go home," she stated.

"Let me—"

"No. Just go."

Harlan stood up slowly and walked over to Evie's chair. She didn't look at him. He placed his hand on her shoulder; she brushed it away. He looked at me sadly, as if in a silent plea for understanding. I didn't know what to do.

After he left, Evie sat in silence for several minutes, blinking back tears. I said nothing, just waiting for her to talk.

"My brother killed my grandmother," she said dully. Then, with an uncharacteristic vehemence, "I hate him! How could he do this?"

I didn't know what to say. She wiped her eyes.

"What do you think I should do?" she asked beseechingly.

"About what?"

"Should I tell anyone what he said, or should we keep it between us?"

"I can't really help you with that. I think you need to make that decision yourself."

"What would you do?"

"I honestly don't know. If you tell people what you know, Harlan will be devastated, and so will everyone else. If you keep it a secret, it may eat you alive. Plus you and Harlan will have to pretend this conversation never took place. It's a lose-lose."

Evie buried her head in her hands, just like Harlan had done just a few minutes before. Her voice was husky when she spoke. "I wish I had never seen that business card."

She looked at me with reddened eyes and then spoke tentatively. "Carleigh, do you think he's telling the truth?"

That was the question I hoped she wouldn't ask. "It's a strange story, no doubt, but there's nothing to suggest that he's lying."

"But why would he have the card with him when he went in to talk to her?"

"Maybe he just had it in his hand absentmindedly. It's entirely possible that he really did put that card in the pocket innocently and then forgot about it."

"Hmmm."

"Evie, I'm sorry, but I really need to call Lucy. She waits for my call each night, and it's almost her bedtime. I can come back in to talk some more after I'm off the phone."

She shook her head, sniffling. "No, that's okay. I'm going to bed. I think that before I make any decision about Harlan, I'll just sleep on it and see how I feel in the morning."

I hugged her and left. It was a welcome change to hear Lucy's high-pitched voice on the phone, explaining all she and Brad had done that afternoon and evening. Another trip to the park, chicken fingers and mashed potatoes at a restaurant for dinner, a walk, and a game. It sounded like she was enjoying her time with Brad, which made me happy—and jealous, if I was being honest with myself. Luckily, she only had a couple more days and I would get her back at Peppernell Manor.

It was a quiet evening. I read a book and fell asleep early. The next morning I got back to work on the dining room wallpaper. The job was progressing well and I spent most of the day on it. Then I moved all the furniture back to where it belonged in the drawing room and took the "after" pictures for the portfolio I made for all my clients. It was exciting for them and for me to see the before and after shots of the rooms I restored.

That evening as the dusk gathered I went for a walk by myself over to the slave cabins. I wandered slowly among them, poking my head in each doorway to gaze at the places where people lived so long ago in poverty and unhappiness. In the semidarkness I was surprised to find Phyllis sitting in the doorway of the last cabin. She waved a hand to indicate that I should sit down next to her. We sat together in silence for several moments until Phyllis said, "Why did you come out here tonight?"

"I was out for a walk and I wanted to see the cabins again."

"Why?"

I didn't really have an answer for that, but I tried to put some of my thoughts into words. "I feel almost guilty looking in the cabins, like I'm invading someone's privacy. But I'm fascinated by them. I love learning about history, and these cabins are a place where history happened to everyday people. They probably didn't even know it. They were just living here, trying to survive the conditions and the violence and the exhaustion and the sadness. I just try to imagine it."

"Sarah was here before you got here."

"What did she have to say?"

"She hates this place. It holds very few good memories for her. And for my ancestors. My family. They didn't care about making history. They cared about surviving to raise their babies and live until the next day. They cared about having no place to go when they were finally freed."

"But you told me she has some good memories, too."

"She does," Phyllis acknowledged. "But you can't really compare the few good ones against all the bad ones."

"I know Sarah doesn't approve, but I'd love to talk to Graydon about restoring these old cabins to the way they used to be."

"Sarah and I *both* think that's a bad idea. Why show people the way the slaves used to live? What good would that do?"

"People would be able to see up close how terrible the living conditions were for the slaves who lived and worked on the plantations. We could even make it interactive to make the experience more real for visitors. It could be very powerful for people, especially children, to learn about slavery that way."

Phyllis shook her head. "I've told you. Sarah would not appreciate a bunch of people—tourists—coming through here poking their noses where they're not welcome. I don't care what they would learn." She got up and walked away toward her apartment.

I wasn't getting anywhere with Phyllis. She was dead-set against the restoration of the slave cabins, especially since Sarah apparently refused to give her blessing to the idea. I decided to take up the subject with Graydon. I returned to the house slowly, lost in thought.

The next morning Heath was at the house for breakfast by the time I went downstairs. He and Evie sat at the kitchen table with Graydon and Vivian.

"So the house belongs to you and Aunt Ruby, Dad. Free and clear," Heath was saying.

"I guess Cora-Camille never had a chance to change her will to leave the management of Peppernell Manor to the state of South Carolina," Vivian said. She smiled. "I'm glad. God rest her soul. Now the family doesn't have to worry about the state kicking us out of our home."

"Mother, Gran wouldn't have let the state do that," Heath informed her. "She would have drawn up the will so that the state managed the property while the family still lived in it."

"Well, just the same, I'm glad she didn't tinker with the natural laws of inheritance," Vivian replied.

"Mother, there's no such thing as a natural law of inheritance."

"There is at Peppernell Manor."

Heath sighed and rolled his eyes.

"My mother isn't even cold yet. Can we talk about something else?" asked Graydon.

This was the perfect opening for me. I cleared my throat. "Uh, Graydon, I have an idea that I wanted to discuss with you."

"Yes, Carleigh? What's your idea?"

"I was wondering how you'd feel about restoring the old slave cabins on the property." I waited for an answer, not knowing what to expect.

Graydon placed his hands together, matching up his fingers carefully. "Well, I hadn't considered that. I guess I'd have to give it some thought."

Vivian spoke up. "Graydon, honey, I think Harlan wants to talk to you about those cabins. You'll want to hear his idea, too."

I already knew what Harlan's idea was—tearing down the slave cabins and building a gift shop. I had hoped that the talk of investors was over, but apparently Harlan hadn't given up yet and now would make his appeals to his father rather than his grandmother. And Vivian appeared to be firmly on Harlan's side.

"Okay. I'll wait to hear what Harlan has to say, then we'll decide what to do," Graydon answered. "Carleigh, when is that little girl of yours coming back here?"

I grinned. "Tomorrow. I can't wait to see her."

Vivian looked surprised. "Haven't you seen her while your ex-husband has been visiting?"

"I saw her the first couple of nights, but then he asked if he could have Lucy to himself for the rest of his time here. It was the only fair thing to do."

"I suppose you're right."

I excused myself and walked into the kitchen. I was rinsing my breakfast dishes when Heath poked his head in.

"I'm just leaving. Say, I've missed Lucy, too. Suppose the three of us take a horseback ride when she gets back here tomorrow?"

I knew I looked as skeptical as I felt. I had told Evie that I wouldn't allow Lucy on a horse.

Heath must have guessed what I was thinking. "We wouldn't put her on her own horse. You and Lucy can ride together if you'd like. Or I can even take her on my horse if that makes you more comfortable."

"I don't know. Let me think about it. She would love it, but I'm just not sure I'm ready to have her ride a horse. It's such a big animal and she's so little."

"I understand completely. Just let me know."

I spent the rest of that long, hot, grimy day working. I finished the wallpaper late in the afternoon. Harlan joined us that evening for dinner. Ruby was there, too, as well as Graydon and Vivian, Evie, Heath, and me. I suspected that Vivian had called Harlan to advise him to get to Peppernell Manor to discuss his gift shop idea with his father before Graydon had a chance to think too much about a possible restoration.

"Dad, here's my idea for the slave cabins," Harlan said excitedly after Phyllis had served the meal. "You know we've talked about getting investors involved in the manor so that it can become a destination for people visiting South Carolina."

Graydon nodded.

"Well, my idea is to tear down the cabins and build a gift shop in their place. What do you think of that?"

Silence. Ruby's eyes bulged. Vivian watched her out of the corner of her eye. Before Graydon could answer, there was a tremendous crash from the entry hall.

Evie was up in an instant. She rushed into the hallway and by the time I arrived, only a second or two later, she was on her knees, helping Phyllis to pick up the remains of a porcelain tray that she had evidently been carrying.

"Phyllis, are you all right?" called Graydon, who had followed me from the kitchen.

"I'm fine," she said angrily. It was then I realized that Phyllis had heard Harlan's words. She was obviously upset by the very idea. She didn't say anything, though. She shooed us all back into the kitchen and she went to get a broom to clean up the mess.

Vivian had not accompanied us to the entry hall. When Graydon sat down again next to her, she asked acidly, "Don't tell me. She broke your mother's best porcelain tray." He nodded and she shook her head in disgust. "Honestly, Graydon, I don't know how much longer we can keep her on here."

"Vivian, it was an accident. You know that. The tray is just a thing and can be replaced."

"Can we get back to my suggestion?" Harlan asked.

"Oh. Yes. I don't know, Harlan. Your grandmother was not keen on the idea of bringing investors into this project. I think she might object to the idea of a gift shop on the property."

"But the manor doesn't belong to Gran anymore," Harlan pointed out. "It's yours now and you can do what you think is best."

I shot a look at Ruby, who remained silent though her lips were a thin white line.

"I'm not sure what's best," Graydon answered.

"Someday the family money is going to run out. What will happen to Peppernell Manor then?"

"I don't really worry about the family money running out. What I do worry about is making the wrong decisions when it comes to this house."

"I think I should set up a meeting for you and Mother to talk to the investor group I've put together," Harlan advised. "I think they'll set your mind at ease."

"I'll think about it. Who's ready for dessert?"

Evie said very little throughout the meal, only looking up from her food now and then to stare at Harlan as if she didn't recognize him. He seemed to have forgotten his admission about his involvement in Cora-Camille's death and was forging ahead with his financial projects. Evie and I went into the drawing room later that evening.

"What do you think of Harlan's big idea?" she asked me as soon as I sat down.

"I don't know that it's any of my business. But since you asked, from the perspective of a person who restores old buildings for a living and loves history, I disagree with him."

"He's flat-out wrong, that's what," she said hotly, slapping her hand against her knee. "I just hope Daddy can see that."

"Don't you think you can trust your dad to make the right decision when it comes to Peppernell Manor?"

"Carleigh, you don't know my father. He cares about writing books. Period. He'll sit down in that room with all those investors and they'll run circles around him. They'll have him signing contracts before he knows what hit him."

"I don't think you're giving him very much credit," I told her.

Evie looked ashamed. "I know. I just can't help it. He has to see that what Harlan is proposing is ludicrous. I need to talk to him."

"If that would make you feel better, then just go do it. But your mother agrees with Harlan, and I'm not sure you want to start a full-scale family war."

"I definitely don't, but Daddy has to be made aware that not everyone agrees with Harlan and Mother. And I think Phyllis heard Harlan; that's why she dropped that tray. She was that surprised. Can you imagine? If someone suggested tearing down your family's old home to make room for a store? She must be beside herself."

"I'm sure you're right. She's talked to me about those cabins and she doesn't want to see anything happen to them. Sarah is against it, too."

Evie smiled for the first time in hours. "Sarah." She shook her head. "Phyllis listens a little too much to Sarah, if you ask me. But I agree with them both in this case."

"What do you think about having them restored?"

"Now *that* might be a good idea," she conceded. "I think I can understand why Phyllis doesn't want them restored, but if this property ever was to be used for teaching, restored slave cabins would be a great learning opportunity. We certainly couldn't show them to anybody in their present condition. Do you think you could do it?"

"I know I could. And I'd love to do it if I could talk Phyllis into the idea and if your father agrees. But I don't want to force him to make a decision, especially since he's the one who signs my paychecks. I've got enough to keep me busy around here without adding more work at this point."

"I'll talk to him in private. I hate to go behind Mother's back, but for some reason she just can't see that Harlan's idea is a bad one."

"Has anyone asked Ruby what she thinks?"

Evie looked surprised. "I don't think so. I assume she's left the decision-making to Daddy."

I wasn't so sure, but I didn't say anything.

The next day flew by. Graydon helped me move the heavy dining room furniture and I was able to sand the bare half of the floor. I was anxious to get cleaned up and pick up Lucy from school. Brad had called me after dropping her off that morning, just to let me know that all her overnight things and books and games were in the office of the school and that he was headed back to Chicago.

When I picked up Lucy that afternoon, she raced into my arms and hugged me for a full minute before letting go and agreeing to get into the car. She chattered all the way back to Peppernell Manor about the fun she had had with Brad. For all his faults, it sounded like he had been a model father while he visited. He took her to fancy restaurants, to family restaurants, to parks and playgrounds, to a movie one evening, and even to a place where she got her first manicure. When we got out of the car she splayed her fingers for me to examine her bright pink little nails. Then she ran into the house in search of Ruby and Evie so she could show them, too. I was thrilled to have her back, even with the uncertainties hanging over us in the manor.

Right before dinner that evening Heath walked in. Lucy raced to see him, show him her nails, and tell him all about the things she did while she was in Charleston. He acted suitably impressed, then turned to me and asked quietly, "Did you give any thought to taking a horseback ride this evening? We could go right after dinner before it gets dark out."

I grimaced. "I don't know, Heath. She's so small."

"What better time to introduce her to horses, when she's too small to be afraid of riding them?"

I smiled. "Oh, all right. But I'm no expert on horseback riding, so I think you'd better let her ride with you. Your horse is gentle, right?"

"Of course. All of our horses are gentle. We'll find you a good one, too."

So after dinner Heath and I and Lucy drove my car over to the stables we had visited on our first day at Peppernell Manor.

"Lucy, how about you and I ride Indigo?" asked Heath.

"Which one is that?"

Heath pointed to a huge horse, dark brown, munching on some hay in a roomy stall. Lucy looked up at Indigo with wide eyes.

"Okay. Can I pet him?"

"Sure." Heath hoisted her up and showed her where to put her hand to rub the horse's strong neck. She stroked the beast gently and beamed.

Heath looked into the stall adjoining Indigo. "This is Chuck. I think he'll be perfect for you, Carleigh."

I looked dubiously at the animal. He was positively gigantic up close. "Mama, I want to pet him, too," Lucy informed me.

Heath picked her up again and she carefully rubbed Chuck's neck. He didn't seem to mind.

"So how does this go?" I wondered aloud, thinking I would never be able to get up onto Chuck's back.

"Just a minute while I saddle him up," Heath said.

He walked over to where a saddle hung on the wall and slung it over his shoulder. It looked heavy. It took him a few minutes to get it on the horse. When he finished, he pulled a stepladder over to where the horse stood patiently. He indicated to me that I should climb up the stepladder. I did, a little tentatively, and swung my leg over Chuck's back when I was at the top. I grinned at Lucy and Heath as I sat there, feeling like I was on top of the world. Heath handed me the reins and gave me a very brief lesson on how to use them to get Chuck to move. I fervently hoped that Chuck knew what he was doing.

Next I watched as Heath put Lucy on top of Indigo and then jumped up himself in back of her.

"Why no saddle?" I asked.

"With two people, it's easier for me to ride without a saddle. And Indigo's used to it." Lucy clapped her hands, then decided she better hang on. She clutched Indigo's long mane. I worried that her hands might hurt and spook the horse, but Heath assured me that it was okay.

We rode slowly out of the stable and into the field just outside the door. I had a hard time figuring out how to use the reins to get Chuck to do exactly what I wanted, but I found that he was perfectly content to follow Indigo if I just left him alone. The two horses walked side by side as the three of us looked around at the twilight colors of the field. Lucy squealed with delight every time Indigo whinnied. I was glad Heath had talked me into letting her go riding. The horses skirted a small grove of trees and kept walking. After a half hour we turned around to head back to the stable. It was getting close to Lucy's bedtime, and I was anxious to get her back into the routine we had enjoyed before her visit with Brad.

We all dismounted with only one minor injury—my pride. As I was trying to gracefully descend from Chuck's back, I misjudged the distance to the ground and ended up on my backside on the stone floor of the stable. Heath ran over to where I sat on the ground.

"Carleigh! Are you all right?"

And Lucy, in chorus, shouted, "Mama!"

I smiled ruefully and stood up slowly. "I'm fine. Just very embarrassed." I rubbed my hand where I had hit it trying to stop my fall. Lucy ran over and kissed it, pronouncing that it was now "all better." I tousled her hair and thanked her.

To Heath I said, "Please let's never discuss this."

He laughed and asked, "Discuss what?"

I nodded and winked and then, taking Lucy's hand, followed him out of the stable. Back at the manor, we thanked Heath for taking us out with the horses and headed inside. As we entered the manor, Heath called me back for a second.

"Would you like to come over to the carriage house for a drink after Lucy goes to bed?" he asked.

I didn't know what to say. I didn't want anything to do with men. But I liked Heath. Was this like a date? As the seconds ticked by and the panic started to swirl around in my head, he must have wondered why it was taking me so long to answer him.

I was just about to decline politely when suddenly I heard myself accepting his invitation. He smiled and turned to go. "See you in a bit."

What was I thinking? I'm over men! But I found myself looking forward to seeing him after Lucy was asleep.

I knocked on Evie's door before leaving. "Would you mind watching Lucy for a little while?"

"Sure. Where are you going?"

"Just outdoors for a bit."

"No problem."

I wandered through the soft night air, heavy with the scent of jasmine, roses, and honeysuckle, to Heath's carriage house. I knocked on the front door, suddenly feeling shy. He answered the door and led me to the small patio behind the house. We sat at an uncomfortable set of wrought iron chairs and a small, round table. He had placed a tray on the table with two glasses and a pitcher of something icy.

"Do you like gin and tonic?" he asked.

"Sure," I replied.

"I like it when it's warm out like this." He seemed as nervous as I felt.

I nodded.

"What did Lucy think of horseback riding?" This was a safe enough topic.

"She loved it. She wants to be an equestrienne now," I answered with a laugh.

"If she really wants to do that, then she's starting out good and early."

The conversation stalled for a moment as we sipped our drinks.

"It's beautiful out here," I told him.

"You mean out here on the patio?"

"Yes. I didn't even know the patio was here. It's hidden by the garden walls." Honeysuckle vines and Confederate jasmine climbed the brick walls that surrounded the patio on three sides.

"I like to garden. Those vines took a few seasons to train, but they're growing well now. They require a little bit of upkeep, but I like the way they look. I've got some rosebushes over here," he said, standing up and walking over to a corner of the patio. "There are some gardenias, too."

He stopped talking.

"Did you hear that?"

"Yes," I answered slowly. "What was it?"

From the other side of the patio wall came a sound like a low growl. Heath crouched down, peering under the bushes that grew along the wall.

He turned to me and said quietly, "There's a dog under there. I think he's scared."

"Come here, boy," he said, holding out his hand.

No sound, no movement.

"I've got an idea," he said softly. He stood up slowly. "I'm going to run in the house and get some meat. That ought to get him out of the bushes."

I could see light reflected in the dog's eyes under the shrubs. He and I watched each other warily while Heath went into the kitchen. In the dim light from the patio lights, he looked like a cross between a golden retriever and an Irish setter. Heath came back carrying a large bowl of water and a crinkly plastic bag from the deli.

"All I have is salami, but that should work." He placed the bowl of water on the patio stones and set a slice of salami on the ground next to it. He motioned me back to the table.

"Let's see if he'll come out of there," he whispered.

As we watched, the dog cautiously poked his head from around the patio wall and eyed the food and water. He looked at us, then back to the meal again, apparently unsure of the situation. After several seconds of indecision, he walked slowly over to the water and salami. He wolfed down the meat—inhaled, actually—and then set about slurping the water. He looked at us eagerly, obviously waiting for seconds.

"He acts like he hasn't had anything to eat or drink in ages," I commented.

Heath pointed to the dog's fur, which seemed to be hanging from his bony frame. "I don't think he has." The dog's fur, the color of ginger, was long and matted, but I could tell he would be beautiful with a bath and a brush.

"Poor thing."

The dog pushed against Heath's hand with his muzzle. Heath stroked its head and ears. "Where'd you come from, boy?" he asked, as if expecting an answer.

"He doesn't have a collar. Maybe he's a stray."

Heath put down more salami next to the water. The dog ate the food quickly, then curled up on a patch of grass near the base of the gardenia bushes and lay his head down on his front paws. He looked content.

"I wonder if he'll be there in the morning," Heath commented.

"You'll have to let us know," I answered. "Maybe you've found yourself a pet."

"Maybe a pet found me," he replied with a smile.

Heath walked me back to the main house. At the door, I thanked him for inviting me for a drink and he smiled broadly. "We'll have to do it again," he said.

I went inside with a smile on my face. *That wasn't bad at all.*

The next morning I was in the kitchen when Heath appeared in the doorway. "The dog stayed under that shrub all night," he told me. "I've been working on the patio this morning and he hasn't left my side. He's a real friendly guy."

"Do you think it would be all right if I took Lucy to see him?"

"Of course! That's why I came over here. To see if you wanted to come to my place and bring Lucy."

I smiled. Lucy would love the dog. I ran upstairs to get her and together the three of us walked outside. To my surprise, the dog was waiting for us by the back door of the manor. He turned and took several long, loping strides toward Heath's home before looking over his shoulder to make sure we were following him.

"Doggie!" yelled Lucy, running to pet him.

"Wait, Lucy!" I called to her. "We always walk up to a dog slowly. And let Heath go with you."

She slowed down long enough for Heath to take her hand, and the two of them approached the dog slowly as he stood waiting for us to catch up with him. Lucy touched his back very gently, mimicking Heath's movements, and the dog licked her face. She giggled uncontrollably, making me and Heath laugh out loud.

"I'm going to take him to the farm's vet this morning," Heath told us. "I'm also going to call the SPCA and the newspaper and the other vet offices to see if he's missing from someone's family. He seems pretty happy to be here, though. If I can't find an owner for him, maybe I'll keep him."

After Lucy had played with the dog for a little while on Heath's patio, I took her into Charleston for school. When I returned to the manor to work I started trying to remove some of the wallpaper in the ballroom. It was dirty work and I was filthy by the time I needed to pick Lucy up from school. But I was excited to have started in the ballroom. It was huge and beautiful, even in its careworn state. This room, too, was going to be a vibrant hue when it was done and I hoped the family liked the color Cora-Camille had chosen, a deep peacock-blue.

When Lucy and I turned into the Peppernell Manor drive that afternoon, we followed Heath in his pickup truck right up to the house. Through the back window of his truck we could see a second head, with floppy ears, looking out at us.

"Look, Lucy," I said excitedly, "Heath has the doggie in his truck!"

When Heath pulled to a stop, he jumped out of the cab and the dog followed, tail wagging, his long ginger fur shining and lustrous.

"He's a she," Heath told me, laughing. "And I haven't been able to find anyone missing a dog of her description, so I think I'm going to keep her. If she'll stay. She's already enjoyed her first bath."

"She's gorgeous!"

"Isn't she?" Heath looked at the dog with affection, then looked at Lucy. "What should we name her?"

"Hmmm," Lucy said, her expression turning serious as she put her finger to her chin. "Let me think." Heath winked at me and said to her, "You take your time and come up with a really good name, okay?"

"Okay."

He whistled for the dog to follow him as Lucy and I went inside for a snack. Over apple slices and a glass of milk, Lucy suddenly looked at me and said, "Addie."

"What?"

"Addie."

"What's Addie?"

"The doggie."

"What a nice name for a dog!" I praised her. "I think Heath will like that name."

He did. "Addie it is, then. She'll love it," he told Lucy with a smile at dinner that evening.

"I know," she replied happily.

I let her play outside with Addie after dinner. Heath watched the two of them on his patio. Addie loved playing with her new friend, and when I went to get Lucy for a bath, the two of them were rolling together on the grass, Addie barking and Lucy giggling uncontrollably.

Heath smiled when he saw me. "These two are already best friends," he said.

"It sure looks that way," I answered with a grin.

I took Lucy back to the manor for a bath and saw Phyllis beckoning me from the kitchen doorway.

"Carleigh, we need to talk about something."

I turned to Lucy. "You go wait for me upstairs. I'll be up in a jiffy."

She nodded and hurried up the stairs.

"What is it, Phyllis?"

"It's about that dog," she said, wrinkling her nose.

"Addie?"

"You've named it?"

"It's a she."

"Stray dogs are bad luck. Sarah has always said so. Even the slaves who lived here a hundred and sixty years ago knew that. Stray dogs bring nothing but bad luck to the people who take them in."

"But Addie needed a home. And she hasn't brought any bad luck. In fact, she's brought only good things. Heath and Lucy love her already. I'm very fond of her, too."

"You mark my words. Bad things will come to Peppernell Manor because of that dog."

"I think that's just a superstition, Phyllis."

She looked at me darkly. "You just wait and see," she warned, then returned to her work in the kitchen.

I went upstairs to give Lucy her bath. I was becoming frustrated with Phyllis and Sarah and their opinions. Addie had brought nothing but happiness in her short time at Peppernell Manor, and I couldn't imagine anyone believing that such a sweet dog could bring bad luck to anyone.

CHAPTER 10

I spent the next day completing the work on the dining room floor. Its surface gleamed in the soft light coming in from the tall windows. That floor might have been lovely when it was brand-new back in the 1800s, but now, with its long history of manor families and visitors peopling the room through the years, of parties and funerals and dinners, of debates over the issues of slavery and Reconstruction and Southern survival and dying farms, it was somehow even more beautiful.

The next few days were a whirl of work and play. Between taking Lucy to and from school, playing with the dog after school, and working on the walls in the ballroom, I had no time to stop for a breath. I was close to completing the prep work on the walls.

Heath came over after dinner one evening and invited me to the carriage house again. I accepted happily, and Evie watched Lucy after I put her to bed.

Sipping cold drinks, Heath and I talked in the dim light of his patio. He was funny and interesting, and I loved his stories of growing up on the farm with Evie and Harlan. He walked me back to the main house a couple hours later.

We walked side by side through the darkness. Twice his hand brushed mine and each time I felt a little thrill in the pit of my stomach.

"Would you like to have dinner with me tomorrow?" Heath asked suddenly.

"Sure," I told him with a smile.

He squeezed my hand when he dropped me off in front of the manor house. "I'll pick you up here at six," he said as he turned to walk back home.

I smiled to myself as I walked into the entry hall and I fairly skipped up the stairs to my room. It had been such a long time since I had had such a comfortable feeling in the presence of a man.

Evie was reading in my room while Lucy slept. "I thought I heard you coming up the stairs," she whispered. "What's got you in such a good mood?"

"Nothing in particular," I answered, grinning.

"Yeah, right." She smiled knowingly and I knew she was happy for me.

The next day I worked on the walls of the sitting room until lunchtime, then Evie asked me to take a break to go shopping with her in Charleston. "I'm going to Atlanta this weekend," she explained. "Boone and I are going to a charity event. I need the perfect dress. We can shop until it's time to pick up Lucy."

I agreed to go with her as soon as I got a shower and changed my clothes. When we got to Charleston, Evie knew exactly the place she wanted to start hunting for her dress. We parked my car in front of an expensive-looking boutique on a street full of expensive-looking shops. We went in and Evie tried on dress after dress until she finally decided it was time to look elsewhere. We went into another shop two doors down.

"What's wrong with the shop in the middle?" I asked.

"Nothing. It's a great little store, but Heath's ex-wife, Odeile, works in there and I can't stand her."

"Is that where she works? Heath told me she worked in a clothing store in Charleston, but he didn't tell me the name of it."

"She's awful."

"Why didn't you ever mention that Heath was married?"

"I made a pact with myself never to talk about her."

"How grown-up of you," I said with a smirk.

"Maybe so, but I just couldn't help it."

Luckily Evie found a dress in the third shop we visited. It was an adorable lime-green sheath with bright white tropical accents. She also found some chunky white costume jewelry and a matching handbag. She would be the belle of the ball in Atlanta. We still had some time before picking up Lucy, so we decided to stop at an outdoor café for a cup of coffee. We were chatting when Evie's phone rang. "It's Harlan. Let me get this," she said before speaking into the phone. "Hello?"

Her brow furrowed. "Hello? Harlan?"

She put her hand over the speaker and said quietly to me, "I can hear some noise, but Harlan's not talking."

"Harlan? What do you want?"

She put the phone on speaker so we could both listen.

"Please, please. No." It was Harlan's voice. It sounded strange.

"Harlan! This is Evie. What's the matter?" she asked urgently.

A different voice, lower, came across, but we couldn't hear what was being said. Harlan replied to the voice, "I'll tell you everything. I promise. Please put that away." He spoke calmly, but there was a tension in his voice.

"Harlan! I'm right here! Put what away?" Evie asked tensely.

His voice issued from the phone again. "Yes. Just put that down and I'll tell you exactly what happened. I did go into her bedroom that night. I was dressed in one of his suits."

The other voice said something. Harlan answered. "Yes. I wanted to get her to agree to my investor idea. I showed her the business card because I wanted her to think that he approved of the idea."

The other voice again, more urgent. Then Harlan again. Evie was yelling his name into the phone and people were staring at us.

"Evie, be quiet and listen to what he's saying," I told her. "You can't help him if you can't hear him. You don't know where he is or who he's talking to."

She fell silent. She had missed Harlan's last remark. He was speaking again. "I got it from a friend of mine who's a chemistry professor. I took it from his lab. I just gave her one dose in her tea one night when I was at the manor. You're right. I wanted the thallium to work before she got a chance to change her will, but she had a heart attack first."

Then, "Please! Please don't!"

We heard a faint popping sound. Evie stared at me and shrieked into the phone, "Harlan! Harlan! Are you all right? What happened? Harlan!"

No answer. Silence. Then a shuffling noise, then nothing.

"We've got to get home, Carleigh. We've got to pick up Lucy right now and head back to the manor. We have to find Harlan!"

She dialed the phone. "Daddy? Have you seen Harlan? He just called me, but he wouldn't talk and he was talking to someone else and I couldn't understand them and I think something terrible has happened!"

He must have told her to slow down and speak so he could understand her. She took a deep breath and relayed the conversation she had just heard. "Okay. We'll be there as fast as we can."

She hung up and looked at me. "Daddy's going to look for him. He'll call Heath, too, and Heath can look at Harlan's office. We have to go back to the manor. Right now."

We hurried back to the car and made a beeline for Lucy's school. I raced in and, after hurriedly explaining to her teacher that Lucy needed to leave a few minutes early, we left together. I picked her up and carried her to the car. Something very ominous was happening, and I needed to get home and make plans for Lucy to go away.

I broke every speed limit driving back to Peppernell Manor. Lucy remained silent in the backseat, seeming to understand that it was not the time for chatting. Evie said nothing on the way home, just staring out the window. When we arrived at Peppernell Manor, I screeched to a halt in front of the house. Evie ran in through the front door and I whisked Lucy upstairs. I shut the door behind me.

"Lucy, how would you like to go visit Grandma June and Grandpa Silas?"

"Yay!" she cried, clapping her hands.

I gave her a coloring book and crayons and, promising to find her a snack very soon, I picked up my phone and dialed my parents, who lived in Florida.

My mother answered.

"Hi, honey. What's wrong?" Moms always know.

"Nothing," I lied. "I was just wondering if you'd like to have Lucy stay with you for a while. I'm pretty tied up here with work, so it would be a big—" My mother agreed to take Lucy, with great enthusiasm, before I even finished talking.

We made plans to drive to Florida the next day. I would alert the school that Lucy would be out for a while, and she would stay with my parents until she could safely return to Peppernell Manor. I ran downstairs for a snack for Lucy, as I had promised her. Before I returned to our room, Evie came looking for me in the kitchen.

"Mother and Daddy can't find him, and Heath is on his way here. Harlan wasn't in his office," she told me breathlessly.

"I'll help as long as someone can watch Lucy for me. Shouldn't someone call the police?"

"Daddy doesn't want to call them until we know where Harlan is. I'll just go ahead and call them myself if we don't find him soon."

Ruby came into the kitchen just then, carrying a plate. "I'm going to make a pie," she said. Then she noticed Evie's drawn expression. "What's the matter, Evie?"

"Aunt Ruby, have you seen Harlan? I can't seem to find him anywhere and I'm afraid he's hurt."

Ruby shook her head. "I haven't seen him. Why do you think he's hurt?"

"It's a long story. I just think he is. Would you come find me if you see him?"

"Yes." Evie left and Ruby turned her attention to making a pie crust. I took Lucy's snack upstairs.

Not long after Lucy finished her snack, Evie knocked on the door. "I'll watch Lucy for you. Would you mind moving your car? I think I'm going to call the police, and I want them to be able to get their cars up to the front of the house. And an ambulance, too, if we need one."

I grabbed my car keys and ran outside. I pulled the car slowly into the garage.

That's when I saw him.

CHAPTER 11

I slammed on the brakes. Harlan lay crumpled on the floor of the garage, a pool of blood collected around him. I jumped out of the car, screaming for someone, anyone, and ran toward Harlan. I knelt on the floor of the garage next to him and reached for his hand. His eyes were closed and blood radiated from a small hole in his chest. I fervently hoped Harlan was still alive, but I knew instinctively that he was gone.

I could hear people running toward the garage, yelling my name. I couldn't answer. I was too horrified to speak. I couldn't think clearly.

A moment later strong hands were gently guiding me away from Harlan. I looked up into Graydon's face. His skin had a chalky pallor. Vivian was behind Graydon, screaming, and Evie was running from the front of the manor. Graydon stopped her before she entered the garage.

"Evie, don't go in there."

"Why not?" she demanded. "Why is Mother screaming?" Her voice had risen an octave.

"Harlan's in there," Graydon answered grimly. "I don't want you to see him."

"I have to see him!" she yelled. "Let me go!"

"Evie, I am your father," Graydon told her sternly. "You will listen to me and do as I say. Go back into the house this instant and call the police. On the house phone."

He wanted her away from the garage. That's why he told her to use the house phone instead of her cell phone, which she no doubt had with her. My mind was slowly starting to work again.

Just a moment later Ruby came running from the house. "What's going on in there?" she asked me.

"I found Harlan," I answered. "Graydon and Vivian are in the garage with him and Evie went back into the house to call the police."

"Is he okay?"

I shook my head. Vivian had stopped screaming. I could hear her retching in the garage.

Heath drove up to the front of the manor just then and jumped out of his truck. "Did someone find him? Evie called my cell and I could hear it ring but couldn't find it. It was under the front seat."

"Yes. I found him. He's in the garage."

Heath ran into the garage. I heard nothing, but he came out a few minutes later with his arm around Vivian. He walked with her to the front door of the manor and hugged her before she went inside and shut the door. He walked slowly back to where I stood, his eyes downcast.

"Harlan didn't make it," he said hoarsely. Ruby gasped nearby, her hand over her mouth and her eyes wide. Heath went over and hugged her. When he held her away from him, her eyes were moist. She used a handkerchief to dab at the tears that were starting to flow.

"I'm so sorry, Heath. I wish we could have found him sooner," I replied.

"So do I."

Evie came back outside and stood with us. Heath told her that Harlan had died, and she stood silently, shaking her head ceaselessly, tears coursing down her cheeks. She put her hand over her mouth. Heath put an arm around her shoulders and I held her other hand. It wasn't long before a police car, followed closely by an ambulance, came up the driveway. Two police officers got out of the car and ran over to the garage. I could hear them ordering Graydon out of the way. Graydon stepped backward out of the garage, then stood at the doorway with his hands clenching and unclenching, helpless and watching. One of the officers came to the door and put yellow police tape across the doorway. Two paramedics then pushed a stretcher to the garage and under the police tape. It was several moments before they appeared again, this time with Harlan's body, covered entirely by a white sheet, on the stretcher. They placed Harlan carefully in the back of the ambulance and left slowly, lights flashing, but without a siren.

The three of us watched it until it turned onto the main road, then Heath put his hand on Evie's shoulder. "I'm going inside," he told us, wiping tears from his eyes. "I've got to see if Mother's okay." Evie stared at him as if she couldn't comprehend what he had said.

Ruby had stood by herself a short distance from us. "Heath, can I get you anything?" she asked.

He offered her a half smile in appreciation. "No thanks, Aunt Ruby. I'll be all right."

She shook her head as she watched him walk away. "That poor boy. To lose a twin. I can't imagine what that must be like."

I shook my head. "I can't either."

"Are you all right, Evie?" she asked. Evie shook her head in reply and Ruby hugged her as their tears mingled.

Two more police cars then drove up to the house, and four officers got out and went directly to the garage. I turned to Ruby and Evie. "Lucy's alone in the house. I need to get back upstairs." They nodded in reply.

I raced up the staircase inside the manor and practically flew to my room. Inside, on the floor and surrounded by dolls, sat Lucy.

"Hi, Mama. Where were you?"

"Putting the car away."

I chatted to Lucy for the next several minutes with the door closed so she wouldn't hear the crying from down the hall. It was Evie. I wished I could be there for her, but I needed to be where Lucy was. I was scared for her. She was blissfully unaware of the sadness and violence that had visited Peppernell Manor, but I was acutely mindful of it and afraid. I decided not to wait until the next morning—I wanted to pack her up quickly and leave for Florida that evening, as long as the police would allow me to go.

I called my parents again and told them of the change of plans. We would be arriving sometime the next morning, and they couldn't wait to see us. Then I called Brad. I didn't want to tell him about the events that had transpired, so I told him instead that I needed to take a short trip for my work. He surprised me by graciously agreeing to let Lucy go to Florida. I would have taken her even without his consent, but it was nice to have it. I hurriedly packed Lucy's clothing, including (as Lucy reminded me) her bathing suit. She loved swimming at Grandma and Grandpa's house. It took me quite a while to pack her bags, since I didn't know how long she would be staying in Florida. I ended up packing most of the things that we had brought with us from Chicago.

My packing was interrupted when Evie knocked on the door to whisper that the police needed to see me downstairs. She stayed with Lucy while I went to the drawing room to be questioned for the second time since arriving at Peppernell Manor. The police wanted to know all about the phone call from Harlan, my actions after hearing the phone call, how I found Harlan, and what I did after I found him. They were apparently satisfied with my answers and gave their permission for me to take Lucy to Florida, as long as I provided them with my cell phone number, license plate number, and my parents' address. They advised me to be back within forty-eight hours. I was grateful to leave them to the rest of their questioning.

Twilight had arrived by the time we were ready to leave. I found Heath and Evie in the kitchen and told them good-bye. It was then I remembered that Heath and I had made plans for the evening; the plans of course had evaporated the minute Evie received the phone call from Harlan. How I wished the evening had unfolded as originally planned. I had packed a meal for Lucy; we told everyone good-bye and then I helped her climb into the car with Cottontail.

It was a ten-hour drive to Florida, and I had some trouble staying awake. I pulled off the interstate twice for large cups of coffee, thinking ruefully that as much as I wanted to be spontaneous, this trip to Florida was not what I had in mind. Lucy fell asleep shortly after we ate our dinner, and amazingly, she slept soundly for most of the trip. I was completely exhausted as she was waking up, full of energy, and we pulled into my parents' driveway at dawn.

My mother and father appeared together on the front steps.

"Grandma! Grandpa!" Lucy shrieked as she tried to wriggle out of her car seat. "Mama, help me get out!"

My mother laughed and came around to give me a big hug, and my father followed suit. I helped Lucy out of her seat and she threw herself into my parents' arms. I don't think she stopped talking for the next two hours, as my parents showed her where she would sleep in their house and helped her unpack her things. After the four of us had breakfast together I finally told my mother that I needed some sleep.

"Dad and I will take Lucy out this morning. She can go swimming, too," she said. "You rest as long as you want. If we get home and you're still asleep, we'll either be quiet or leave again and go somewhere else."

Lucy was jumping up and down. "Swimming! I want to go swimming! Can Cottontail go?"

My father smiled at her. "Of course Cottontail can go. I don't think he should swim with you, though." He was very indulgent of Lucy and would have taken Cottontail even if the little rabbit had weighed a thousand pounds.

Lucy looked at him very seriously. "Cottontail doesn't know how to swim." He patted her head, laughing.

Knowing she was in good hands, I practically fell into bed. I don't know how long I slept, but the sun was making its way westward when I woke up. Lucy and my mother were coloring in the kitchen.

"Mama! Grandma June is coloring with me!"

I tousled Lucy's wet hair, still groggy.

"It's almost time for dinner," my mother said. I had forgotten how early they ate dinner.

"Dad went to get us some subs at the sandwich shop downtown. You like turkey, don't you?"

I nodded as I sat down at the table with them. I felt like the goings-on at Peppernell Manor were starting to take their toll.

My mother looked at me with concern. "Are you all right, Carleigh? I think you're working too hard at that job."

I smiled wanly. "I'm really not, Mom. I'm just tired, that's all. It was a long drive."

"Evie cries," announced Lucy. I didn't know Lucy had heard Evie crying.

My mother looked at her in surprise. "Why does Evie cry?"

Lucy looked at me, as if indicating that I should answer the question.

"She's upset about something to do with her brother. No big deal," I replied airily.

"We'll talk about it later," my mother promised.

The four of us spent a very pleasant evening. We played one of the games Lucy brought, and I took her swimming just for a few minutes. It was nice to be away, if only for a day or two, from the stress that was building at Peppernell Manor. I could relax and let my parents take care of Lucy and me, just as they had when I was little.

Lucy was exhausted and cranky at bedtime, and it took all three of us to persuade her to go to sleep without further screaming. After she had finally quieted down, I dropped into a chair in my parents' living room. They sat on the couch opposite me.

"So what's really going on at Evie's house?" my mother asked. Mom was never one for subtlety.

"What makes you think something's going on?"

My father answered. "For one thing, you left there on short notice and drove through the night to get here. You wouldn't have done that unless you wanted to get away from there in a hurry."

"Plus Lucy mentioned that Evie cries," added my mother. "Why is Evie crying?"

I took a deep breath. "Evie's brother Harlan passed away yesterday."

My mother gasped. "How?" she cried. "He was quite young, wasn't he?"

"He was in his early forties, I think. And I'm not exactly sure how he died." *Not a lie, really. Just a little misleading.*

My mother arched her eyebrows at me. "What do you mean you're not exactly sure?"

"Just what I said. I'm not exactly sure how he died." My tone stopped the barrage of questions that I was sure she was going to lob at me. She changed her approach.

"Is there anything that your father and I should be worried about? Are you safe there?"

"Of course! I've known Evie's family for years. Don't worry about me at all. The job is going well—I've accomplished a lot in six weeks—and I love the plantation and the city of Charleston. You should take a few days and go up there sometime."

I hoped I had successfully steered the conversation in another direction, but my mother was not to be deterred. "Why do you have to go back there so quickly?"

I sighed, exasperated. "Mom, I have a job to do. I need to get back to it." Then I repeated the lie I had told Brad. "I have to go away for a few days for the job, and I didn't want to leave Lucy there. I couldn't take her with me, so I thought this might be a nice opportunity for you and her to have a nice extended vacation."

"What about her school?"

"Mom, it's preschool. It's not like she's missing physics or European history. I thought it would be a great opportunity for her to see you. That's all."

Mom studied me for a moment. "All right, if you say so. But if anything goes wrong at that house, I want you to come straight back here."

I smiled at her. "I will. I promise." I would have loved to stay, but I needed to get back. And I didn't believe that I was in any danger at Peppernell Manor. Whatever was going on didn't seem to involve me at all.

CHAPTER 12

I said a reluctant good-bye to Lucy and my parents the next morning and made the long drive back to Peppernell Manor that day. I hated to leave, not just because I would miss Lucy and I didn't know how long it would be until she could return to Peppernell Manor, but also because I longed for the simplicity and tranquility of my parents' home.

It was with a heavy heart that I turned up the Peppernell Manor drive late that evening. I couldn't even look forward to seeing Evie or her family, since I knew they would be consumed with their own grief.

When I went inside, it seemed that a quiet pall had settled on the house. I peeked into the drawing room and found Ruby in there by herself, sitting in a rocking chair and staring out the window at the darkness beyond.

"Hi, Ruby. I'm back."

She seemed startled to see me.

"Oh. Hi, Carleigh. Did you leave Lucy in Florida with your parents?"

"Yes. I think she's going to have a nice vacation."

"We'll all miss her."

"Thank you. I miss her already."

Ruby nodded and fell silent. She continued rocking and after a moment I went upstairs. I knocked on Evie's bedroom door.

"Come in," she called.

She was sitting on the bed with her phone in her hand. "I just hung up with Boone," she said glumly. "I wish I could go to Atlanta to see him. We're obviously not going to that charity event."

"Will he be visiting for the funeral?"

"Yes, but he can't stay long because he has to go to Tokyo in a few days. He'll be here the day after tomorrow for the funeral, but I'll be so busy that I won't be able to spend any time with him."

"What are the police saying about Harlan?"

"They don't know who did it, but they think it was someone he had financial ties to. Like someone he worked with."

"What about the things he said about your grandmother?"

"Someone in that group of investors was probably upset that he hadn't been able to convince her to sign on with them to finance the restoration of the manor. The police think that when she died suddenly, the person became more upset because there was no longer an old lady to try to take advantage of. Upset enough to kill Harlan.

"They think the phone call was a setup. They think the person who killed Harlan made him dial the phone and wanted me to think that the reason he was being shot was because he poisoned Gran. But they don't believe that. They think it had something to do with money."

"Do they have a name?"

"No, they're still investigating. They've been here nonstop since you left. I gave them permission to search your room. I hope that's okay."

"Of course. I trust they didn't find anything?" I said, trying to get her to smile.

It worked. She smiled. "Not that they mentioned."

"How are you doing?"

"Not good. The police told Mother and Daddy what we heard Harlan say on the phone. About him poisoning Gran. I was hoping they could keep that information to themselves, but I guess they figured Mother and Daddy were entitled to know. Mother doesn't believe it. She says he made that story up out of fear for his own life."

"What about your dad?"

"He hasn't said whether he believes it or not. I think he believes it, even though he doesn't want to." She passed her hand across her forehead. "I have such a headache. I think I'm going to go to sleep early."

"Okay. I'll see you in the morning."

I wasn't ready for bed, so I went downstairs to look for a snack. I was surprised to see Phyllis in the kitchen.

"What's up, Phyllis?"

She was seated at the table, an untouched cup of tea in front of her.

"I told you that dog would bring bad luck. But you wouldn't listen. Now Harlan's dead."

I was shocked. "Phyllis, you can't seriously think that Addie is somehow responsible for Harlan's death."

"I didn't say it was responsible, I said it brought bad luck to this house."

"So you think Harlan would still be alive right now if Addie weren't here?"

She shrugged. "Things will only get worse until that dog goes away."

Suddenly I didn't want a snack anymore. I turned on my heel and stalked upstairs. I was furious with Phyllis for believing such nonsense.

I read for a long time in my room, trying to forget Phyllis's words. Slowly I calmed down and was eventually able to fall asleep. It was strange to sleep in the room without Lucy. I hadn't liked it when she was in Charleston with Brad, and now I liked it even less because she was so far away, even though she was with my parents. I would have to throw myself into my work to forget about missing her so much.

That's exactly what I did the next morning. After only nodding to Phyllis in the kitchen at breakfast and refusing to let my thoughts wander in the direction of Phyllis and Addie, I got started on the walls of the ballroom and sitting room. I worked so hard and for so long that day that I figured I would be able to complete the prep of the walls in both rooms the following morning. The funeral for Harlan was in the afternoon, so I could be done in plenty of time to prepare for that. I was exhausted, but I had kept my mind busy all day and hadn't felt overwhelmed with thoughts of missing Lucy.

I had just come downstairs from a shower when Heath walked through the front door.

"Hi, Carleigh. Doing anything for dinner?"

"Nothing special. Are you going to eat here?"

"I was wondering if you'd like to grab a bite in Charleston."

I hesitated. I hadn't spent much time with Evie since Harlan's death, and I was looking forward to talking to her.

"You don't have to," he hastened to add.

"I'd like to, but I was kind of looking forward to spending the evening with Evie. She's so blue."

"Why don't we ask her to go with us?"

I smiled at him. "That's a great idea. I'll see if she's interested."

I ran lightly up the stairs and knocked on Evie's door. She answered, red-eyed, and I drew her into a big hug. Suddenly I knew that if I asked her to go to dinner, she would refuse. So I didn't ask—I ordered her.

"Get some shoes on. We're going into Charleston for dinner with Heath."

"But—" she replied.

"But nothing. You're going. Come on."

She smiled at me as the tears coursed freely down her cheeks. "I don't know what I'd do without you," she sniffed.

"You'd be lost," I said with a grin.

She put shoes on, dried her eyes, and we went downstairs together. Heath was waiting for us in the hall. He wrapped his arms around his little sister and held her for several moments.

"Guys? Why don't you just go into Charleston without me? I'm sure you could use some time alone," I suggested.

"No," came the reply from them simultaneously. "You're going," commanded Heath. Evie nodded, the tears flowing again.

Heath drove. He had a country station on the radio even before we left the driveway and he and Evie hummed along to the music in unison. I was never a huge fan of country music, but it was nice listening to them.

Driving into Charleston, it felt like a curtain had lifted in the sky. We had left Peppernell Manor's melancholy behind us. We were just three people trying to escape our fear and grief with dinner and conversation.

After we were seated at dinner and had ordered drinks, I thought I saw someone I vaguely recognized watching us from across the restaurant.

"Don't turn around just yet, but isn't that Odeile over there?" I whispered to Evie, nodding my head in Odeile's general direction.

She waited several seconds and then discreetly turned her head slightly. She scowled. "Yes, that's Odeile. What are the chances that we'd end up at the same restaurant as her?" she asked in disgust. "Heath," she continued, "your delightful ex-wife is glaring at us from across the room. Can we go to a different restaurant?" she whined.

"Don't be silly," he replied. "We've already ordered drinks. We're going to sit here and drink them and ignore her."

"She's headed over here," I warned. Odeile made me a little nervous.

She appeared at our table. Again, she looked beautiful. She was dressed in a breezy navy-blue dress, those same red high-heeled shoes, and her jet-black hair hung loosely in a bun at the nape of her neck. Several long strands of hair had escaped and hung gently around her face.

"Heath! It's wonderful to see you! Who's this girl with you again?" she cried in a low sultry voice. She pointed at me.

"Odeile, this is Carleigh. Carleigh, this is Odeile. She won't be staying long." He glowered at her.

"Carleigh. What a pretty name," she went on sweetly, ignoring Heath's look. "What brings you to Charleston with that darling little urchin of yours? You don't look like you belong here."

I looked at Heath. I felt obligated to answer her. "I've been hired to restore Peppernell Manor," I told her.

"I just loved the manor," she told me. "You know I was there all the time with Heath when we were married."

"Odeile—" Heath began.

"We had some wonderful times there, didn't we, Heath?"

He glared at Odeile, refusing to answer.

"He's embarrassed," she informed me. "Doesn't want his new little girlfriend to compare herself unfavorably to the ex-wife." She smiled at me. She looked like a snake.

I could tell that Evie was writhing on the inside, just dying to say something to Odeile. Finally she obviously couldn't stand it anymore. "Odeile," she said through clenched teeth, "Carleigh is ten times the person you are. I suggest that you leave us alone now."

Odeile laughed lightly. "Evie, you haven't changed a bit. Still unable to hold your tongue. Bless your heart."

That quintessential Southern woman's expression, which meant exactly the opposite, was enough to send Evie rocketing out of her chair, her hand in the air, waving for the maître d'. He came scurrying over.

"How can I be of service?" he asked Evie solicitously.

"Please bring us the bill. Something has come up and we need to leave."

"Right away, miss."

Odeile graced Evie with a crocodilian smile. "I'm not making you leave, am I, honey?"

"Of course not," Evie spat.

Odeile smiled again and placed her hand on Heath's cheek. "Bye, darlin'. I hope I see you soon." She gave me one last look, said nothing, and went to sit down again at her own table.

"Evie, why'd you do that?" Heath complained. "That's exactly what she wanted us to do. You played right into her hands."

"I can't *stand* that woman!" she answered shrilly. "I don't care if I played into her hands or not. We're going somewhere else for dinner. There are a hundred restaurants to choose from."

"I'm sorry about that, Carleigh," Heath told me. "Odeile is jealous. I'm sorry she was unkind to you."

"That's okay," I replied cheerfully. "She doesn't bother me."

But she *did* bother me.

"It's not okay," he said, "but let's try to forget about her."

We walked up the street slowly, three abreast, and ended up at another restaurant, far more casual than the first.

"This is perfect," Evie declared. "Odeile wouldn't be caught dead in here."

It *was* perfect. I hated to return to Peppernell Manor. A palpable sense of sadness descended upon the car as we drove up to the front of the house.

"Thanks for inviting me out tonight, you two," Evie said as we climbed out of the truck. "I know I was sort of a third wheel, but I really needed to get out."

"Nonsense," I told her. "It was great having you." Heath nodded his agreement.

"But," he said to Evie, "I hope you don't mind if I invite Carleigh over for a drink and not you." He grinned.

She tilted her head back and laughed. "Of course not!" She winked at me as she turned around to walk into the house.

"Shall we?" Heath asked me.

"Sure."

He held my hand as we walked slowly back to the carriage house. The night was warm and clear. There were thousands of stars in the darkness above, and I wanted this evening to last. I hated to think of the funeral the following day.

When we walked around the back of the carriage house to the patio, I was surprised to see that Heath had set up a beautiful wicker glider.

"Oh, I love it!" I cried. I walked over to it and sank down in the cushion. "This is so comfortable. I could fall asleep here." The glider slid back and forth gently.

Heath got wine from the kitchen and poured two glasses. He sat down next to me.

"To Harlan," he said, clinking his glass against mine.

"To Harlan," I repeated. I assumed Heath had not yet been informed of Harlan's attempt to poison his grandmother or he wouldn't be making this toast. I suppressed a twinge of guilt over the truth that obviously had not been revealed to him, but I felt it was not my place to inform Heath of his brother's actions before his death.

Heath settled back against the cushion and sighed. "I hate funerals."

"Me too."

"There have been two too many around here."

I nodded.

We sat in silence, rocking back and forth in the glider. He put his arm around my shoulders and I leaned my head against him. It was very comfortable. He pointed out several constellations, and I loved that he knew the night sky.

Addie jumped onto the glider and curled up next to me, her head on my lap. The three of us sat for a while longer before I reluctantly told Heath that I had to get back to the manor.

"Do you have to go?"

"I do. Sorry."

He walked me back to the manor and kissed me gently at the front door. "You're special," he said, holding me close to him.

"So are you."

I went indoors with a wonderfully warm sensation. Besides feeling so right when I had been with Heath, I had spoken to Lucy on my cell phone earlier in the evening, and even though I missed her, I wasn't consumed with sadness. I slept well that night.

I got to work before sunrise the next morning so I could finish the prep work on the ballroom and sitting room walls before I had to clean up for the funeral. I felt an exhilarating sense of satisfaction despite the sorrow that pervaded the house that morning, and I looked forward to being able to start painting the next day.

After I had cleaned up my materials and had a shower, I went downstairs to the drawing room to wait for Evie. We were going to drive together to the funeral in Charleston. Boone was planning to meet her there. She came in just a few minutes later; I gave her a hug and we walked out to my car. She didn't say much as we drove into Charleston. But as we drew closer to the church where Harlan's service was to be held, she spoke.

"I feel guilty."

"Why?"

"Because I miss Harlan. He admitted to trying to poison Gran, and I feel like I'm being disloyal to her by missing him so much."

"Evie, he was your brother. It's only natural that you miss him and mourn him, even if he did something during his life that was . . . that was . . ." I searched for the right word.

"Bad," she finished my sentence.

"Exactly."

"You always know the right thing to say," she told me. I smiled at her.

When we arrived at the church, Evie took a deep breath and got out of the car. A crowd was gathering out front and we took a side path to get inside without having to talk to anyone.

Graydon and Vivian were already inside, talking with the minister. Ruby sat in one of the front pews, her head bowed. Heath arrived shortly after Evie and me, and Phyllis came in just after Heath.

"When is Boone getting here?" I asked Evie.

"He should be here anytime now."

We all stood talking quietly in the hush of the church when a tall blond man appeared in the narthex and walked slowly up the center aisle. Evie's eyes lit up when she saw him.

"Boone!" she cried, running to him. He caught her in a long embrace and they stood like that for several moments. Graydon and Vivian watched them and smiled. They must have known Evie needed to see Boone.

Boone walked up to Vivian and kissed her cheek, then shook hands with Graydon and Heath. I had "known" Boone for a long time from all the stories Evie told me, but I had never met him. When Evie introduced us, he hugged me and thanked me for being such a good friend to Evie. I liked him right away.

The mourners started to file into the church, and the family sat in the front two rows in the sanctuary. They would form a receiving line following the funeral.

It was a lovely service. The church was full of people, reminiscent of Cora-Camille's funeral. Many of Harlan's business associates were there, as well as friends from his days in Atlanta. I waited at the end of the line following the service as guests greeted family members and filed out the front doors of the church. A large crowd of mourners dawdled on the sidewalk in front of the church. As I passed among them to get to my car, I could hear faint whispers of speculation as to the identity of the person behind Harlan's untimely death. I tried not to listen to the gossip. This was certainly not the time or the place for it. I got into my car and followed the rest of the family to the cemetery for the burial.

It was solemn and quiet as the eight of us stood above Harlan's grave and said our final good-byes. Vivian was distraught and held on to Graydon's arm. Evie, encircled by Boone's arm, cried silently, and Ruby stood with her eyes closed. Phyllis's lips moved as if in silent prayer, and Heath just stood over the hole in the ground, stone-faced, while the coffin was lowered. I saw him clench and unclench his jaw several times. I was glad when the ordeal was over. We all filed back to our cars and made the short trip back to Peppernell Manor. A lunch had been set up there by friends and neighbors, and the family spent the rest of the afternoon reminiscing among themselves as well as with a few friends of Harlan who dropped by. I tried to make myself scarce since I wasn't part of the family, but eventually Evie came up to my room in search of me.

"Why don't you come downstairs with the rest of us?"

"This is a day for just family."

"You *are* part of the family."

"Thanks. But wouldn't you all rather just spend time together yourselves?"

"No. Come on."

I accompanied her downstairs and went into the drawing room, where the family was assembled. Graydon was talking to Phyllis and Ruby in one corner, and Vivian sat with Heath on a couch. She was nursing what looked like a tall glass of water, but I suspected it was something much stronger. Heath looked up as Evie and I walked into the room. "Hi, Carleigh. We thought you had disappeared."

"I was up in my room. Vivian, how are you doing?"

She sniffled and waved a small handkerchief in my direction. "About as well as can be expected," she answered. Her normally cultured Southern drawl sounded a bit ragged and she looked terrible. Her hair, which was always coiffed and in place, was limp and dull. She wore mascara that had run, giving her the look of a hunted raccoon.

"He was too young," Vivian said to Heath, evidently continuing a conversation they had started before I appeared. "There were so many things he wanted to do. To accomplish." Heath nodded in sympathy.

"Mother, why don't you go lie down?" asked Evie. "I think you'd feel better if you could rest." She looked at me as if seeking my help somehow, but I didn't know what to do. It was clear that Vivian needed a respite from grief. I shrugged slightly at Evie.

Vivian shook her head. "I don't want to rest. I want to stay down here with everyone else."

Graydon glanced up from his conversation with Ruby and Phyllis. He excused himself and walked over to sit next to Vivian. He put his hand on her knee. "Let's you and me go for a horseback ride," he suggested. "That would get us out of here and give us something to do." She looked at him gratefully and gave him her hand. He pulled her up and together they walked out slowly, arm in arm.

Evie watched them go with sad eyes. "Mother is devastated. I wish there was some way to take away her sadness."

"There isn't, though. She'll work through it. Once she gets back into the swing of things at work, she'll have more to occupy her time and her mind, and she'll start to heal," Heath said.

Evie sighed. "I hope you're right."

Ruby and Phyllis came over to join us. "We're going to make something light for dinner," said Ruby. "Is anyone hungry?"

"Thanks, ladies," said Heath. "I could use a bite to eat. All I have at the carriage house is cheese. And maybe some graham crackers." His remark broke the sadness for a few moments and we all trooped into the kitchen to talk while Phyllis and Ruby cooked. All the casseroles that the delightful Southern neighbors had brought to help the family in their time of mourning were delicious and greatly appreciated, but they were very heavy and rich. A light meal would be just the thing.

Phyllis put together a salad of chilled salmon, greens, and lemon dressing, while Ruby took a loaf of homemade bread from the freezer, warmed it up, and sliced it. She had made a bowl of honey butter earlier in the week, and she put it out for us to slather on our bread. While the bread was warming, she whipped up a batch of benne wafers for a treat after the salad. Benne wafers, a delicacy made famous in South Carolina, are a sesame seed–coated cookie with brown sugar and salty notes. I had sampled both sweet and savory wafers, and I preferred the sweet. I hadn't tried benne wafers before coming to South Carolina, and I had decided I never wanted to be without them again. They were caramely and nutty and simultaneously chewy and crunchy, and I loved them. They were Lucy's favorite snack, and Ruby had very kindly made sure that she had two boxes of them to take to Florida— one for Lucy and one for my parents.

We spent an easy time together, the five of us, and we carefully stayed away from the topic of Harlan's violent death. I'm sure each of us was wondering about the perpetrator, but no one spoke about it. We talked instead about hurricane season and past storms and the tourist business in Charleston. When Graydon and Vivian came in from horseback riding, Vivian's despair seemed to have lifted a bit and she was even able to join us for a bit of salad and some wafers.

Heath stayed for a little while after dinner to talk to me in the drawing room, but he was very tired and wanted to get a good night's sleep. He had to begin the process of working on Harlan's will the next day, and he wanted to be fortified with lots of rest before then.

He was also trying to keep up with all the paperwork and payroll for the farm without Cora-Camille. It was a daunting and time-consuming task. He said good night and promised to stop by to see me soon. He looked bone-weary.

I went upstairs and wrote a letter to Lucy. She would love receiving mail at my parents' house. I drew her a picture of Addie in the letter so she could show her grandparents her new best friend.

CHAPTER 13

The next day I started on the walls of the ballroom. I couldn't wait to see them finished in their deep peacock blue. I wondered how the rest of the family would react when they saw the color Cora-Camille had chosen before her death.

But Graydon and Ruby were now the owners of Peppernell Manor. I could have consulted them regarding the color of the walls, but I had a theory. If I showed them a swatch of the jewel tone that Cora-Camille had chosen, they might panic and think the color was too dramatic for the ballroom. If I went ahead and restored the walls with the rich hue, then they could see it in all its glory before forming an opinion of the color. At that point, if they didn't like the color and wanted to change it, then at least they could have a chance to see the room as Cora-Camille had envisioned it.

So I decided to go ahead, paint the room, and *then* ask everyone's opinion. I got started right away. I spent the entire day taking down all the wooden trim around the windows and doorways in the ballroom and sitting room, just as I had done in the drawing room and the dining room. I sent them to the same shop in Charleston that had resanded all the other woodwork, then set up sawhorses in the basement to paint them when they were completed and returned.

I would normally have kept the sawhorses in the garage, but no one had been allowed in there since the day of Harlan's death. The police were still investigating and the space was still considered a crime scene. I hoped I would never have to go into the garage again, even after the crime had been solved and the person responsible had been brought to justice.

When I was done working for the day, I found Heath waiting for me in the drawing room. "Want to go for another horseback ride after dinner? I need a couple hours off," he told me.

"Sure," I replied happily. It would be nice to go horseback riding without having to worry about Lucy falling off and getting hurt.

The family and I had dinner together in the dining room. It was slightly less gloomy than the previous days had been. Vivian had gone into her store that day and received a new shipment of antiques. She described them as "exquisite" and told us all about them and where they had come from. Graydon had spent the day locked in his office, working on some ideas for a new book. He bounced ideas around at dinner and we gave him our input and critiques. In all, it was a relatively normal meal, albeit without Harlan and Cora-Camille. Their absences were felt, but it was nice to talk of things other than death and violence.

After dinner Heath and I drove over to the stables. I rode Chuck again and Heath climbed up onto Indigo's back.

"There's a story behind every horse's name," I said. "What are the stories behind these two?"

Heath held Indigo's reins lightly and steered the giant horse down a dirt path that ran along the woods beyond the stable. I followed, a little less expertly.

"Chuck is named after my grandfather. Gran called him Charles from the time they were first introduced, but all of his friends called him Chuck. Gran didn't like the nickname and refused to acknowledge it. The horse's name was kind of a joke. Gran loved Chuck."

"That's a good story."

"And Indigo got her name because long before Peppernell Manor was a farm, it was a rice plantation. And before that, it was an indigo farm. Indigo used to be a very popular crop in South Carolina, but the industry eventually died out and lots of indigo fields became rice fields instead over the years. Indigo is sort of a nod to Peppernell Manor's history."

"I like that."

"Everything around here is symbolic of some aspect of Peppernell Manor's past."

"That's why I love working here. I love learning the history of a place. And when I can incorporate it into my work, it's even better. That's part of the reason I've talked to Graydon about restoring the slave cabins."

"I don't know whether Dad has made up his mind about that," Heath replied. "You should ask him again."

"Well, with all that's gone on lately, that issue has sort of been put on the back burner. And that's fine with me. I have lots of other work to keep me busy."

"I don't agree with the plan that Harlan had for the slave cabins, but I know Mother agreed with him. You may want to talk to Dad before Mother has a chance to persuade him to do what Harlan wanted simply for emotional reasons. If you'd like, I can talk to him," he offered.

"No, thanks. I'll talk to him." We rode along in silence for a while, listening to the quiet noises of the twilight. From a distance, a dog barked. Nearby, invisible frogs and crickets were croaking and chirping in a cacophony of rhythmic, peaceful sounds.

"What a beautiful time of day," I sighed. "Especially now since the evenings are a little cooler."

He nodded in agreement. "It's a lot easier to work on the farm when the weather gets cooler. It's brutal out there in the heat of the day in summer."

We rounded the far end of a field behind the stable and headed back along the other side of the long rows of autumn vegetables. The stable was barely visible in the darkness that had fallen. Its old-fashioned lamp glimmered faintly in the distance. Heath led the way through a narrower part of the path, then turned on Indigo's back to wait for me.

"I've been meaning to ask you something," he said.

"What is it?"

"What are your plans for Thanksgiving?"

I hadn't even thought about Thanksgiving. "I suppose I'll spend it with my parents in Florida. I'm hoping that by then everything here has gotten back to normal and Lucy is back with me. My parents will be dying to see her again."

"Oh."

"Why?"

"I was wondering if you'd like to spend it here with me. With my family."

He had taken me by surprise. "I don't know," I answered truthfully. "I think we'll have to wait and see what happens here and when I'm able to get Lucy back."

"Would you spend it here if you could?"

"Sure. I'd like that." I could see him smiling at me through the semidarkness. I marveled at how, so recently, I had shied away from any involvement with men. Suddenly I was talking about spending the holidays with Heath's family, and it felt right and comfortable.

We rode the rest of the way back to the stable in the quiet, and I dismounted into his arms, more gracefully than I had "dismounted" the first time I slid off Chuck. "Much better than last time!" Heath said, then he kissed me and laughed.

I looked at him sternly. "You were never supposed to mention that again!" He took my hand and we walked back to the truck.

Once again at the manor, I told him good night. He asked me to come to the carriage house for a bit, but I wanted to talk to Evie. I went straight up to her room.

"What's up?" she asked.

"You coming downstairs?"

"Sure. I thought you were out with Heath."

"I told him I needed to talk to you tonight instead."

"Wow—I must rate!"

I grinned. "Come on. Want a glass of wine?"

A few moments later we were seated facing each other on the sofa in the drawing room. Evie sighed. "This is just like the way it used to be. Just us girls."

"I feel almost guilty without Lucy here," I told her. "But she's safer with my parents."

"Are you going down to see her this weekend?"

"Yes. I'll leave at about three o'clock Saturday morning and be there by midmorning."

Evie changed the subject. "So, what's up with you and Heath?"

I could feel my face turning red. She laughed. "I like him," I told her almost conspiratorially.

"He is nuts over you," she replied. "If you knew him as well as I do, you'd realize it. He has been totally anti-dating since he divorced Odeile. He never wanted to have to put up with another woman again. But now you're here and all of a sudden he's going horseback riding and finding excuses to come over to the main house and he bought a glider and you two are having these little chats under the stars on his patio . . ."

"I came to South Carolina not wanting to date anyone because of my experience with Brad. But I feel so comfortable with Heath, it's impossible to keep my promise to myself about no dating."

"Heath is great," Evie told me. "He's a gentleman, he's respectful, he's kind, he's funny. Plus, he thinks the world of Lucy—what more could anyone ask for?"

"Not a thing," I answered truthfully.

We engaged in girl talk for a while longer before going upstairs to our respective rooms. I could hear Addie barking outdoors as I got ready for bed. Once she quieted down, I listened to the sounds of the night through the open window. A breeze fluttered the curtains and the room felt cool and comfortable. I think I fell asleep almost instantly.

I worked steadily for the next several days on the painting in the ballroom. When I stood back to look at the walls at the end of each day, I was very pleased with the progress. The room was vibrant—perfect for holding parties and balls, just as it had been in the 1800s. It took several coats of the peacock blue paint to completely cover the plaster, and then I got to work on the window and door trim, which had been returned from Charleston. The trim for this room wasn't just paint; in consultation with Cora-Camille, I had ordered special strips of gold leaf and thin strips of brightly patterned rich blue fabric to add to the trim and complement the walls. The new strips would be fitted around the existing window and door trim and I was excited to see them completed. The textile shop owner had been out to the manor to make precise measurements, and she came out again, this time with several staff members, to supervise the hanging of the strips. When her crew had finished, she beamed with pride and took lots of pictures that she intended to display in her store.

When the week came to a close, I was exhausted. Heath ordered takeout and he and I ate a quiet dinner on his patio. Evie had to work through dinner that evening, so it would have just been me, Graydon, Vivian, and Ruby in the dining room. Having dinner with Heath—just the two of us—was a much more appealing option.

We went for a short walk around the property after dinner. Addie joined us, jumping and barking the entire way. She would run off, then return, then repeat her antics. Heath left me at the front door of the manor. He wrapped me in a huge hug before kissing me and letting me go inside. I was going to miss him while I visited Lucy, but I was so excited to be spending the weekend with her that I could think of little else.

I left very late that night. I sped along the interstate to my parents' house in the total darkness with no other cars to keep me company. My thoughts kept returning to Harlan and his plan for Peppernell Manor. It didn't seem right to have the house and property managed by some impersonal group of people who were only interested in a return on their investment. I also needed to have a discussion with Graydon regarding his ideas for the slave cabins. The more I thought about it, the more I really wanted to get my hands on those slave cabins and restore them to their original condition and appearance. If Graydon consented to the restoration, I would have a heart-to-heart with Phyllis and try again to make her understand how crucial it was to preserve such important remnants of American history. Transforming those old cabins into a gift shop was unthinkable and, in my opinion, a desecration of the manor's past.

I pulled into my parents' driveway midmorning and was greeted by Lucy flinging herself out the front door and into my arms. I caught her up and spun her around, as happy as I'd ever been. I had missed her very much while I was back at Peppernell Manor, but I hadn't realized just how much until she was with me again. Lucy and I and my parents spent the day together, taking walks and swimming.

The next day the four of us went to a state park. We spent hours there, taking a short hike and enjoying a picnic. We took a boat ride to see the manatees lounging in the warm water, and Lucy was thrilled to see the slow, lumbering sea cows. She was delighted to watch them devouring fat heads of lettuce and leafy bunches of beets and carrots. I was sorry when our time at the park ended, because it meant I would be leaving soon to return to South Carolina. Lucy and I read a couple of books while my mother made dinner, and we enjoyed our visit together until it was time for me to head back to the manor. I promised to return soon, and I left with tears in my eyes. Lucy, in my father's arms, waved at me until I turned the corner, and I let myself pull over and cry for a few minutes before continuing on my trip.

I turned down the allée of Peppernell Manor at dawn. With only a short time to sleep before I needed to get to work in the sitting room, I went straight upstairs and fell into bed.

A few hours later I was eating breakfast when Heath walked into the kitchen. He smiled and scooped me up from the table and wrapped his long arms around me.

"I sure missed you," he said into my hair. "I didn't realize how much I would miss you until you were gone!"

He held me away from him and stared at me for a few moments. I could feel my cheeks getting hot. "I missed you, too," I told him.

He gathered me to his chest again. "Don't leave without me anymore, okay?"

I gave him a big smile. "Whatever you say."

"What are you working on today?"

"I need to get started in the small sitting room next to the ballroom. I have the paint and I've prepped the walls, so I'm going to start painting this morning. Have you seen the ballroom?" I was eager to hear his thoughts.

He cocked an eyebrow at me. "Maybe I'm just too traditional, but it's about the brightest room I ever saw. Gran picked that out?"

I grinned. "She sure did. And the funny thing is, that *is* a traditional color for a ballroom. So many places now are painted in pastels and neutrals that bold colors look out of place sometimes, but bold colors were very popular when this house was built. Cora-Camille wanted to go back to the manor's roots."

"Well, if that's what she wanted, she sure got it," he said and smiled. "What color is the sitting room going to be? I almost hate to ask."

I laughed. "I think you'll like it. At least you'll like it more than the ballroom. It's going to be a light shade of coral. Almost like a pink."

He winked at me. "We'll see. Now, not to change the subject, but will you have time to go out to lunch with me today?"

I shook my head. "I'm sorry. I took the whole weekend off to see Lucy, and now I'm feeling the pressure to get the walls started in the sitting room. I have to finish the walls and the trim, do the floors in the ballroom and sitting room, and finish the entry hall before the holidays start. They'll be here before I know it."

"Okay. I'll be here for dinner, then. How's Lucy?"

I smiled. "She's having a great time with my parents. And I think they're having just as much fun as she is. I can't wait to bring her back here."

He smiled back at me. "I'm glad you got a chance to see her. I'll talk to you later." He left then and I got to work in the sitting room. The paint was indeed a delicate and soothing shade and actually complemented the color of the ballroom nicely. My plan, in keeping with Cora-Camille's wishes, was to keep the sitting room simple and free of "fuss," as she called decorative adornments. I was able to paint the entire room with a first coat before hurrying upstairs to shower before dinner.

All six of us were there for dinner that night—Graydon, Vivian, Heath, Evie, Ruby, and me. The atmosphere was slightly livelier than it had been before I left for Florida. Vivian wanted to talk about the ballroom, which she loved. I sat next to her and we discussed ways to decorate the ballroom for her Christmas open house. Graydon listened to our chatter briefly and decided he'd rather talk to Heath about the farm. He did give his blessing to the color of the ballroom, but he said he would need some time to get used to it. Ruby liked it. She said the color was happy and cheerful. She even chimed in with some ideas of her own for the open house, such as what types of finger foods should be served. She indicated that she would love to be involved in cooking the desserts. I thought they were good ideas, but Vivian tactfully indicated her distaste for Ruby's input, saying that she hadn't decided whether the entire party should be catered by *professionals*. I don't know if Ruby felt the sting of Vivian's rejection, but if she did, she didn't show it.

After dinner Heath and I went for a walk. I steered him over to the slave cabins and we went inside the first one we came to.

"How long has it been since you've been in one of these cabins?" I asked him.

"A long time," he replied absently, looking slowly around at the inside of the tiny dwelling.

"Is this the way you remember it?"

"Yeah, but it's a little more run-down than the last time I was in here. And there are more leaves and twigs in the corners."

"I like visiting these cabins. They're so quiet. They're so different from all the fancy trimmings in the manor house," I said. Heath reached for my hand and we walked out the door into the South Carolina twilight. The soft scent of pine wafted around us as we wandered slowly among the cabins.

"Not many people would choose to come out and visit these old slave quarters to find quiet. They'd go to the river or out on the veranda. That's one of the many things I love about you. You're so connected to history. You have a strong sense of place and respect for things that no longer exist. Are you sure you weren't born in the South?"

I smiled at him. "Do you think I'm spontaneous?"

He looked surprised. "I guess I never really thought about it. I don't know . . . it's probably not a word I would use to describe you. Why do you ask?"

I blushed. "It's silly, really. My ex-husband accused me of not being spontaneous."

"You say that like it's a bad thing."

"He said I was boring."

"Now wait a minute. Just because you're not spontaneous doesn't mean you're boring. I happen to think you're exciting. You're smart, you're fun, and you're a wonderful mother to that little girl of yours. Spontaneity is not all it's cracked up to be, if you ask me. Maybe your ex-husband needs to grow up a little."

It was as if Heath knew exactly what I wanted to hear, but more than that, I knew he was telling me the truth. He really didn't care that I wasn't wild and unpredictable. He seemed to like me just the way I was. His next words confirmed it.

"I love you, Carleigh. Just the way you are."

I was speechless for a moment. I looked up at his handsome face, those dark eyes looking at me from behind his tortoiseshell glasses.

"I love you, too, Heath."

CHAPTER 14

I floated on air the next several days. I worked steadily in a happy fog, completing the walls of the sitting room and beginning the floors in both the ballroom and the sitting room. Vivian and Graydon were pleased with my progress and Vivian began planning her holiday open house in earnest. One evening as we gathered in the dining room for dinner, I noticed that there were two extra places set at the table. I knew Heath was in his office in Charleston, working late on a case that was going to trial, so he wouldn't be around.

I nodded at the extra place settings and asked Evie, "Who's joining us for dinner?"

She shrugged. "I have no idea. No one told me anything."

Graydon came in then and sat down. "Girls, why are you standing around?"

"There are two extra spots at the table and we were just wondering who's going to be here besides us," answered Evie.

"Oh. I don't know. Maybe your mother invited some friends over. Sit down. You're making me nervous."

Evie smiled at her father. We sat down and waited for Ruby, Vivian, and the dinner guests. Ruby came downstairs shortly and took her place at the table, and then we heard the front door open. Along with Vivian's, we could hear other voices, but I didn't recognize them. Vivian swept into the room and beckoned to the people standing behind her in the doorway.

"Graydon, I'd like you to meet James and Abigail, two of the people that were part of Harlan's Peppernell Manor investment group. I thought it was high time that we had a talk with them about the manor and its property and what the plans are for it. As far as the group is concerned, that is."

I quickly looked at Evie, who was staring at her mother. Graydon betrayed nothing, though I suspected that he wished Vivian had informed him of this meeting. He stood up, smiling, and shook hands firmly with James and Abigail. He then introduced the rest of us at the table. He insisted upon small talk and friendly conversation during dinner, then when Phyllis had served dessert he finally asked James and Abigail what the investment group had in mind for Peppernell Manor.

James answered first. "As you know, it was Harlan's vision to convert this property to a commercial destination. The group is interested in furthering his goal by possibly looking into having an inn on the property, as well as a restaurant and a small conference or event center."

"That's right. Our preliminary research has shown that there is a desire in this area for a facility that can host intimate parties, weddings, corporate retreats, and other events. Not large ones, mind you, but fairly small ones," Abigail added.

Vivian was beaming. "Graydon, doesn't that sound wonderful? Imagine Peppernell Manor used as a backdrop for social events and weddings! I think it's a delightful idea!" she gushed.

"This is where we live."

The words came from Ruby. She hadn't spoken since James and Abigail had been introduced, and I think we had all forgotten she was there.

James and Abigail clearly didn't know how to respond to her statement.

"Well," James began, looking to Vivian for help, "well, don't you agree that it would be nice if other people could use Peppernell Manor for important events?"

"No."

"But they would pay for such a privilege, and your family would be the beneficiaries of some of that money. A little bit extra never hurt anyone."

Ruby stared at him without speaking.

Vivian jumped in, apparently trying to help James. "Ruby, we obviously wouldn't use the main house for the bed and breakfast. We'd continue to live here and build the inn elsewhere on the property."

Ruby ignored her and turned her attention to Graydon. "You know this isn't the way Mother wanted her home to be used."

"Well, I think it's only fair to at least consider what these people have to say."

"What about the farm? What about the cabins? What about all the other special buildings, like the carriage house and the barn?"

"That's what we need to hear them talk about, Ruby," Graydon answered.

She sat sullenly in her chair like a chastised child. James continued. "We think the carriage house would be a perfect spot for a small restaurant."

I raised my eyebrows. Heath's home. They couldn't turn that into a restaurant! I desperately wanted to say something, but it wasn't my place. I wasn't part of the family and this wasn't my home. I looked beseechingly at Evie. She cleared her throat.

"Daddy, don't you think that Heath should be here to listen to these plans? After all, it's his house they're talking about."

Graydon rubbed his eyes. "Yes, Evie. I think you're right. Vivian, we can't make any decisions without Heath."

Abigail hastened to chime in. "You understand, of course, that these are just preliminary discussions. We're not looking to have anyone move out yet." I exchanged glances with Evie. *Yet?* "Harlan talked to the group about it a little bit, but we never had the opportunity to learn more about the property before his untimely death."

Vivian didn't seem to know when to stop talking. "James," she began, "tell Graydon what your ideas are for those awful cabins."

"Yes. Well, we had a look at those cabins and they are not in good shape, obviously. If we tore them down and replaced them with a shop, we could sell all kinds of Peppernell Manor–themed gifts in there. Heck, we could even sell pieces of the old cabins, and photos, too. People love that kind of thing. The shop could be the same shape as the current cabins, but of a much larger size."

I found myself staring at James, mouth agape. I couldn't believe what I was hearing. I tried to catch Graydon's eye. After what felt like an eternity, he finally looked at me.

"Oh, yes." He cleared his throat. "Carleigh is living here while she works on restoring the manor to the way it was back in the 1800s. She's got an idea for the slave cabins, too."

Vivian made a scoffing noise. "She wants to restore them. I don't think anyone cares about them. I certainly don't."

James looked from me to Graydon. Ruby spoke again.

"What about Phyllis and Sarah?"

James and Abigail looked at each other, obviously wondering who Phyllis and Sarah were, while Vivian wheeled on Ruby.

"Do not mention that woman's name again, Ruby," she seethed between thin lips.

"Which one?" Ruby asked.

"I was referring to Phyllis's ancestor," Vivian answered tightly. She turned to James and Abigail and said, "You've already met Phyllis. She's just the woman who served your dinner."

James and Abigail looked thoroughly confused, but they wisely did not ask about Sarah.

James made a display of looking at his watch. "I didn't realize it was getting so late. Abigail, we should probably get going." They thanked Vivian and Graydon for a delicious meal and shook hands with Evie, Ruby, and me again.

After they had left, Phyllis came into the dining room to clear away the dessert plates. She looked darkly at Vivian, who noticed.

"Don't be impertinent, Phyllis," Vivian warned. "I assume you were listening, and I don't want to hear one word. You've already made your views known. Well, let there be no mistake. You are the help in this house, and no more. We will do what we feel is best for our family and for Peppernell Manor. If that means your apartment and those awful cabins are torn down, then so be it. You'll just have to find another place to live."

Phyllis said nothing and left the room. We all looked at Vivian, shocked at her words. I didn't think there was much love lost between Vivian and Phyllis, but this was unexpected.

Graydon put his hand on Vivian's. "Viv, you and I need to talk about a few things. First, you cannot speak to Phyllis like that. I'll go talk to her. I hope she doesn't quit after your outburst, because she's needed around here. And second, don't ever invite those people here again without warning me first."

Vivian let out a "humph" and stormed out of the dining room. The rest of us sat in silence, staring at one another. After a few moments

Graydon got up and walked into the kitchen. Ruby followed. Evie and I sat there a while longer, lingering over our coffee.

"Wow," was all Evie said.

"Do you think Phyllis will quit?" I asked.

She sighed. "I hope not. I'm sure Daddy is trying to smooth her ruffled feathers right now. Ruby, too. She and Phyllis get along and Mother is nasty to both of them, so they have lots in common."

"What do you think your dad will say?"

"It's hard to know. It sounded like he was expressing some interest in what James and Abigail had to say, but I don't really believe he wants that for Peppernell Manor. I think he was just being polite."

"I'd like to sit down with him and talk to him about my ideas for restoring those cabins."

"Sounds like you'd better do it soon, before Mother forces her plans on him. Want me to come with you to talk to him?"

"Yes," I answered gratefully. "I'd appreciate that."

"Wait until he's done talking to Phyllis, then we'll have a little discussion with him." We remained at the table until Graydon came back in after several minutes.

"There," he said, addressing Evie. "I have spoken to Phyllis and assured her that your mother spoke out of turn and that the rest of us do not share her ideas of a caste system around here. I think she'll stay."

"Daddy," Evie began, "I know Carleigh has spoken to you before about restoring the slave cabins, and this might be a good time to discuss that with her. I mean, now that you've heard what James and Abigail are planning. I think Carleigh's onto something. Maybe you should hear her ideas before you go deciding about anything the investment group has to say."

"Of course you're right, Evie." He looked at me intently. "Carleigh, what do you propose?"

"Well," I began a little nervously, "the slave cabins are an important part of the history of Peppernell Manor."

"Agreed."

"When I first spoke to Cora-Camille about restoring the manor house, it was very important to her that we stick as closely as possible to the original aesthetic of the house to keep it connected to its history."

Graydon nodded, but said nothing. I continued.

"It seems a shame to put such care into the historical accuracy of the great house only to ignore the historical accuracy—and importance—of the other houses on the property. That is to say, the slave cabins. I think it's essential to remember that people lived in those homes, too.

"I know I could restore them as closely as possible to their original state. And once that's done, you could take your time deciding what to do with the property. You could keep it and just live in it the way you do now, or you could give it to the state of South Carolina for use as a cultural center and park, or you could turn it over to the investors, who might even appreciate having restored slave cabins on the property since they could use that as a marketing tool. And they could still have their gift shop if that's what you decide—they'd just have to build one elsewhere on the property."

Graydon was silent for a moment. "Carleigh," he drawled, "I think you make some very good points. I think Vivian needs to hear your reasoning before she goes and makes foolish decisions on my behalf about Peppernell Manor. But tonight isn't the time to discuss this with her." He chuckled. "She's hoppin' mad at me. I'll let her cool down and talk to her about it tomorrow. Are you going to be here in case she has any questions?"

I nodded eagerly. "Of course. I'll be finishing up the floors in the ballroom and the sitting room."

"All right, my dear. We'll find you if Viv wants more particulars. You have my vote."

I wondered briefly about Ruby's vote, but I didn't say anything. I was just happy to have persuaded Graydon. I suppose I should have mentioned that Phyllis was opposed to the restoration of the slave cabins, but that could wait until Graydon had spoken to his wife.

I went to bed that night with a feeling of elation. First Heath, now the slave cabins. The only thing preventing my happiness from being complete was Lucy's absence. As soon as we heard from the police that Harlan's killer had been apprehended, I would drive down to Florida and pick her up. And the farther from his murder we got, the more likely it seemed that it had been an act perpetrated by an angry business associate. It's funny that we never considered any other options.

CHAPTER 15

The next morning I woke to a beautiful day. The air was cooler and dry, and the windows were flung open to let in the soft breeze. *This was the way the South was meant to be enjoyed*—with gentle warmth and sunny days in the autumn.

I went downstairs with a lightness in my step that hadn't been there recently. I ate breakfast by myself and paged through the newspaper. Nothing happened to suggest that anything was amiss in the great house.

But when I left the dining room to get started for the day, I walked into the ballroom and stopped short with a gasp.

The ballroom walls, which the previous day had been a vibrant, deep blue, were now scarred with long, jagged streaks of black paint. There was paint on the floor and paint on the ceiling. That beautiful ceiling, which I had worked on for so many days! Looking at all the droplets on the walls, some of which were dripping in long scraggly lines, it was obvious that someone had taken a brush and flung paint all over the room. I walked quickly to the sitting room, trying to avoid stepping in any drops of black on the floor. The sitting room had thankfully been left untouched. I was confused, shocked, dismayed. I ran to the doorway of the ballroom and took off my shoes. I was going to run upstairs to find Evie and Graydon when the front door swung open. Heath peeked his head around the door. He smiled when he saw me.

"Good morning!"

Then he saw the look on my face. He came inside quickly and closed the door. "What's wrong?"

I couldn't speak. I pointed to the ballroom and he looked through the doorway. He turned to me, his face mirroring my own. "What happened?"

I shook my head and finally found my voice. "I don't know." I gulped. "I don't know. It was like that when I went in there just a minute ago."

"When did it happen?"

"I don't know," I repeated. "Sometime between yesterday afternoon and this morning. I haven't been in there since then."

"Does Dad know?"

"I doubt it. I just found it myself."

Heath went to the stairs. "Dad!" he called up, a sense of urgency in his voice. "Dad!"

We could hear doors opening upstairs. Graydon's head appeared over the railing upstairs. "What is it?" he asked with concern.

"Come down here, quickly. There's something you need to see."

Graydon came downstairs, tying his robe. Evie clattered along behind him, still in her pajamas. Graydon looked from Heath to me, glancing at my bare feet. "What's wrong?"

Heath pointed grimly in the direction of the ballroom. Graydon walked to the doorway, followed by Evie, and let out an expletive.

He turned to me. "What on earth happened?"

I threw my hands in the air. "I have no idea. It was like that when I walked in there just a few minutes ago."

"Is the paint still wet?" Evie asked.

"I don't know. I'll go see." I walked into the ballroom and ran my finger down one of the drips of paint on the wall. It was still a bit wet. I bent down and did the same with the paint on the floor. Same result.

"It's not completely dried, but it's not fresh, either. Someone must have done this a few hours ago," I informed the group.

"That doesn't really help us much," noted Graydon, "unless someone was down here in the middle of the night and saw it happening."

"Saw what happening?" asked Vivian. She had come down the stairs and was standing in the entry hall with the rest of us.

"Someone vandalized the ballroom," Graydon informed her grimly.

"There are streaks of black paint all over the walls and drops of paint on the floor and the ceiling."

"What?" she exclaimed, her eyes widening. "Who did it?" she asked as she looked into the ballroom.

Graydon shrugged. "We don't know."

"What about the sitting room?" she asked.

"The sitting room is untouched," I answered.

"Thank heaven for that," Vivian remarked. "What do we do next?" Everyone looked at me.

"I guess we wait for the paint to dry and then I redo the ballroom," I said simply. "I'll try to remove as much of the black paint as I can from the walls, but it's going to be hard to do that without damaging the plaster. I may just end up having to paint over the black. The same is true for the ceiling.

"And as for the floor," I continued, "I'll scrape it off as best I can and restain it." I shook my head. "This will take some time. I guess I'll get started in the front hall while I'm waiting for all the paint to dry."

Just then Ruby came in the front door. She looked around at everyone, confused. "Is something the matter?"

"Ruby, do you know anything about the black paint in the ballroom?" Graydon asked.

"No. What happened?"

"Someone splashed black paint on the walls and floor and ceiling of the ballroom. It's ruined and now Carleigh is going to have to do the entire room again."

Ruby went over to the ballroom doorway and peered in. She turned around, her hands over her mouth, and stared at me with wide eyes. "This is terrible!"

"I know," I sighed resignedly. "I'll get started today on the entry hall. Normally I like to work on walls first, but I think I'll work on the floor first this time."

"It had to have been someone in this house," Vivian said conspiratorially to Graydon loudly enough for us all to hear. "My money's on Phyllis. She's disgruntled."

Graydon turned to her angrily. "If she's disgruntled, then we have you to thank for it. So don't go around making accusations like that. We have no idea who did it."

Vivian stared at him stonily for a moment and then said, "Well! I guess we know where your loyalties lie!"

He rolled his eyes. "Vivian, don't start. You know my loyalties lie with my family. But you can't go around treating Phyllis like that! She's worked for us for many years, and her mother for many years before that, so I think we owe her a certain amount of respect."

"Where is Phyllis, anyways?" Evie cut in, probably to stop her parents' bickering.

"She wasn't in the kitchen when I came down to eat breakfast," I answered. "I imagine she's in her apartment."

"Maybe I should go look for her," Ruby said.

"You do whatever you want," Vivian replied sourly. "I'm going to work." She walked out the front door, closing it quietly behind her. Ruby went into the kitchen, presumably in search of Phyllis.

"Carleigh, I'm real sorry this happened," Graydon said. "You're a good girl to keep working on this house." Evie, smiling, rolled her eyes and jerked her thumb toward her father at his antiquated chivalry. Her reaction lightened the mood.

"Daddy, for heaven's sake, don't call her a good girl. She's not a child."

He looked at me sheepishly. "Sorry, Carleigh."

I grinned at him. "That's okay."

"I think we need to notify the police about this," Graydon said. "I'll call them and I'm sure they'll be over here before long."

He went upstairs, leaving Heath and Evie and me standing in the entry hall.

"Who do you suppose did it?" asked Evie.

"I can't imagine," answered Heath. "Why would anyone here want to vandalize the house? We all live here."

"Do you agree with Mother?"

"That is was Phyllis? Could be. Mother sure made her angry last night."

"I don't blame Phyllis for being mad, but she needs to find a better way to express herself," Evie replied with a sigh. "Carleigh, what do you think?"

"I have no idea who did it. That doesn't seem like something Phyllis would do, but I really don't know her very well."

"Carleigh's right. It seems out of character for her. Do you suppose someone could have broken in and done it?" Heath asked.

Evie shivered. "I hope not. That's a scary thought. Don't you think we'd see evidence of a break-in if someone from outside had done it?"

I shrugged. "I don't know. I'm sure the police will check that out once they get here."

"I wish I could stay here to help you," Heath told me. "But I need to get into Charleston to work. I've got court this morning."

"That's okay. This is my job, remember? Just because there's been a setback doesn't lessen my responsibility to complete it. Go on. Have a good day." I shooed him toward the front door.

He smiled at me and kissed my forehead. "I'll see you tonight," he promised.

"I'll come down when the police get here," Evie said, heading up the stairs.

I sighed and stood looking into the ballroom. *Who could have done the damage to the ballroom? Phyllis? Even Vivian? She was pretty angry last night. Maybe she vandalized the room out of spite.* But I didn't want to be the one to suggest to Heath and Evie that their mother might have been the culprit.

I gazed around at the entry hall for a few moments. Some areas of the marble had become discolored through the long years, and I wanted to try to clean them before thinking about having the floor replaced.

I was gathering the supplies I would need to tackle the marble when the police arrived. After looking around the ballroom, they examined the doors and windows on the rest of the first floor. Evie and Graydon and I waited for them in the drawing room. Then they questioned us in turn in the kitchen. They left after explaining that they could find no evidence of a break-in and that this appeared to be a domestic problem. They suggested that we keep our eyes and ears open for anything suspicious, but there appeared to be nothing they could do about it. I was discouraged, as were Evie and Graydon.

I threw myself into my work that day, scrubbing the marble until my arms hurt. I think I was trying to forget about the scars in the ballroom. By late afternoon I was starving and ready for a break. Phyllis came into the entry hall to offer me a glass of sweet tea.

"Ruby told me what happened in the ballroom. The police questioned me, too," she told me. "It's too bad your work was ruined. I saw how hard you worked in there and it looked nice."

"Thanks," I replied. "I wish I knew *why* someone threw paint in there."

"You know what I think?" she asked.

I looked at her askance. I knew where this conversation was headed. But I answered anyway. "What?"

"It's that dog."

I shook my head at her. "Phyllis, I hope you aren't suggesting that Addie came into the manor house and threw paint on the ballroom walls."

She arched her eyebrow at me. "I didn't say the dog did it. But I warned you about stray dogs. They bring nothing but bad luck to a house. It wouldn't have happened if Heath hadn't adopted her."

"Don't talk like that. Addie doesn't even live in this house! She lives with Heath!"

"Doesn't matter," she answered, shaking her head. "She lives on this property, doesn't she?"

Apparently there was no reasoning with her. I was exasperated. "Thanks for the tea, Phyllis. I have to take a shower." I went upstairs and as I reached the top I looked back down out of the corner of my eye. Phyllis was watching me. I shivered. The very idea—that Addie could be responsible for Harlan's death *and* for vandalizing the ballroom! Between Phyllis's superstitions and her belief in ghosts, I was beginning to think she was more than a little creepy.

CHAPTER 16

During dinner my cell phone vibrated. When I looked down at the number and saw that it was from Florida, I excused myself to take the call.

"Carleigh? It's Mom." Her voice sounded strained.

"Mom? What's going on? What's wrong?"

"Lucy's okay, but Dad is sick."

I was shocked. "Is he all right? What's the matter?"

"We don't know yet. He wasn't himself when he woke up. Then this afternoon he fainted and when he did, he fell and hit his head. He's bleeding internally and has a broken wrist. He's in the hospital right now and they're running tests. He'll probably be there for several days.

"I think it would be best if you took Lucy back to South Carolina so I can concentrate on taking care of him."

"Absolutely. I'll be there as soon as I can get there. I can leave right away. Do you think Dad's going to be okay?"

"I think he'll be fine. But it's going to take some time to figure out exactly what's wrong and how to treat him."

"I'll be there by tomorrow morning. Tell him I'll see him then. And Lucy, too. Bye."

I hung up and returned to the dining room. I told everyone that I would have to leave to pick up Lucy as soon as possible. Everyone was concerned about my father, but happy that Lucy would be returning to Peppernell Manor.

I ate a little of my dinner and ran upstairs to pack for an overnight. Before long I was in the car heading south.

My emotions were scattered in all directions. I was worried about both of my parents. I knew they had lots of friends in their neighborhood, but what if something happened in the night and there was no one close by to help Mom? What if he fell getting out of the car or out of bed? The *what ifs* were starting to whirl around in my mind until I felt my chest start to tighten.

And besides worrying about my parents, I was very concerned about having Lucy back at Peppernell Manor. As much as I wanted her with me, there was always the nagging reminder that Harlan's killer still hadn't been caught. I didn't want to expose my daughter to the very grown-up things that went along with a police investigation, but my choices were limited. I felt that I couldn't leave Peppernell Manor with the restoration incomplete. My job and my reputation were on the line. Besides, the police wouldn't let me return to Chicago anyway. Also, I was starting to feel at home in South Carolina, and I didn't want to leave Heath behind.

I felt a little better knowing that there were enough people at Peppernell Manor to help me watch Lucy every minute that she wasn't sleeping or in school. They would be happy to help me, I knew. There would surely be days when I would have to devote most of my time to the restoration, and the knowledge that she wouldn't ever be alone in the manor or on the property if I couldn't be with her put me more at ease. I felt some disquiet about the paint incident, but there was nothing I could do except trust that Lucy would be in safe hands while I worked.

I was exhausted when I got to my parents' house. My mother met me on the porch with a big hug. Her eyes looked tired and worried; she appeared to have aged in the short time since I had seen her last. Lucy was still asleep, having gotten to bed very late the previous night.

"How's Dad this morning?"

She passed a weary hand over her eyes. "Okay, I guess. Now that you're here I'm going over to the hospital to see him. I'll be back later and then I'll watch Lucy and you can go visit him. He'll be happy to see you."

"Do you want to rest a bit first?"

"No, I just want to get over there."

"Okay." I watched her get into her car and drive away. I went indoors and sat down in the living room while I waited for Lucy to get up. I didn't have to wait long. She appeared in the doorway just a little while later and within just a few seconds she was sitting on my lap, her arms wrapped tightly around my neck.

"Grandpa's sick," she told me.

"I know. Grandma is going to have to take care of him when he comes home, so you and I are going back to Peppernell Manor together. Would you like that?"

She nodded, her head against my chest. We spent a quiet morning eating breakfast and watching cartoons. I had just sent Lucy into the bedroom to pick out her clothes for the day when Mom came home.

"How's Dad?" I asked.

"He's still in a lot of pain, but he's very anxious to come home. They've found something wrong in his intestines, but apparently it's treatable," she said. "He's making friends with all the nurses." She rolled her eyes and smiled and I had a feeling she and Dad would both be okay.

"I'll go see him right after lunch," I told her. "I'm taking you and Lucy out." She smiled gratefully and sat down on the couch.

"Why don't you sleep for a bit first?" I suggested. "I'll take Lucy out for a walk while you rest and then we'll find a good restaurant."

After Mom got a much-needed nap the three of us had a leisurely lunch together at an outdoor restaurant where the tablecloths were made of paper so Lucy could color to her heart's content. Mom and I talked about the care Dad would need when he got home.

"Carleigh, I don't want you to worry. Dad and I will be just fine. Do you think you could come down and spend Thanksgiving with us?"

"That would be nice. Could I bring someone with me?"

"Lucy? Of course!"

"I don't mean Lucy." I blushed. "I mean Heath, Evie's brother. He and I have become very close, and he just adores Lucy."

Mom grinned. "Why didn't you tell me before? Sure he can come! I can't wait to meet him!" She winked.

"I'm not sure he'll be able to come, but I'll ask him. He actually asked me to stay at Peppernell Manor for Thanksgiving with his family."

"Well, maybe you can visit after Thanksgiving, then."

"Let's just see how it works out. I'm not going to decide just yet."

She patted my hand. "We'll be here if you want, but do what works best for you."

I dropped Mom and Lucy at the house before going over to the hospital to see Dad. He was sleeping lightly when I got there, so I waited in a chair next to his bed until he woke up.

"Hi, Dad. How are you feeling?"

"Carleigh! What are you doing here?"

"I came to pick up Lucy and take her back to Peppernell Manor so Mom can devote her time to you when you get home."

He snorted. "Your mother. I don't want Lucy to leave!"

I smiled at him. "Tell you what. I'll bring her back for a visit if you get better soon and don't give Mom a hard time."

"Deal."

We talked sports for a little while until he started to look tired again. I left after promising to see him again before returning to Peppernell Manor.

Before we left early the next morning, I went over to the hospital to see Dad one more time. He looked better than he had the day before, and he couldn't wait to get home. My mother was going to have her hands full keeping him from overdoing it once he was released. I didn't take Lucy to see him since I thought she might be afraid once she saw him in his hospital gown with all the tubes that were hooked up to him. She and I left Mom late that morning with a promise to be back soon. Lucy waved at her until she was out of sight.

On the long drive home, Lucy alternately napped and chattered about the things she did with Grandma and Grandpa. She asked countless questions about the people at Peppernell Manor, and we sang and told stories.

We arrived at Peppernell Manor that evening. When Lucy burst through the front door everyone was there to greet her: Heath, Evie, Graydon and Vivian, Ruby, and Phyllis. She was thrilled with the attention and talked nonstop until she finally fell asleep on the sofa in the drawing room. Heath carried her upstairs for me. I tucked her in and fell into bed myself, happy to have her back with me once more.

I let her stay home from school the next day, since both of us were still very tired. I wanted her near me as much as possible, so she spent most of the day in the drawing room, playing dolls with Ruby and napping, while I worked on the floor in the entry hall. Most of the stains were coming out with a lot of elbow grease on my part. I had already spoken to a specialist who could come in the following day and finish removing the stains from the floor. I was very happy that the marble floor could be saved. That floor had witnessed so many generations of family and guests and important visitors that I hated to think that it might have to be replaced with brand new marble.

That evening Lucy begged me to take her over to see Heath and Addie. I happily obliged her since I wanted to see them, too. I had seen Heath briefly after Lucy and I returned from Florida, but it would be nice to spend time together, just the three of us and Addie. I hadn't told Heath what Phyllis said about Addie; I wasn't sure I wanted to. He might not be thrilled to learn that Phyllis thought of Addie as an omen of bad luck. And Addie was overjoyed to see Lucy at the carriage house. She ran tirelessly in circles around Lucy until we were all dizzy just watching her. She licked Lucy's face until she couldn't stop laughing. We took a walk together in the gathering darkness, Lucy and Addie running ahead of Heath and me. It was a short walk, since Lucy had to be in bed early. She was excited to be going back to school in the morning to see her teachers and her friends again.

As we walked back toward the carriage house, Addie started behaving a little strangely. She crouched low to the ground and began to growl, a low throaty sound that was a bit scary. Lucy tried to walk over to her and pet her, but I took her hand and led her away. I didn't want Addie to bite her. After all, we didn't really know much about Addie. And in spite of myself, I thought briefly of Phyllis's warnings.

Heath suggested that I take Lucy back to the manor and put her in bed. He said he would text me later if Addie was feeling more like herself so I could go over to the carriage house.

"Heath, maybe you could come over to the main house tonight. I really don't want to leave the house while Lucy is alone in the bedroom."

"Sure," he agreed.

About an hour later, I did get a text from him: **ADDIE'S FINE. COMING OVER.**

I went downstairs to meet him in the drawing room.

"Thanks for coming over here tonight. I know you're more comfortable in the carriage house, but I need to be near Lucy until the police have told us that they have the person who killed Harlan."

"I agree completely," Heath said. "I haven't heard anything lately. Maybe I'll give them a call tomorrow to see where their investigation stands."

"What do you think was wrong with Addie?"

"I have no idea. Probably just some small animal spooked her."

"I wasn't going to tell you this, but Phyllis has a theory about Addie. She says stray dogs bring bad luck. She's positive that Addie is going to bring all kinds of mayhem to Peppernell Manor."

He shook his head. "Sometimes Phyllis's superstitions are a bit much."

"I sort of told her that was silly."

"Good. Want to sit outside? We may not be able to go out on my patio, but we can at least enjoy the sky and stars. It's nice and clear out tonight."

I followed him out to the veranda. We sat on a wicker loveseat from which we could see out over the trees lining the front allée. I sighed and laid my head on his shoulder.

"It's beautiful out tonight."

"It is," he agreed.

From the direction of the carriage house came the sound of barking. Heath mumbled, "I wonder what the problem is now."

"Should you go see?"

"I think she's all right. She's probably mad that I left her alone tonight." He chuckled. "This is my punishment."

I hoped being left alone was Addie's only problem. We sat hand in hand for a short time, just enjoying the night sky, while Addie's barking continued. Evie poked her head out the front door after a little while.

"What's the matter with Addie?"

"She misses me," Heath answered with a smile. Evie rolled her eyes and went back inside.

"I probably should go check on her."

We said good night and Heath left. The barking stopped just a few moments later. I smiled to myself. *That dog is spoiled already!*

The next morning Lucy and I were at breakfast when Graydon joined us in the dining room.

"Goin' back to school today, little one?" he asked Lucy.

"Yes," she replied happily, her mouth covered in jam.

"Looks like there's a storm brewing way down south in the Caribbean," he told me. "I was watching the television in our room. They say we may need to keep our eye on this one."

"You mean an h-u-r-r-i-c-a-n-e?" I asked.

He nodded.

"Lucy," I said quickly, "let's clean you up and get ready for school." I didn't want to have any discussion of a hurricane in front of her.

We left for Charleston a short while later. I stopped at a few stores after I dropped Lucy off, then headed back to Peppernell Manor. I turned on the radio while I drove. The news program had a brief mention of the storm churning off the coast of Hispaniola. I had never been in a hurricane and had no desire to experience one. And I was worried about my parents in Florida. I fervently hoped it would skirt the East Coast.

The marble specialist had arrived by the time I returned to the manor. She worked steadily for most of the day and was able to complete the stain removal on the floor of the entry hall. When she was done, we stood together in the front doorway and surveyed our work. It was beautiful. As usual, I took pictures to compare with the ones I had taken before I started work. I showed them to the woman who had finished the floor and she was amazed at the difference.

When I picked up Lucy from school she was tired and a little cranky. She was weepy on the way home and fell asleep as soon as we got back to Peppernell Manor. While she napped I worked on trying to remove some of the black paint from the floor in the ballroom. I hadn't had a chance to work on it since I had to retrieve Lucy from Florida. It was hard work to remove the paint without damaging the floor. It was a job that would take many hours. I planned to repaint the walls after the dried paint was removed from the floor.

Dinner that night was a little strained. Lucy was grumpy and there was obviously something up between Graydon and Vivian. They apparently did not want to discuss it during the meal, and I suspected it was because of the presence of a child in the dining room. Evie kept glancing at them, as if she knew what was going on. I was anxious to get Lucy upstairs for a bath and bedtime; I knew Evie would fill me in later.

Lucy fell asleep as soon as she was in bed. I tiptoed out of the room and knocked softly on Evie's door.

"You going downstairs?" I asked.

"Yeah. Meet you in the drawing room."

I went down and waited for her. She looked keyed up when she came in.

"What's up?" I asked her.

"The police called Daddy today. They think they've got the person who killed Harlan."

"Who?" I asked eagerly.

"Some new guy in that investment group. I guess he had a falling-out with Harlan over money about a week before Harlan's death, and he was just arrested on a domestic violence charge."

"Are they sure?"

"Sure enough that they're going to charge him with Harlan's murder."

"You and your parents must feel such a sense of relief."

She nodded absently. "We do. We wanted to tell you at dinner, but we really couldn't discuss it with Lucy there."

"I know. Are you okay?"

She gave me a half smile, her eyes glistening. She blinked several times before answering. "I guess so. I really miss Harlan. I'm feeling so many things right now. I just wish he was still here, that's all." Large tears began to slide down her cheeks and I went over and sat down next to her on the sofa. I held her hand in mine.

"I'm so sorry, Evie." I didn't have to say anything else. All she needed was for me to sit there with her in the semidarkness and hold her hand. She cried quietly for several minutes before sniffling and saying she was going to go upstairs and call Boone.

"Thanks for being here, Carleigh," she said as she left the room.

"What are friends for?"

Just then my cell phone buzzed with a text from Heath. YOU BUSY?

No, I texted him.

CAN I COME OVER?

SURE.

I waited for him on the veranda. He came up the steps and held me in a big, long hug.

"Are you thinking about Harlan?" I asked.

"Yes. I can't believe it's finally over. All the worrying and the waiting to find out who did it."

"I was just talking to Evie about it."

"How are Mom and Dad doing?" he asked.

"No one talked about it at dinner because Lucy was in the room. But they seemed subdued."

"I haven't had a chance to talk to them about it. Evie called me earlier at my office and gave me the news."

"I'm sure they're trying to deal with the outcome, just like everyone else. I can't imagine losing a child. And to such a senseless act of violence."

"Let's do something fun tomorrow," Heath suggested suddenly. "I need a break from everything. From the talk about Harlan, from the firm, from the farm. Let's pick up Lucy from school and take her to the aquarium in Charleston."

"Okay," I agreed. "She would love that!"

After I dropped Lucy off at school the next morning I returned to Peppernell Manor and spent the day working on the ballroom floor again. The day passed quickly as I made measurable progress, and by the time I was ready to leave for Charleston to pick up Lucy, I estimated that I could remove the rest of the paint stains on the floor by the next day. Then I could start repainting the walls to cover up the ugly scars made by the black paint.

I could see Heath's lanky figure standing outside Lucy's nursery school before I parked my car. His face lit up and he grinned at me as I walked toward him.

When I had brought Lucy outside, Heath and I explained to her that we had a trip planned. She was immediately excited.

The aquarium, located on the Charleston Harbor, was incredible. Lucy loved everything, from the salt marsh aviary to the touch tank to the ocean tank to the turtle hospital. We hated to leave at closing time, but Lucy was exhausted. She fell asleep on the way home. I was carrying her into the house when I heard Addie barking again. I smiled to myself, thinking that Addie must be beside herself when Heath wasn't around. I was beginning to understand the feeling.

The next day I was able to finish removing the stains from the floor and begin applying a coat of the peacock blue paint on the walls. Standing back to look at it as it dried, I could still see black streaks underneath the paint. It would need at least one or two more coats. I hoped that the person who had ruined my first paint job would stay away from the ballroom after this.

That night after dinner Evie took Lucy upstairs to look through a trunk that held dress-up clothes from Evie's childhood, complete with high-heeled shoes and fancy hats. I knew this would keep Lucy busy for days, but all I asked was a half hour to go for a short walk with Heath.

As much as I wanted to stay outside and continue walking in the cool dusk, I returned to the manor and found Lucy draped in a pink chiffon dress that was way too big for her. Her little feet teetered in a pair of high-heeled strappy sandals. She wore a feather boa around her neck. I snapped a few photos with my cell phone to text to my parents and maybe even Brad.

Evie was having fun, too. She had dressed in a long green gown with sparkly straps. The two of them explained that they were getting ready to go to a party.

"Can I come?"

"Yes, but you have to bring Heath, too," Lucy informed me.

"Well," I told her, laughing, "Heath has gone to bed and now it's almost your turn."

"I think she's getting used to having Heath around," Evie whispered to me.

I grinned. "I think she is, too."

Evie let out a little squeal. "That is sooo exciting!"

I had to agree.

CHAPTER 17

Over the next three days I finished touching up the ceiling and painting the walls of the ballroom. The color was deep and rich and there wasn't a trace of the black paint that had so marred the room. It was time to get started painting the walls of the entry hall. The downstairs was really coming together nicely and it would be finished in time for Graydon and Vivian's open house soon after Thanksgiving. As long as no one tampered with it again.

One night at dinner Graydon and Vivian announced to everyone at the table that they were thinking of going out of town for Thanksgiving. This evidently came as a surprise to Evie and Heath. Evie protested that the family always had Thanksgiving together at Peppernell Manor.

"This year is different, Evie," Graydon explained quietly. "With Mother and Harlan both gone, we thought we might take a little vacation to get away from Peppernell Manor for a short time. Your mother thinks it might be too difficult around here without them. Just this year, you understand. By next year maybe we can be together again at home."

"I guess I could celebrate Thanksgiving with Boone's family," Evie said with a pout. She turned to Heath. "What about you?"

He looked at me. "I don't know yet," he answered. "It kind of depends on Carleigh and Lucy."

Graydon smiled at him. Heath actually blushed.

"My parents have invited me—us—to have Thanksgiving with them," I ventured. "That is, if you're interested."

"I guess I'm having Thanksgiving in Florida this year, then," Heath said with a grin.

"With us?" Lucy asked him.

"Yup."

"Yay!" she squealed.

Evie looked troubled. "What about Ruby? And Phyllis?"

"Ruby is going with us," Graydon replied.

"And Phyllis will just have to find family or friends to visit while we're all gone," Vivian stated flatly.

"Well," Evie began doubtfully, "I guess we don't have much choice this year. But please, can we all be here for Christmas? You too, Carleigh. And Lucy."

I laughed. "Let's get through Thanksgiving first before we start worrying about where Lucy and I are going to be for Christmas."

Over the next several days I finished the floor in the sitting room, touched up several places where the paint had removed the stain from the ballroom floor, and painted the front hall. In contrast to the other rooms on the first floor, Cora-Camille had chosen a soft ivory color for the walls in the front hall. She had told me she didn't want to startle anyone who walked into the entry hall with a great swath of color. I thought the ivory would be beautiful with the grand staircase and the marble floors. Cora-Camille's idea had been to find portraits of Peppernell ancestors in the basement and attic and have them cleaned, reframed if necessary, and hung in the front hall to greet guests. I initially thought the idea was a little morbid, but she thought it was a great way to give a nod to the Peppernell ancestors.

Cora-Camille had taken me up to the attic one day to find the portraits she had in mind. There were several. Large, severe-looking portraits of men, women, and children in the Peppernell line had been wrapped in cracked brown paper and stacked against each other. But those portraits weren't sufficient to cover the walls as Cora-Camille had wished, so I needed to look for more portraits in the basement. Unfortunately, Cora-Camille had passed away before she had gotten a chance to go down there with me.

I went down to the basement by myself one afternoon while Vivian was looking after Lucy for me. As fascinating as the cellar was, my imagination sometimes took charge when I was down there alone. The echoes of my footsteps reached me from the dark recesses of the huge space, and I couldn't wait to locate the paintings and get back upstairs to daylight and other people.

I poked through several of the small rooms in the basement before I finally found the portraits stacked on the floor in an old storage area. Like the ones in the attic, these were wrapped in brittle brown paper. I took them upstairs to the large table in the kitchen to unwrap them and have a good look at them. I was amazed at what I found.

Looking up at me from the top of the stack was a portrait that could have been taken of Heath. Or Harlan. Some old Peppernell ancestor stared from the canvas, his spectacled eyes bright and intelligent. I was thrilled with my find and couldn't wait to have it reframed and hung up in the front hall.

I also found a portrait of a woman seated in what looked like the drawing room. I was very pleased to note that the color of the walls behind her was a deep coral, just like I had painted it so recently. What interested me most about the portrait, though, was not the subject herself, but a person standing behind her and to the very edge of the painting. It was a woman—one who looked just like Phyllis, but younger.

Could that be Sarah? I wondered. How wonderful it would be if I could have this painting restored and given to Phyllis as a gift. I didn't know if she had ever seen the portrait, but I doubted so. I would ask Evie before broaching the subject with Graydon or Vivian. And if the person in the background of the painting was Sarah and I could get the portrait restored, maybe Phyllis would forgive me for forging ahead with the restoration of the slave cabins.

I could hear Phyllis coming to the back door of the kitchen from her apartment, so I quickly covered up the portrait and picked up the unwieldy stack of paintings. I took them all into the drawing room and placed them against a wall.

I hadn't even asked Graydon about his ideas for the entry hall, but I assumed he would accede to his late mother's wishes, as he had done since her passing. I asked him about hanging the portraits in the entry hall that night at dinner.

"I guess so," he said a little doubtfully. "What do you think, Carleigh?"

"When Cora-Camille first suggested the idea, I thought it was a little macabre. Like something you'd find in a haunted house. But the idea has grown on me, to be honest with you. Having old Peppernell ancestors looking down on the people coming and going through the front hall might be a really interesting way of keeping history alive in the manor."

"I think it's a good idea," Ruby said. Again, I had forgotten to address her in my inquiries regarding the restoration of the manor. It was easy to forget that she was one of the owners, too.

"Well then, let's go ahead with it," Graydon boomed. "If we decide we don't like it, we can always take the portraits down, but they might look very good up there."

Later that evening, I sat in the drawing room with Evie. Lucy had fallen asleep on the sofa, so I would just carry her upstairs when I went to bed. "You wouldn't believe two of the paintings I found in the basement this afternoon," I told her. "There's one that looks exactly like Heath and Harlan and one is of a person who I think might be Sarah."

Her eyes widened. "You're kidding! I'd love to see them."

I got up to unwrap the paintings I had stacked against the wall earlier. She was amazed by the resemblance between the old Peppernell gentleman and her brothers.

"Hey," she said excitedly. "How about having this restored and giving it to Heath for Christmas? He could hang it in the carriage house instead of in the front hall. What do you think?"

"I didn't even consider that," I admitted. "I assumed it would hang in the front hall in the manor. But he might like it in his own house. Could I give it to him for Christmas? I'd pay to have it restored myself."

"He'd love it!"

"Now you have to see this other painting," I told her. She couldn't believe the resemblance between the woman in the painting and Phyllis. I told her my idea of having the portrait restored and given to Phyllis as a gift.

"Is there a date on the back of the portrait? I guess we can figure out whether that's Sarah if we can figure out when the portrait was done." We checked the back and sure enough, there was a date that corresponded with the time Sarah would have worked as a slave inside the great house at Peppernell Manor.

"As long as we can assume this is Sarah, I think it's a good idea to give Phyllis the painting as a gift. But don't tell Mother what you're planning," she cautioned. "You know how she feels about Phyllis."

"I don't want to hide anything from your mother."

"Then maybe I can suggest to Daddy that *I* pick out a gift for Phyllis for Christmas this year. We always get her a nice gift, and if he puts me in charge I can see that this painting is restored and given to her. Mother will be more likely to keep her mouth shut if she thinks she might hurt *my* feelings by saying something uncharitable about Phyllis's gift."

I grinned. "That's a great idea. Thanks."

I carried Lucy upstairs that night and could hear Addie barking again as I drifted off to sleep. The next morning Heath came over to the manor for breakfast.

"Heath, can't you keep that dog of yours quiet at night?" Graydon asked grumpily. "She kept me up long past my bedtime."

"Sorry, Dad," Heath replied. "At first I thought she was barking because she was lonely, but now I'm beginning to think that she's barking because she likes the sound of her own voice."

"Can't you keep her inside your house?"

"Usually I do, but I have to let her out once in a while."

"All right," Graydon grumbled. "Thank the good Lord she doesn't bark all day, too, or I'd never get any work done."

Heath grinned at his father. "I'll have a talk with Addie."

I noticed Phyllis looking at me out of the corner of her eye as she served breakfast. She raised her eyebrows at me as if to say *I told you that dog is bad luck.*

"Phyllis," Vivian said, "we need to start pulling decorations out of storage for the holiday open house."

"I'll start that today," Phyllis answered.

"Any word on that storm?" Heath asked Graydon.

"It's a slow-moving one," Graydon replied. "The last I heard it's supposed to miss Florida and move in farther north toward the Atlantic coast of the U.S."

"What are they saying about timing?" Heath wanted to know.

"Still several days off," Graydon answered. "We need to keep an eye on the radar."

I didn't like listening to talk of any storm. "What happens if the storm heads this way?" I asked no one in particular.

"We batten down the hatches," Graydon said. "I'm going to keep my radio on today and see what the meteorologists are saying. We'll have to get some work done around here on the outside of the manor if the storm is headed for us."

"What kind of work?" I asked.

"We'll need to shutter all the windows on the manor and on the dependencies," Heath said. "Anything outside has to be fully secured. I'll have to make sure the stables are good and tight and we'll have to make sure all the farm machinery and tools are put away and secured."

"Has there ever been a hurricane here before?"

"Oh, sure," Graydon told me. "Lots of them. Some are worse than others, of course. There have been some storms that caused terrible damage, and others that haven't turned out to be that bad. It just depends on the track of the storm."

I hated to talk about this in front of Lucy, but I needed to know for my own peace of mind that there was a plan in place if a hurricane were headed our way. Besides, she seemed preoccupied with a bird that was hopping around on the ground outside the window.

But she had been listening. On the way into Charleston just a short while later, she asked, "Mama, is there a storm coming?"

"I don't know. We have to wait and see."

"Soon?"

"Maybe. But don't worry. It's just rain and wind." I hoped I sounded more confident than I felt.

"I love rain and wind," she responded cheerfully.

I spent much of that day in several Charleston shops, gathering information about the best place to drop off all the paintings that needed to be restored. I eventually decided on a small shop off the beaten path in the city, and left the paintings there. Unfortunately, though, they would not be ready in time for Vivian's open house.

After I picked up Lucy that afternoon, we went back to the manor and Evie looked after her for a short time while I painted some touch-up spots on the walls in the front hall. The walls looked clean and elegant in ivory. I spoke to Graydon and Vivian that evening about artwork that could go on the walls temporarily while we waited for the portraits to be restored.

Vivian snapped her fingers. "I have just the thing," she said excitedly. "A collection of antique Lowcountry oil paintings just came into the store. I could bring them back to the manor for a temporary display on the walls in the front hall.

"There are twelve paintings in the collection and they're quite large," she said. "They won't all fit in the front hall. Why don't you come into the store tomorrow and we'll decide together which would look best?"

When I arrived at Vivian's store the next morning after dropping Lucy at school, she was with a customer. She smiled at me when I walked in and turned back to the man so I had a chance to watch them interact. She seemed very knowledgeable about the antiques in her store. I was impressed, as was the customer. He bought two large pieces of furniture and several smaller knickknacks.

After they had made delivery arrangements, the man left and Vivian walked over to me.

"I didn't even put any of the paintings on display," she told me conspiratorially. "I wanted you to see them first to decide if they'll work at the manor. I think they'll be perfect." She led me to a large back room that was chock-full of antiques. I could have spent hours wandering around that room and the front of her store. She walked straight to a large wooden crate and bent over its side. She beckoned to me and I joined her. Inside the crate were at least twenty wall hangings, presumably paintings, all generously wrapped and stacked on their sides. She was busily unwrapping a painting.

She stood back so I could see it. It was a gorgeous oil painting done in light greens and yellows and blues. The sun rose in the background and pathways of water wound through marshland in the foreground. The sun twinkled on the water. The effect was idyllic and serene.

"I love it," I told Vivian. "Can I see some of the others?"

"Of course."

I took my time perusing the artwork. There were several pictures that were similar to the one I had seen already. There was a stunning painting of an allée of trees just like the ones at Peppernell Manor. That painting would definitely have to go in the front hall. There was another picture of a narrow waterway snaking its way toward the sunset between two stretches of land. The clouds, colored pink and purple by the sunset, looked real. The painter had done a beautiful job.

And I especially liked one of Lowcountry tree silhouettes under a full moon.

"What do you think?" she asked excitedly.

"I think it's going to be hard to narrow down our favorites!"

"How about this? You pick four and I'll pick four. Then we can see if they go together and will fit in the front hall. Did you bring the measurements?"

I laughed. "I don't go anywhere without all the measurements of every room. You pick your four first."

"All right."

I watched as she chose her favorites. Sure enough, she picked the allée painting that looked like Peppernell Manor. She also picked out a marshy-looking painting as well as one with several shorebirds walking among the reeds and one of the open ocean with a beach in the foreground.

"My turn?"

I chose my four carefully. I ended up with the first painting I had seen—the one of the sunrise—plus I chose the one with the silhouettes under the full moon, one with a field of wildflowers in the foreground and a watery marsh in the background, and another ocean painting, this one with a faraway sailboat. All eight paintings would indeed look striking grouped together in the front hall of Peppernell Manor. In fact, they looked better than the portraits would—too bad these were only on loan until the portraits were restored.

Vivian was very happy with the entire ensemble. She told me she would do the necessary paperwork to take them home for a loaner display and then get them to the manor as soon as possible.

I went back to the manor and walked around slowly in the rooms I had finished thus far, taking a few more photos and noting whether there were any finishing touches that I needed to complete. I was pleased with the progress of the restoration and was anxious to get started in the withdrawing room. All of the other public spaces downstairs were complete, with the exception of some furniture for the ballroom and the paintings for the front hall.

I walked into the withdrawing room. It was a small room, paneled entirely in cypress, as was the custom in the grander homes of the mid-nineteenth century. Though there had been some staining, I could see that the wood, once restored, would be the color of a fine cognac. A large fireplace stood along one wall, with a green-and-black marble hearth. The carved details on the cypress were astonishing. They looked like they were still in very good shape, so I might not need a special woodworker to finish this room.

I had completed the work on the ceiling weeks ago, but now I would have to get to work refinishing the walls due to the discoloration from cigar smoke almost as old as the manor. It would probably take a couple of long days to completely remove the stains. This room was carpeted, too. A dark blue carpet with a gold fleur-de-lis design covered the floor. It looked rather worn and dingy and I wondered whether I would be able to save it.

I got to work on the walls right away. It would be great to have this room finished in time for the open house in case anyone wanted to use it. Lucy even "helped" me after I picked her up from school during the afternoon. She had her own cloth to wipe down the walls; she had fun and I didn't have to worry about her or ask someone else to watch her for me again.

Heath joined us at dinner that night. Vivian was focused on the open house and the plans that she had made so far. Phyllis tried to speak once when she was serving the meal, but Vivian shushed her and waved her away imperiously. "Not now, Phyllis. When I need your advice, I'll ask." Phyllis looked daggers at her but said nothing.

Heath had more important things to discuss. "Dad, it's looking more and more like that storm is going to make landfall along the Carolina coast. When do you want to start buttoning things up?"

"Tomorrow morning, first thing," was Graydon's swift reply. "The weatherman is saying that there's a strong possibility that the hurricane is going to make a direct hit not far from here. We need to get everything secured within the next twenty-four hours."

Just then I got a text from Lucy's school. All nursery school classes were cancelled the following day to allow families time to prepare for the storm. I was starting to get nervous. Living in Chicago, I was never much concerned about hurricanes. They were something that I followed from thousands of miles away on cable news. Now it looked like I might be in the middle of one, and I was very anxious, especially for Lucy.

My phone vibrated. Brad. I knew what he was calling for and I excused myself from the table and went into the drawing room to take the call.

"Hello?"

"I assume you've heard about the hurricane heading for South Carolina," he began. "When are you leaving?"

"What are you talking about? We're not leaving."

"You have to. If you don't I'll take back my permission for her to be there with you."

"Don't threaten me, Brad. She and I are staying here and she'll be just fine."

"How do you know?"

"The owner of Peppernell Manor has assured me that this house has been through lots of hurricanes and there's never been so much as a broken window," I lied.

"Sure," he sneered.

"Brad, I think it's safer for us at this point to stay here than it is to go running off somewhere else." It wasn't true, but I couldn't think of anything else to say.

"How long will it be before the storm makes landfall?"

"Could be any time now. Could be by tomorrow."

"You're lying, Carleigh. I've heard that it won't be for a couple of days."

"Why did you ask, then?"

"You have plenty of time to get out of there."

"Brad, why can't you just trust me to keep her safe? If it seems like the storm is too strong, there's a huge basement. We'll go down there."

He was quiet for a moment, probably thinking.

"Besides, I frankly think we're safer in the basement than we are driving out on the road to get somewhere else."

"Well," he began, "are you sure you'll be with her the whole time?" Good. He was starting to come to his senses.

"Of course! What else would I do?"

"Hmm. I guess it would be all right if you stayed there, as long as you promise to keep her right with you all the time."

"You know I will. I don't want anything to happen to her, either."

"Have Lucy call me as often as you can."

"I will," I promised.

The next day we were all busy getting the manor ready in case the hurricane made landfall nearby. Graydon and Heath took a ladder all around the outside of the house to make sure each set of shutters was in working order and to put large X shapes in each windowpane with strong masking tape. Then they closed the shutters, leaving each room in near-complete darkness. Walking around indoors was eerie, like walking around in the twilight, even though the weather outside was sunny and, to my eyes, beautiful. Lucy trotted along beside me as I helped Evie and Phyllis move lawn furniture down into the basement. The garage, now free of its police tape, would have been a more logical destination for the furniture, but we all agreed that we didn't want to go in there. We also put Heath's patio furniture inside the carriage house. Vivian had gone into Charleston to supervise hurricane preparations at her store. I shuddered thinking of all the beautiful historic artifacts that could be ruined or damaged by a hurricane.

After the lawn furniture had been stored safely, Evie and Lucy and I went indoors where our assignment from Graydon was to make sure that the manor's emergency kit was completely stocked. Evie assured me that it remained fully stocked at all times so our job was just to double-check.

The kit was kept in a large storage closet in the basement. I couldn't believe all the things that were necessary in case of an emergency requiring the residents of Peppernell Manor to evacuate or live without electricity for an extended period. There were the things I expected: lots of water, a first-aid kit, flashlights, a large supply of batteries, candles, matches in waterproof containers, canned food and a can opener, a battery-operated radio, and a supply of personal items like toothbrushes, toothpaste, and deodorant. But there were other things I never would have thought of: powdered milk and sports drinks, sunscreen, bug spray, a camera for insurance purposes, paper and pens, a waterproof and fireproof box for any important documents that were kept upstairs in the house, a tool kit, bedding, and even a supply of books and games to play when boredom set in. The emergency items couldn't really be called a "kit." It was more like an entire room filled with items that might be necessary in case of a dire emergency. Evie told me that the only things missing were cash and travelers' checks, which Graydon always kept in a safe upstairs.

I was astounded by the amount of work that went into preparing for a hurricane that might or might not strike.

"Do you guys do this every time there's a hurricane in the forecast?" I asked Evie.

"Only when it looks likely that the hurricane is going to hit nearby," she answered.

"This is pretty late in the season for a hurricane, isn't it?"

"Yes. There were a couple of close calls over the summer, but nothing like this. We only shuttered the windows for those."

We went upstairs where Phyllis and Ruby were busy making quick breads and some cookies for the "kit" in the basement. Lucy wanted to help them, but Heath called me and asked me to put together a kit for Addie in the carriage house. Lucy decided she'd rather visit her furry friend than bake.

We went over to the carriage house, where Addie greeted us excitedly. People say animals know when a storm is coming, but Addie acted the same as always, running around in circles, barking, and jumping with sheer joy. We found a large box and filled it with dry food, treats, towels, fresh water in gallon jugs, and an extra leash. Lucy was in charge of choosing a number of Addie's toys to keep in the box. She took a photo of Addie with my cell phone and I wrote down the name and address of Addie's veterinarian and put the paper in the box for Heath. We didn't want to leave Addie again, so we stayed for a little while to play with her on Heath's patio. She must have been confused by all the activity around her, so we wanted to give her some special attention.

After a little while we went back to the manor to help with additional preparations. Graydon insisted that the radio and television stay on to keep track of the storm; there now seemed to be a general consensus among the weather experts that the storm was headed right for the Charleston area. I was getting more and more nervous, but I tried to stay busy to keep my mind off the hurricane and to keep Lucy occupied.

We worked around the property for the rest of the afternoon and then went over to the stables with Heath to check on the animals there. We made sure the animals had plenty of food and water in case no one was able to get there during or right after the storm, though Heath indicated that he would make every effort to get to the stables to tend to the animals. He put tape on each stable window while Lucy and I made sure that the chickens were secured inside their coop.

Then we went back to the manor to wait through the long hours before the hurricane was due to come. It would be at least twenty-four hours before we would begin to feel the first hints of the storm. We all had dinner together in the dining room, darkened due to the covered windows. It was really rather cozy, with the lights shining warmly and the silverware clinking quietly in the subdued atmosphere. Lucy thought it was fun.

After dinner Heath went to the carriage house where Addie was no doubt anxious to see him, and Lucy and Evie and I went upstairs to read and play with her dolls. We spent a very pleasant evening, just the three of us and the dolls.

The next day I worked on the main staircase of the manor. The steps were worn and scuffed, and I wanted to clean them as much as possible before refinishing them. I planned to refinish every other step first, then let them dry and refinish the remaining steps. Otherwise there would be no way for everyone to get up or down the stairs.

Lucy played with some of her toys in the drawing room while I worked. Evie was busy up in her room, making calls and doing some work on her computer that might not be possible if the storm knocked out power. Heath and Vivian were both in Charleston making final storm preparations. I knew Vivian was very nervous about the antiques and artwork in her store and she was spending as much time as possible there to make sure the artifacts would be safe.

It was a day of waiting, of apprehension. The weather outside was strangely calm and only a little cloudy. There was no rain, no wind. I took Lucy over to the carriage house for a little while to play with Addie on the patio and it was actually pleasant sitting out there. It truly was the calm before the storm.

We were at dinner that evening when the rain started spattering on the windows. The storm had arrived. Though it started with raindrops hitting the shutters, it became strong quickly as the wind picked up. Heath had joined us, but planned to go back to the carriage house right after dinner to stay with Addie. Strangely, Vivian had not yet arrived from Charleston. Graydon tried calling her cell phone, but it went right to voicemail. He excused himself from the table and went into the kitchen to leave her a message, which we could all hear clearly from the dining room.

"Viv, have you been paying attention? There's a hurricane coming! Get home now! Quit worrying about the things in that store of yours. They're only things. Your family is waiting for you."

He came back to the table and looked around sheepishly. He must have realized we could all hear his raised voice. He spoke to Evie and Heath.

"I don't know where in the world your mother is. She knows better than to be out in this weather. I'm starting to get worried."

Evie spoke soothingly. "Daddy, I'm sure she knows what she's doing. It isn't as if she's never been in a hurricane before. She isn't going to do anything stupid."

Heath nodded. "Don't worry, Dad. She probably forgot to turn her phone on. Or maybe she forgot to charge it. I'll bet she's on her way home now."

I hated for Heath to leave after we finished dinner. He gave Lucy a big hug and then held me in his strong arms before he went back to the carriage house.

"Stay safe," he said, his lips against my hair. "I'll see you sometime tomorrow." He kissed me good night, and I knew I would be a nervous wreck after he left.

The rest of us went our separate ways after dinner. It wasn't long before the wind started groaning around the house and the rain began slashing against the windows, and each of us gradually made our way to the drawing room, where we could be together. Vivian still wasn't home yet. Graydon had a portable radio with him and he kept an ear to the weather all the time. Every time there was a noise outside, he would jump up and walk to the front door, peering outside into the storm. And every time, he would return to the drawing room and announce, "That wasn't her." For all they seemed to get on each other's nerves, Graydon was clearly worried about his wife's absence.

As time dragged on, the storm worsened. The wind shrieked outside, slamming into the house with tremendous force. It was amazing to me that the manor didn't buckle under its strength. As Graydon explained, many people think a hurricane is a big thunderstorm, but it's really the wind that does such a massive amount of damage. The rain was relentless, but it was the keening sound of the wind that I knew I wouldn't be able to forget. The house shuddered each time a gust roared past, and I could tell Lucy was afraid. She buried her head in my lap and I stroked her forehead as I tried to get her to relax and perhaps even to sleep.

From somewhere in the house came a thunderous crash and the sound of breaking glass.

"Broken window. Must have blown the shutter off," Graydon

mumbled. "She can't be out in this." He got up and walked out of the drawing room. Evie followed him and turned to the rest of us saying, "He's going upstairs. He'll find out what the noise was." She yelled to him, "Daddy, do you want some help?"

"No," came the reply from upstairs. "Just stay where you are."

He returned several minutes later, his hair disheveled and shirt-sleeves rolled up.

"One of Ruby's shutters blew off and the glass in one of her windows broke. I tried to stuff it with a sheet. We'll get the window fixed as soon as we can once the storm is over, Ruby."

"Thanks, Graydon," she said gratefully.

She and Phyllis had been playing a card game by lamplight. As the game finished, there was a noise from outside that was different from the screaming wind to which we were quickly becoming accustomed. It was more of a crashing sound, accompanied by the raw crunch of crumpling metal.

Phyllis was the first to reach the window, followed closely by Graydon.

"It's Vivian!" Graydon announced grimly. "What is she doing out there?"

He ran to the front door and yanked it open. A tremendous gust of wind knocked him right off his feet as he stepped out into the howling hurricane. Phyllis, who was right behind him, knelt down and tried to help him up. He was on his hands and knees, cursing, when Evie rushed up behind him in the doorway.

"Daddy, are you hurt? Let me see!" Evie took her father's arm and helped him stand up. They turned and went into the house, Graydon protesting that he needed to help Vivian.

Phyllis looked up at the figure lurching across the front lawn of Peppernell Manor.

It was Vivian. She was obviously trying to make her way to the front door while carrying a very large, bulky box. She stumbled and sprawled onto the ground.

Phyllis ran out into the wind and rain and bent down over Vivian's prostrate body. She tugged at Vivian's arm and helped her to stand up. Lucy and I watched the scene from inside the doorway. As Phyllis began leading her back into the manor, Vivian began to gesticulate wildly, yelling something, but I couldn't hear her words over the roar of the wind. Phyllis evidently understood what Vivian was trying to say, because she turned around. I could see her gesturing to Vivian and they both returned to the manor, heads bent, slowly making their way through the storm to the front door. The wind was blowing so hard that they were both clearly having trouble staying upright.

When they finally reached the door, Vivian saw me and reached for my arm. "I dropped the box with some of the paintings for the front hall!" she gasped.

I looked at her, mouth agape. "Vivian, what were you thinking? Who cares about the paintings?"

"We have to go back out there and get them! They'll be ruined!" she insisted.

Phyllis was listening and turned around, her hair bedraggled and water dripping from the tips of her fingers. "I'll get them," she stated quietly.

Vivian stared at her, eyes wide. "Would you, Phyllis?"

Phyllis nodded and headed back out into the wind and rain. With a slight limp, Graydon charged into the front hall in a rage.

"What were you doing?" he demanded. There was a loose bandage over one eye and he was holding his right arm close to his side, as if it pained him to move it.

"Graydon, just listen. You know those paintings that Carleigh and I planned to hang in the front hall. I had to bring them home with me to protect them from the hurricane."

"That was the stupidest thing you've ever done!" he bellowed. "And now you've probably wrecked your car, too! Was that the crunching sound we heard?"

"Graydon, I simply refuse to discuss it with you until you've calmed down. Yes, my car was the crunching sound you heard. And Phyllis is out there right now retrieving the box with the paintings."

"You've got to be kidding!" Graydon yelled. "How can you send someone outside in a hurricane?!"

"She volunteered," Vivian said quietly.

I stood at the front door, waiting for Phyllis as she struggled to the door with the large box that Vivian had dropped. I wanted to help her, but Lucy was clinging to me and whimpering, terrified that I would leave her to go out into the storm. I could see Graydon and Vivian out of the corner of my eye.

Graydon was looking into Vivian's eyes. "Thank God you're all right," he told her. She smiled at him. "But you shouldn't have sent Phyllis out into the storm. She deserves better than that from you."

"I'll apologize, Graydon," said Vivian with a pout.

"That's my girl," he said. They joined me in peering out into the storm. Phyllis was lugging the box of paintings up to the front of the house. I ran out to help her and together we got the box up the stairs. She pulled and I pushed it through the front door.

"There's your box," she told Vivian.

"Thank you, Phyllis," Vivian replied. She glanced at Graydon. "I'm sorry I let you go out into the storm."

Phyllis nodded her head in acknowledgment.

Vivian continued. "And thank you for coming to my rescue out there." She looked at her feet. Vivian, who was usually so poised and confident, was clearly not used to apologizing.

"You're welcome," Phyllis stated.

I turned to Phyllis. "Let's get you out of those wet clothes and into a bathrobe," I told her briskly. "You go change and I'll make you something hot to drink." She looked at me gratefully. Lucy trotted behind me into the kitchen and watched while I made Phyllis and Vivian cups of hot sweet tea.

Hot sweet tea during a hurricane ... I was getting to be a real Southerner.

I set up a tray with the tea and a plate of benne wafers and knocked on Phyllis's door, Lucy still following me silently.

"Come in." She sat in her living room in a bathrobe and slippers.

"You okay, Phyllis?"

"I am now. Thank you for bringing me tea. That's some storm out there."

"With the exception of Ruby's shutter and window, the house seems to be making it through the hurricane just fine."

She settled into her armchair. "This house has been through plenty of hurricanes. Sarah told me about the Great Hurricane of 1893. It made landfall in Savannah, Georgia, and devastated the coast from Georgia to New York."

"It sounds awful."

"That's what Sarah said. But you know what? This manor house has survived them all. And you know why? Because slaves built it, that's why. They were craftsmen. They took pride in the work they did. They were good at what they did. Their work has stood for almost two hundred years, through hurricanes and storms and climate and weather, and it's still standing because they knew what they were doing."

"I never thought about it that way, Phyllis. You're right. They must have been amazing craftsmen."

"And they built those cabins, too. The only reason the cabins don't look so good now is that they weren't allowed to use the high-quality materials on their homes that they used for the great house." She shook her head in disgust.

"It's amazing that they're standing at all, then. What a testament to their work."

"Unfortunately not everyone sees it that way."

"Maybe we can get them to, Phyllis, if you'll think a little more about my suggestion to restore them. Graydon thinks it's a good idea, and we would do it respectfully."

She stared into space for a full minute, then answered me.

"Maybe. Just maybe. I suppose the family will go ahead and do what they want whether I like the idea or not, so it would be nice if someone could do the work like it deserves to be done, to honor those people who built the cabins."

"I would do that, Phyllis. I promise."

She smiled at me. "Do you think maybe I could help you?"

"I wouldn't want to do it without your help," I told her.

"Then let's give it a try."

I beamed at her. "That's wonderful! Everyone will be so happy to hear that you've given the project your blessing!"

"You go back to the manor now and ride out the rest of this storm in the drawing room with the rest of the family. I'll be fine here."

"By yourself?"

She smiled again. "I won't be by myself. Sarah's here with me."

In spite of myself, I turned around to look behind me. As I had known, I couldn't see anyone standing there, but apparently Phyllis could. "Okay. But come and join us if you want to," I remarked as Lucy and I left.

"Who's Sarah?" my little one asked as we made our way back to the drawing room.

CHAPTER 18

We all camped together in the drawing room that night. Evie and I went down to the basement and brought up several air mattresses, sheets, and blankets that had been in the storage room containing the emergency supplies. Everyone shared a big pot of "hurricane stew" that Phyllis had left in the kitchen. It was delicious mix of tomatoes, zucchini, sausage, onions, and carrots. Even Lucy liked it, and she wasn't usually fond of any red food except pizza.

It took Lucy quite a while to fall asleep because of the noise from the wind, the excitement of having a sleepover with the entire household in the drawing room, and the lamp that we left burning dimly in the corner. But eventually her breathing became deep and regular and I knew she was sleeping soundly.

It was almost midnight when the power went out. I was still awake, listening to the crashing and shrieking of the wind outside. I didn't know if anyone else was lying awake, but when the lamp went out suddenly several voices started whispering at once.

"Daddy, are you awake? The power's out," Evie said. She didn't even sound tired.

"I know," came his reply.

"Hush, both of you," cautioned Vivian. "You'll wake Lucy."

"Should we get the candles?" asked Ruby.

"Nah," answered Graydon. "As long as it's the middle of the night, let's just try to get some sleep. We'll get the candles tomorrow when the storm is over. If it ever ends."

As if in response, the wind outside roared around the house, slamming rain into the windows. I shuddered. The emergency radio bleeped on, warning us of possible tornado conditions nearby. *That* really scared me. I lay next to Lucy, stiff as a board, wishing I could be sleeping as peacefully as she was. Evie stood up and went to the front door. I watched her from my mattress through the doorway of the drawing room. She opened the door and looked out; the noise from the wind reached a deafening pitch with the door open. With an effort, she closed the door again and came back into the drawing room.

"The sky doesn't look any different and I don't hear a tornado," she whispered. "Not yet, at least."

Having lived in the Midwest, I knew all about tornadoes. They touched down often in Illinois, but I had never experienced one in Chicago.

"Is it common to have a tornado during a hurricane?"

"No, but it's happened before," Evie answered.

I don't know how I ever got to sleep, but eventually I drifted off into a fitful rest.

There must have been a lull in the wind for a brief moment in the middle of the night. That's when I heard the blood-curdling scream that jolted me to my feet.

Evie and Graydon heard it, too. The others remained asleep.

We all raced to the front door and stared out into the storm. We couldn't see anything but the slashing rain and the trees near the house, nearly bent over to the ground from the force of the wind.

Another lull, and we heard it again. It seemed to be coming from behind the manor. Graydon grabbed a raincoat from a hook near the rear door of the manor and turned to us.

"I have to see what's making that noise."

"Daddy, you can't go out there! You're limping and your arm is all bandaged, and your eye is hurt, too!"

He looked at Evie grimly. "I can't just ignore that screaming."

There was a tremendous banging at the front door. I hurried to yank it open and Heath stood there, soaking wet.

"What's going on? Were you screaming?" I asked.

"No. But I heard it, too. I went out to see what it was and I didn't find anything." He looked at Graydon's bandages in surprise.

"What happened to you?"

"Never mind. Where's the noise coming from?"

"The pond outside Phyllis's apartment."

"Let's go."

Before Heath could say anything, Graydon had opened the rear door and was headed out into the storm, his body bent to shield his face from the wind. Heath hurried after him.

I could barely see Heath and Graydon as they made their way slowly to the pond. Suddenly Heath bent down and reached for a dark form lying on the ground. He must have called for Graydon, who turned back and knelt down. Together, the two men started pulling the form toward the house. Addie had somehow gotten out of the carriage house and was jumping back and forth between them.

I couldn't stand watching anymore. I ran out into the storm, telling Evie to keep an eye on Lucy. "Heath?!" I cried, lurching toward the dark figures.

"Stay back, Carleigh!" came his voice through the storm's din. I ignored his warning and kept going toward the men. The rain stung as the wind blasted it into my skin.

I stopped short when I heard Heath yell. "Carleigh, go back and call an ambulance! This guy needs help!"

I didn't even stop to ask who the person was or why he needed help. I turned on my heel and ran back into the house.

I burst through the door; and it wasn't long before Evie was at my side as I held the house phone to my ear. She held a flashlight.

"Nine-one-one, what is your emergency?" asked a woman's voice.

"I don't know! There's someone hurt outside, but I don't know who or how," I answered breathlessly.

I told her where I was located. Her voice came back on the line.

"I don't think we can get anyone out there right now because of the storm. Can you describe the injuries to me? I'll tell you what to do to keep the patient stable until help can arrive."

"Yes." I stayed on the line while we all waited for Heath and Graydon to pull the stranger to the safety of the house.

I turned to Evie. "Where's Lucy?"

"She's still asleep. Can you believe it? I'll go back in the drawing room and stay with her. I just heard you come in and I needed to know what's going on."

Vivian and Ruby appeared in the kitchen. "What's wrong?"

Evie turned around. "I don't know. There was screaming outside. Daddy and Heath are out there and they're bringing someone back inside. The person is hurt."

I looked outside again, the phone still clutched in my hand. Heath and Graydon were still tugging on the stranger's arms, making slow progress toward the manor.

I had to help them. I spoke quickly into the phone.

"I'll be right back."

"Okay," came the dispatcher's calm voice.

I ran out again into the fierce storm. "Come on, buddy!" Heath was yelling above the wind. "Try to push yourself along a little. Carleigh, take Addie into the house, will you?" Graydon tried to put his arms around the man's torso to help Heath pull. The man seemed to be having trouble using his legs. I focused the flashlight's beam on the ground behind Heath and Graydon so they wouldn't trip.

I called to Addie, though I doubted she would leave Heath and Graydon with the man. To my surprise, she made her way over to me, checking behind her every couple seconds to see if Heath was all right. I grabbed her collar and made her stay next to me.

I moved the flashlight beam a little by mistake when I grabbed the dog and saw a dark substance covering the man's legs. Blood.

"Heath, what happened?" I yelled.

"Alligator!"

I froze. Vivian was standing behind me and heard Heath.

"An alligator!" she exclaimed, wringing her hands. "What are we going to do? We won't be able to set foot outside!"

The man being dragged appeared to be drifting in and out of consciousness, but it was still too dark to tell for sure. Graydon and Heath pulled him up toward the back of the manor as I ran inside with Addie.

Leaving Addie, I returned to the scene as Heath and Graydon were finally able to drag the stranger into the kitchen and turn him onto his back.

CHAPTER 19

It was Brad. He lay on the floor, eyes closed, his leg bleeding profusely where an alligator had bitten him. I gasped.

"I know. It looks pretty bad," Heath said grimly.

"That's not what I mean," I told him. "That's Brad!"

"Brad? Your ex-husband? What's he doing here?"

"I have no idea. I thought he was in Chicago!"

Brad's eyes fluttered open, then closed again. I stared at him in astonishment then remembered the dispatcher on the phone.

"There's a man here who's been bitten by an alligator!" I told her.

She briskly gave me a list of supplies we would need to give Brad first aid and then waited as we found everything we needed in the emergency kit. Then she walked me through the process of administering first aid to keep Brad stable until the paramedics could get to the house.

We dragged an air mattress into the dining room and placed a heavy sleeping bag on top. Heath and Graydon carefully lifted Brad onto the mattress and he lay there, motionless, as I bandaged his leg, his arm, and his head. There was nothing else we could do but wait for an ambulance to arrive. My thoughts turned to Lucy. I didn't want her to know her father was in the house, and I certainly didn't want her to see him in his condition. I called Evie over.

"Can you keep Lucy occupied in the drawing room and upstairs until the EMTs can get here and take Brad away?"

She nodded. "No problem."

Graydon and Heath had been drying off and getting warm drinks. They both came to stand near me, as did Vivian and Ruby.

"I wonder why he's here," Graydon mused.

I shook my head. "I have no idea. I thought he was in Chicago."

"What do you suppose he wanted?" asked Vivian.

"Your guess is as good as mine."

Heath decided to spend the rest of the night at the manor. He sat with me in the dining room where Brad was curled in a fetal position on top of the sleeping bag. Though it was nearly impossible, I must have dozed out of sheer exhaustion, because I awoke to a strange silence in the house. Mercifully, no tornado had come.

Vivian was opening the door to the EMTs and police. I could see daylight outside. Heath and I stood up quietly and tiptoed to the front door. I showed them where Brad was still lying—either asleep or unconscious, I didn't know—on the dining room floor.

They quickly took charge of the situation. The police pulled Heath and Graydon and me to the side while the EMTs got to work on Brad's leg. I heard one paramedic utter the terse phrase "in shock." I peeked into the hallway just in time to see Evie leading a still-sleepy Lucy upstairs. Thankfully she seemed to be completely unaware of the drama in the dining room.

Heath and Graydon and the police were looking at me. I had missed a question from the police officer.

"I'm sorry. What?"

"Do you know that man?" the officer repeated.

"He's my ex-husband."

"Where does he live?"

"Chicago."

"What was he doing here?"

"I have no idea. I didn't know he was in South Carolina."

"Would he have any reason to be here that you know of?"

I shook my head. "Not unless he was here to check up on our daughter. She's here with me while I'm working on restoring this home. But she talks to him every night on the phone and he never said anything about being in the area."

The officer was writing in a small notepad and turned when one of the paramedics walked up to him.

"We're taking him in," the medic said. "You coming?"

"Yes," the officer answered. He turned to the rest of us. "I'll be back once the other side of this storm moves through." Then he followed the paramedics steering Brad on a stretcher around to the front of Peppernell Manor.

Heath and Graydon were staring at me; Vivian and Ruby had joined them.

"I'm so sorry, all of you. I have the same questions that you must have."

"Brad isn't the only problem," noted Graydon. "There's an alligator on the property that we have to take care of. I'll call Animal Control after the storm ends. They'll know what to do. The gator could have come out of the river, or it could have been in the pond. The storm probably stirred it up and it came out of hiding."

"I hope they don't kill it," Ruby said quietly.

Vivian looked at her in disgust. "Ruby, how can you say that? I only hope it doesn't attack someone else before Animal Control can catch it."

Graydon addressed his sister. "I don't think they'll kill it. They'll probably capture it and release it far away from here."

"Good," she said with a sigh.

"Heath, if you want to get back to the carriage house you'd better do it now before the storm worsens again," said Graydon.

Heath nodded and whistled for Addie. He looked at me, concerned. "Don't worry. We'll figure everything out once the storm is over. Just be glad Lucy never found out Brad was here." Then he kissed me. I smiled wanly.

He descended the front steps, then turned around just as Evie came up behind me.

"What happened to Mother's car?" He nodded in the direction of the garage.

Evie rolled her eyes. "Long story."

"You'll tell me later, I gather."

"Of course. Daddy's mad at her, but I think it's just a mask for his relief. She got home during the storm last night, long after you left."

Heath winced. "Thank goodness she's all right." He turned around and headed back to the carriage house.

"Lucy's asleep in her bed," Evie told me before I even had a chance to ask her.

Ruby brought me a cup of tea, which I drank gratefully. I walked to the front door and looked outside again. It was still. I could see the damage wrought by the wind, but it seemed to be mostly confined to tree branches, plants, and some roof shingles from the garage, at least from where I stood.

As everyone made their way into the kitchen, Phyllis appeared and set out slices of homemade banana bread and fresh fruit. Luckily, there was a gas stove in the kitchen and she had been able to heat up water for tea. She said that there were eggs in the refrigerator but since the power had gone out at least seven hours ago, she was reluctant to use them.

We waited for just a short time before the wind started howling again. The back of the storm had arrived, bringing with it more slashing rain. It was somehow easier to wait through the rest of the storm during the daytime. We played games in the drawing room by candlelight since we still couldn't open the shutters to let in the light, and we read books. Everyone took turns reading to Lucy.

At last the storm was over. The wind petered out slowly, and the rain slowed to a steady drumming. Heath came over and he and Graydon went around the manor, opening shutters to gray misty light. A couple of windowpanes were cracked, but Ruby's shutter and window seemed to have suffered the worst damage. The rest of the house had made it through another storm intact. Phyllis reminded us as we ate a late lunch of bread and fruit that it was the work of her ancestors that had kept us all safe from the hurricane.

The police and paramedics had my number and had said someone from the hospital would call later. I hadn't heard from anyone yet, so after lunch Lucy followed me around as I gathered the supplies I would need to refinish the staircase in the entry hall. I began the tedious job of sanding and restaining each step. Around midafternoon, Heath called.

"Feel like going into Charleston with me?" he asked. "I need to check on things at the office."

"I'd love to, but I assume I'm going to have to talk to the police again and I should probably find out what's going on with Brad. Besides that, I've taken the past few days off and I should really get some more work done," I explained. "Lucy will have to go back to school tomorrow and I have a couple of shops I need to visit after I drop her off. Want to meet for lunch then?"

"It's a date," he said.

The hospital finally called later that evening. Brad was stable, the nurse told me, but he could not yet receive visitors. Someone would call when he was awake and alert. The police called, too, and said they wanted to talk to Brad before they questioned me again.

CHAPTER 20

The next morning Graydon called Animal Control to discuss the alligator that was possibly still on the property. They were quite busy, they said, with displaced animals from the storm, so they would get to Peppernell Manor as soon as possible. I took Lucy back to school, where she was thrilled to be reunited with her friends, all of whom chatted excitedly about things other than the hurricane. It was peculiar—the adults talked of nothing else, but the kids seemed to have forgotten it already.

Another nurse called after I dropped Lucy off and said that Brad was doing better, but he had asked that I not visit him yet. That was fine with me.

I was excited to begin talking with a few shop owners about my ideas for restoring the slave cabins. I felt a twinge of guilt over not working on the stairs that morning, but I needed to get the prep work done on the cabins so I could work on them as soon as the stairs were completed. I stopped first to talk to the woman who had sold me the dining room wallpaper. She loved the idea of being involved. I had done some research on the subject and consulted with Phyllis, and the shop owner also shared some of her knowledge with me. We eventually decided to cover the walls with a special type of reinforced paper printed with reproduction newsprint from the nineteenth century. The paper would look just like pages from newspapers. Phyllis's ancestors would have used newspapers to cover their walls and keep out drafts, and I wanted to be true to the cabins' original interiors.

I went next to the workshop of a steeplejack. I wanted to make sure that the chimneys in the cabins were safe and in working condition before beginning the restoration of the ceilings, walls, and floors. The man offered to visit Peppernell Manor sometime over the next day or two to have a look at the chimneys and make his recommendations. He was familiar with the slave cabins at Peppernell Manor, he told me, and was thrilled to have the opportunity to help in their restoration.

I had a delightful early lunch with Heath before returning to the manor to work again on the staircase. We sat outside a café in the bright sunshine, his hand on mine. It was *almost* easy to forget that we had been in the middle of a hurricane just two days earlier, and that my ex-husband had been seriously injured while trespassing during the storm.

After lunch we walked leisurely around the block hand in hand, talking of things other than my job, his job, Brad, or Lucy. I told him about winter in Chicago and he told me about winter in South Carolina. I was looking forward to spending winter in the South.

I left him at his office and went back to work at the manor; I was actually able to get a lot done before I had to pick up Lucy.

The power was finally restored to the manor that night after Lucy went to bed. Though she was thrilled by the use of candles for light, I had begun to grow tired of it and I was glad when the lights came on again. Evie and I went into the drawing room, each with a glass of wine, and she turned on every lamp.

"Isn't that overkill?" I asked.

She laughed. "Maybe, but I don't care. Now that the power's back on, I intend to use it."

The morning dawned windy and pleasant. The hospital called and said Brad was ready to receive visitors. I called the police and was told that two officers were going to talk to him and that I could talk to him when they were done. After I ate breakfast with Lucy and sent her upstairs to get ready for school, Vivian came into the kitchen.

"Carleigh, are you going to the hospital in the morning to see your ex-husband?" she asked.

"Yes. I'll stop there as soon as I drop Lucy off at school."

"I feel violated," Vivian exclaimed. "To think that an unwanted visitor was on our property!"

"I am very sorry about it," I told her. "If I had had the slightest inkling that he was planning to come here, I would have put a stop to it immediately."

"I'm sure you would, dear."

"Would what?" asked Evie, coming into the room.

"I would have stopped Brad if I had known he was coming here."

"Are you going to see him in the hospital?"

"Yes."

"Are you going to tell Lucy that he's in South Carolina?"

"No way. She doesn't need to see him like that. It would just scare her."

"What are you going to say to him?"

"I don't know," I answered grimly, "but he's got a lot of explaining to do. His leg is going to be the least of his worries."

"I think you'd better take Heath with you," Evie fretted. "I'm not sure it's safe for you to go by yourself."

"There's nothing Brad can do to me in the hospital. He can't even walk. But I'll take Heath if he wants to go. He may not want to be there for my tender reunion with Brad, though."

"Maybe he should go to keep *you* from killing Brad," Evie said with a wry smile.

"That might be a good idea," I agreed.

As it turned out, Heath didn't want me to go see Brad alone, so we dropped Lucy off at school and drove over to the hospital together. I located Brad's room and we went up and stood in the hallway. The police were just leaving. They said they had gotten very little information from Brad and would talk to me later.

Suddenly I was reluctant to go in. Heath said, "You don't have to go in there, you know. You can just let the police do their job and do your talking through them."

I shook my head. "No, I have to talk to him face to face."

"Okay, if you're sure. I'll wait for you out here. Just give me a shout if you need me." I squared my shoulders and pushed Brad's door open. He lay on the bed with his eyes closed. He had IV tubes stuck in his arms and his leg was heavily bandaged. His face was worn-looking and haggard with several days' growth of beard. It looked like he had lost weight.

He looked terrible.

I shook his free arm gently and his eyelids fluttered open slowly.

"Carleigh." The word came out of his mouth dry and sticky.

"Yes. How are you feeling this morning?"

He groaned. "Miserable. The gator got my leg."

"I know. What on earth were you doing out there? And during a hurricane?"

He turned his head slowly away from me and didn't answer. I was about to repeat myself when he turned back toward me. He closed his eyes and spoke in a low voice.

"Checking up on you and Lucy. I was holed up in the outhouse—"

"It's called a privy," I interrupted.

"I was waiting out the storm in there and didn't think the hurricane would be as strong as it was. I just wanted to make sure she was safe, but I couldn't see in the windows of the manor. I thought I would be able to get back to Charleston."

"Why? What's wrong with a phone call? And what do you mean, 'back to Charleston'?"

"I wanted to see everything for myself. And I've been staying in Charleston."

"For how long?"

"About a week."

"A week?! And you wanted to see what for yourself?"

"I wanted to see where you and Lucy are living. I wanted to see what your life is like down here. I wanted to see . . . everything."

"I trust you satisfied your curiosity?"

His form seemed to shrink under his thin sheet. He winced, whether from pain or from shame, I don't know.

"Well, did you?" I asked.

"I guess."

"How long were you at the manor?"

"Several nights in a row."

"What?!" I yelled. I could see Heath's head out of the corner of my eye, checking on me through the window.

"Several nights. I wanted to know who that guy is and what you're doing with him."

"What guy?" I knew perfectly well which guy he was talking about.

"That really tall guy who lives next to the mansion."

"Why do you care who he is?"

"I just do," he said petulantly.

"His name is Heath Peppernell."

"He's your boyfriend?"

"Yes, though that's none of your business."

He turned away again.

"It is my business because of Lucy."

"I don't get it."

"You can't see him if he's not good to Lucy."

"First of all, you can't tell me what I can and can't do. Second, do you think I'd date someone who isn't good to her? Honestly, Brad, do you think I'm stupid? Heath adores her, and she adores him, too."

"You should have told me that you're dating him."

"It's none of your business."

"Are you going to marry him?"

"That's also none of your business."

"I expect you to tell me what your plans are."

"The same way you did when you fell for that stripper?" I jeered. "How is Jiggly—I mean Jilly, anyways?"

"Don't call her that." He turned to face the wall again. "Anyway, she and I are through."

"I'd love to stay here and chat about it, but I don't have time. I've got to get back to work. Listen to me, Brad. The police aren't done with you yet. They're wondering why you were trespassing on my employer's property during a hurricane. They're going to love it when you tell them you were there to stalk your ex-wife and daughter. The family court judge back in Chicago ought to enjoy the story, too. Good luck with that, and don't come near me or Lucy again without telling me first."

I turned on my heel and went out to where Heath was standing in the hallway.

"How'd it go?" he asked.

"He's a jerk," I answered. "He's been spying on me! He's been at Peppernell Manor for several nights!" I paused suddenly, thinking. "I'll be right back," I told Heath.

"Where are you going?"

"I have to ask him something."

I went back into Brad's room. His eyes were closed again, but he opened them when I walked in. "Brad, when did you and Jiggly break up?"

"Around the time you left Chicago. Why?"

"Did you call me at the manor and threaten me?"

He looked away.

"Brad?"

"Yes," he mumbled.

"Why?"

"I wanted you to bring Lucy back to Chicago. Jilly and I had broken up and suddenly I was alone."

"You're unbelievable," I said with a scowl. He didn't answer and I left.

"Everything all right?" Heath asked when I joined him in the hallway again.

"Yes. Brad was the one who called me that night and threatened me. So that's solved."

"He called and threatened you?"

"Yes." I had forgotten that Heath didn't know about the phone call.

"He *is* a jerk."

Heath looked pensive as we walked to the elevator together and he finally said, "I'll bet that's why Addie has been barking so much at night. She knew someone was there."

"Of course! That has to be the reason! Poor thing, she was trying to warn everyone and nobody would listen to her."

"We'll have to give her a treat." He smiled and put his arm around my shoulders, then became serious. "Was it upsetting to see Brad?"

"A little, but I surprised myself. It was easier than I thought to stand up to him. Of course, he *was* in a hospital bed. I don't know that I would have been as brave if he hadn't been an invalid."

"Why was he spying on you?"

I grimaced. "He wanted to know who you are."

"Me? Why?"

"He wants to make sure that you're good to Lucy."

"Does he think you would tolerate anyone who wasn't good to Lucy?"

"That's what I said. He's a stalker, plain and simple. He just wants to keep tabs on me, that's all. He's always been like that—you can ask Evie."

"She doesn't like him?"

"Never did, apparently, in part because he was so controlling. I didn't recognize it as that when I was in college, but I see it clearly now."

"He makes me a little nervous. What's going to happen when he gets out of the hospital?"

"I don't know. I'm going to ask the police how they recommend dealing with him."

"Maybe you and Lucy should stay with me," he said, grinning and waggling his eyebrows.

I rolled my eyes at him, laughing. "I'd love to, but with Brad in town, I think we'd better stay in the manor house. The last thing I need is to be giving Brad ammunition by living with my boyfriend."

"Let's hope he just goes back to Chicago."

CHAPTER 21

Heath went to his office and I drove back to Peppernell Manor. I had a meeting with the steeplejack to determine what had to be done to restore the fireplaces and chimneys in the slave cabins.

He was right on time. I showed him the slave cabins and explained what I had in mind for the restoration. His recommendations were encouraging, and he told me he could start the brickwork immediately. We made plans for him to return the next day to begin. I spent the rest of the day working on the staircase in the manor and I had completed it by the time I had to go pick up Lucy at school. The stairs looked magnificent; the family would be very pleased.

When Lucy and I arrived back at the manor, Graydon was in the kitchen taking a break from his work.

"Any word on the g-a-t-o-r?" I asked him.

"Animal Control should be here tomorrow. Apparently we're not the only property with that problem," he said, recognizing that I didn't want Lucy to know there had been an alligator on the property. "We're the only ones that experienced a casualty, though. How is he?" he asked cryptically.

"I'll fill you in later," I promised him. As we spoke Lucy looked from me to Graydon with a blank look on her face. Graydon tousled her hair and tickled her, making her forget that the adults were having a conversation she didn't understand.

Heath joined the rest of the family for dinner that night. Vivian had evidently spoken with someone during the day who had piqued her interest in once again having investors look at the property.

"Graydon, you have to speak to a man who came into my store today. We got talking about old properties and of course I told him about Peppernell Manor, and he thought his investment group would love to learn more about it," she told him excitedly.

Ruby looked at Graydon. Her mouth opened as if she wanted to say something, but she closed it again. Heath glanced at me as if to say, "Uh-oh. Here it comes."

Graydon raised his water glass to his lips and took a sip, then slowly folded his napkin on his lap as Vivian looked at him expectantly. He seemed to be gathering his thoughts. Finally he spoke.

"Vivian, my dear, I don't want to argue with you at the dinner table, but since you keep bringing up this subject in front of everyone, I feel you've left me no choice. You know very well how I feel about investors coming into this house. Mother didn't want outsiders with a financial interest having a say in how this property is used, and I feel strongly that we should honor her wishes. Not only that, but I happen to agree with her. Now I hope that closes the subject."

"It most certainly does not," Vivian answered in a huffy drawl. "This is my home, too, and I believe *I* deserve a say in how it is run in the future. I am a businesswoman, Graydon, and I know better than you do how to run a successful venture. And I am telling you that we should go with the smartest way to provide a profitable future for this manor!"

She turned on Heath. "Heath, honey, you agree with me, don't you?"

"Mom, you know that I don't like getting involved in these discussions."

"What kind of man did I raise, that won't support his mother?"

"A smart one." Heath winked at me.

"Y'all make me so mad," Vivian seethed. "You need to learn how to run a business."

"This isn't a business, Vivian! It's a home!" Graydon exploded.

"Why you can't—" Vivian began.

From the other end of the table came a sharp, piercing scream. All eyes turned on Ruby, who was sitting with her hands over her ears, her eyes squeezed shut. The scream went on, Ruby only stopping once for a long, ragged breath.

"Stop it stop it stop it stop it stop it stop it!" she screamed, repeating the phrase over and over until, spent, she slumped forward in her chair, sobbing. Lucy started crying and I jumped up and whisked her upstairs. I couldn't imagine what was going on in the dining room, but I was thankful to have escaped. I gave Lucy a bath and read to her, trying to soothe her, until she finally fell asleep in my arms. Heath came up to our room after a while. We talked in whispers.

"What happened?"

"Ruby cried and cried until Evie finally got her to talk. She's upset about the fighting. She feels that it dishonors Gran when Mother keeps insisting on bringing up the subject of money and how Peppernell Manor will be run in the future. And she finally reminded everyone that she is half-owner of Peppernell Manor, too. I'm afraid we've all kind of overlooked that. Dad is such a strong personality, and it's easy to forget that he's not the only owner."

"I've wondered sometimes how Ruby feels when people talk to Graydon as if he's the only one in charge here. I wonder if she's upset or if she's relieved that her brother is the one dealing with the business side of things," I replied.

"I'm embarrassed to say I never really thought about it," he said.

"How did your mother and father react to what Ruby said?"

"Mother was indignant and told Ruby that she can't see beyond the end of her nose. But I think the truth is that Ruby embarrassed her and she was just being defensive. Dad apologized to Ruby and told her that he thought she wanted him to take charge."

"What did Ruby say?"

"She told him she doesn't mind if he takes charge, as long as the people who live here continue to honor Gran's memory and as long as people remember that she is a co-owner."

"I don't think anyone is likely to forget it again," I noted.

He sat down on the bed and Lucy, still asleep, shifted and flung her arm across his lap.

"Isn't this great?" he whispered, nodding down at Lucy.

I nodded, smiling at her chubby face. "She just adores you," I replied.

"We make a great trio," he told me, winking.

"I agree."

He removed Lucy's arm slowly and carefully so she wouldn't wake up, then kissed me. "I should get back to my place," he said. "I have files to review tonight. Court in the morning. I'll see you tomorrow."

When I returned to the manor in the morning after taking Lucy to school, Animal Control was parked in the drive and four men stood around the pond with all kinds of implements that I assumed they would use to try to catch the alligator. They were talking to Graydon. I was thankful they hadn't arrived while Lucy was still there, or I would have been fielding her questions for days. I was surprised when they all got into their van and drove off, leaving their equipment behind.

"What's going on?" I asked Graydon when he came in the house.

"They'll come back tonight and set the traps for the alligator."

"Why don't they do it now?"

"Because they still have other properties to visit and because the gators come out at night to feed. That's the best time to catch them. They'll set up traps by the pond and along the riverbank."

"What happens if they catch an alligator?"

"Do you really want to know?"

I thought for a moment. "I don't know. Just tell me the gator doesn't get returned to Peppernell Manor."

"Don't worry about that. If the gator is alive and unhurt, I think they'll send it to the Everglades, where there are endangered gator populations. If the gator is hurt, they'll have to euthanize it."

I shuddered. I hated to think of the gator being killed, but on the other hand, I didn't want to ever see it alive at Peppernell Manor again.

I went to work in the slave cabins that day, cleaning out the brush and the rubbish that had accumulated in the corners and around the cabins' bases. I couldn't do any more inside the manor until the mason I'd hired to work on the basement floor had completed his work. He said it should only take him a few days. While I worked, the steeplejack arrived and began his work. I took some time to watch him to learn more about his job and the work he was doing. It was fascinating.

By the time I had bagged up all the refuse from the cabin sites, the steeplejack had finished his work for the day and it was time to get Lucy. We spent the afternoon and evening indoors since there was a gator lurking around somewhere outside, but I couldn't wait for the gator to be caught so we could once again enjoy being outdoors, visiting Addie and Heath in the evenings.

The men from Animal Control came back after dark and used large electric lanterns to see as they set the traps. Lucy was in bed, sound asleep. If I craned my neck I could watch their activities from my window. Graydon and Heath were outside with them; they probably were more of a nuisance than a help, but I'm sure they were fascinated with the process of setting an alligator trap.

I watched until everyone dispersed and Animal Control took their lanterns with them. In the morning I was awakened by the sound of voices outside. Moving quietly to the window so Lucy would remain asleep, I peeked outside. It wasn't quite light out yet, but I could see from my perch.

There was an alligator in the trap by the pond. It was attached to a long line that led somewhere—I couldn't see where. The beast was enormous—at least six feet in length. The men from Animal Control were outside and they used some kind of instrument to tranquilize it from a short distance away. I hoped, on second thought, that they hadn't just killed the animal before my eyes, but then when I saw them carefully lift the gator I figured it was still alive. They were probably taking precautions in case it should wake up too soon. It took the strength of all four men to move the alligator onto a large sling that was lying on the ground nearby. I noticed Graydon and Heath standing safely off to one side, allowing the people from Animal Control to do their work unimpeded.

After that the gator was loaded onto a sledge-like contraption and dragged out of my sight. When Lucy and I went downstairs to breakfast a short while later, Heath and Graydon were reliving the experience excitedly over breakfast, but they stopped talking about it when we walked into the room.

"Everything taken care of?" I asked.

"You bet," said Graydon. "Did you see any of it?"

"Yes," I answered. "Some of it."

Heath took one last gulp of coffee, grabbed his briefcase, kissed me, and rumpled Lucy's hair saying, "Why don't you guys run over and see Addie before school? She's been lonely."

Lucy let out a whoop of joy and I told her I'd take her over to the carriage house. Poor Addie hadn't had any visits from her best friend since the alligator attacked Brad. I had been afraid to walk anywhere on the property with her until the gator was caught.

After I had dropped Lucy off at school, I returned to Peppernell Manor, where Graydon was outside talking to the steeplejack and the mason about the alligator.

"Carleigh," he called to me. "I got a phone call from Animal Control. Want to know more about our gator?"

"What did you find out?" I asked. The steeplejack and mason listened with obvious interest.

"It was a relatively young male, healthy, who was probably displaced or confused after the hurricane. He still had a piece of Brad's pant leg in his teeth. The guys from Animal Control think Brad was just in the wrong place at the wrong time. The gator probably thought he was some kind of food and lunged at him from inside the pond."

"I almost hate to ask this, but what are they going to do with him?"

"I asked them about that, and they are indeed going to release him into a threatened population in the Everglades down in Florida."

"Good. I didn't want him to die, but I certainly didn't want to ever see him around here again."

The conversation drew to a close and the hired men and I got to work on our respective tasks. I had a look at the work the mason was doing down in the basement; he seemed to be doing a beautiful job. As soon as he was done I could get started on the walls and storage rooms.

Before picking up Lucy from school that afternoon I went to the hospital to check on Brad's progress. He had shaved, but his eyes still had a haunted look.

"They're letting me out tomorrow," he said by way of a greeting.

"Where are you going after you get out?"

"I'm thinking of staying right here."

"Why don't you want to go back to Chicago?"

"Because my daughter is here. I want to be close to her."

"You're still going to have to deal with the consequences of being at Peppernell Manor, spying on me, the other night. They caught the alligator, by the way."

"Good. Did they shoot it?"

"No. They're sending it to the Everglades to introduce him into a threatened population of alligators down there."

"They should have shot it."

I cocked my eyebrow at him. "You wouldn't have been hurt at all if you hadn't been snooping around where you weren't welcome or permitted."

He looked at me with a hangdog expression and I ignored it. "You are going to have to go back to Chicago to get your stuff," I pointed out.

"I brought it with me. It's all in the back of my car. The rest I put into storage in Chicago."

I was somehow surprised by this. "You were planning to stay all along?"

"Yes."

"Why didn't you just tell me, 'Carleigh, I've decided to move to South Carolina to be closer to Lucy' instead of embarking on this crazy scheme of yours?"

"I don't know. I had to find out if you had a boyfriend and I couldn't trust Lucy to keep her mouth shut if I asked her."

"She's three," I reminded him. "I'm not sure how much information you could have gotten out of her anyways."

"I know," he replied miserably.

"Where are you going to stay?"

"I found an apartment in Charleston."

"Are you going to continue trading?"

"Yes."

"I don't want you interfering with Lucy. I'm not sure you're even going to be allowed near her if you're charged with trespassing or whatever else stalkers get charged with."

"Enough, Carleigh. I'm sorry, all right? Is that what you want? An apology? I'm sorry."

"I don't need an apology from you. All I want is a promise that you're going to leave me alone from now on."

"Okay. I'll leave you alone. I promise."

"And Lucy?"

"What about her?"

"Are you going to promise to leave her alone, too?"

"No. She's my daughter and I want to see her whenever I choose."

"You're forgetting that I have primary custody. That still holds true even if we're not in Illinois anymore."

"Okay. Then we have to work out an arrangement where I can see her."

"Let's work on that after your current troubles are over. I don't even want Lucy to know you're in South Carolina until this whole thing is cleared up."

"All right," he snapped.

"I've got to go." I walked to the door and turned the handle, then looked back at Brad. He looked pathetic lying there in the hospital bed, and I felt an unexpected pang of sympathy for him. "Brad, I hope we can get through all of this and be friends. For Lucy's sake."

He just nodded, avoiding my eyes.

CHAPTER 22

With the weather getting cooler I could finally turn my attention to Thanksgiving, which was only a few days away. I was excited to take Heath to Florida with us to meet my parents. Lucy only had two more days of school before we left.

She and I had dinner with Heath again that evening. Addie was sound asleep in the carriage house. As we sat on the patio and enjoyed hamburgers on the grill, one of Heath's specialties, the talk centered on our Thanksgiving plans. Lucy was thrilled that Heath would be joining us at Grandma and Grandpa's house in Florida for the holiday. She didn't yet understand the full meaning of Thanksgiving, but she understood that it was a time for family to be together, and she was getting excited to see her grandparents again. After dinner Heath walked us back to the manor in the gathering darkness.

He hugged Lucy and kissed me good night. Lucy watched, wide-eyed, and asked Heath, "Do you love Mama?"

He laughed. "I sure do!"

Lucy looked at me and said, "Me too!"

What a wonderful way to end the evening.

The next day the steeplejack and the mason finished their jobs in the slave cabins and the manor basement. I was thrilled to now be able to get started on both projects. I decided to start with the basement's plaster walls; I could work on the slave cabins while the plaster cured. I didn't need the assistance of the Charleston plasterer to do the basement walls because it wasn't a public space and there were not many spots that had to be repaired.

The police visited me on Lucy's last day of school before Thanksgiving vacation. They had a few follow-up questions for me. They told me that Brad was out of the hospital and settling into his new apartment. He had been charged with trespassing and stalking, since he had been on the Peppernell property several times spying on me, but was out on bail. They asked me if I was taking precautions to avoid dealing with him. I told them that I had spoken to Brad, that he had promised to leave me alone, and that we had agreed to work out an arrangement for him to spend time with Lucy after his legal troubles were over. The police clearly placed little faith in Brad's promise to leave me alone and advised me to stay away from him. They gave me a list of steps to take in case he continued to bother me. I really didn't think there would be any further trouble, but I took the papers they offered me and assured them I would take the necessary precautions.

That evening we packed for our trip. Lucy reminded Heath to pack a bathing suit so we could use the pool. A friend of Heath's had promised to look after Addie while we were gone.

Finally, Heath and Lucy and I were on our way to Florida. We left early in the morning the day before Thanksgiving and arrived in time to have dinner with my parents. We had phoned them on the road telling them that we would take them out when we arrived, since there would be enough cooking to do on Thanksgiving Day. We met them at one of Lucy's favorite restaurants. She would be occupied coloring while the grown-ups talked.

When Lucy saw my parents, it was a noisy and sweet reunion. My father's health had continued to improve in the month since he became ill, but he was still a little pale and he moved slowly. He and Mom were thrilled to see Lucy and very happy to meet Heath. I stood by, beaming, as I watched all of my favorite people meet and talk. We had a wonderful time at dinner, and Lucy fell into bed when we got back to my parents' house.

Heath and I stayed up for a little while, talking to my parents. He and my dad talked farming and law while my mother and I talked about the progress I was making at Peppernell Manor. Clearly, they already loved Heath.

And Thanksgiving Day was just as nice. Heath and Dad took Lucy out to a playground while Mom and I prepared dinner, and the five of us had a happy, low-key Thanksgiving meal. Over the next two days Mom and I did a little bit of Christmas shopping and the others relaxed. Lucy showed Heath how she was learning to swim, and he indulged her many requests to return to the pool.

We were all sorry to leave on Sunday morning, but Heath and I had to get back to work and Lucy had to return to school. We left with promises to return soon and waved at my parents until they were out of sight.

The ride home was a little subdued because Lucy and I missed my parents. Heath seemed to understand our melancholy and tried to entertain us with stories from his childhood. When we arrived back at Peppernell Manor, everyone else had just arrived home from their various Thanksgiving jaunts.

Evie and Boone had good news—they were engaged.

"I thought you were married to your job!" I accused her, laughing.

"I am, but I'm cheating!" she replied.

Graydon and Vivian had apparently known this was coming—Boone had asked Graydon for Evie's hand weeks ago. They were all smiles as Evie showed us her ring and gushed about the proposal.

"It was in this tiny botanical garden in a park we visited the day after Thanksgiving," she told us breathlessly. "He got down on his knees and everything! I wanted to surprise you all together, so I waited until I got home to tell everyone!"

Graydon uncorked the champagne and it flowed freely while we all talked at the same time about our trips and Evie's wedding. Lucy got white grape juice and settled down to enjoy her treat before it was time for bed.

When Heath left that night I stood with him out on the front porch for several minutes. Lucy had fallen asleep on the couch in the drawing room and everyone else was still in there.

We watched the stars in silence, his arms wrapped around me. "Boone's given me a great idea," he whispered.

"What do you mean?"

"I mean, I think we should visit a botanical garden, too. I love gardens!"

I punched his arm, laughing, and he said seriously, "I mean, I've been thinking the same thing."

I turned to face him. "Are you serious?"

He smiled, his features soft in the light from the porch lamp. "What do you think?"

"I think you'd better give me a proper proposal, that's what."

"You shall get one, naturally. But not yet. I have to find the perfect ring."

We stood together for a while longer, caressed by the cool evening breeze. His arms around me felt exactly right. I was over the moon and I know he was, too.

When he returned to the carriage house several minutes later I went indoors with an ear-to-ear smile on my face. Evie took one look at me and gasped.

"Don't tell me that you and Heath . . ."

"Not yet," I admonished her. "When it happens, you'll be the first to know. I promise. For now, enjoy your own engagement!"

I crawled into bed with a feeling of indescribable happiness. I fell asleep with visions of Heath and Lucy and me riding horses, walking Addie, having dinner together. We were going to be a real family.

CHAPTER 23

The next morning after I dropped Lucy off at school, I stopped at the shop where I had ordered the wallpaper for the slave cabins. It had arrived, and the shop owner and I gazed at it with pleasure, reading aloud to each other some of the old newspaper stories that were reprinted on its surface. There were stories about what land had been bought and sold, what had been planted, and even where slave auctions were being held. The articles were riveting. I took the paper with me, excited to get started hanging it in the cabins.

I began hanging the wallpaper as soon as I got back to the manor. I got three sheets hung in the first cabin that day. As I stood back admiring the walls, Phyllis walked by outside. I called to her.

"What do you think?" I asked her as she walked up the steps into the cabin.

She looked around thoughtfully.

"How did you find those newspapers?" she asked.

"I found a shop in Charleston that could print old newspaper articles onto durable sheets of wallpaper. Do you like it?"

"I think so."

"Do you think Sarah will like it?"

"I don't know. I don't know if she wants to be reminded of her old surroundings. Like I've told you before, there were a lot of unhappy memories in these old places."

"Will you ask her?"

"Yes."

Phyllis wandered slowly around the inside of the cabin, touching the walls here and there, pausing to read some of the articles printed on the paper. I wondered what could be going through her mind.

She turned to me, pointing to one of the articles on the wall. "This auction was for slaves that were from a house not far from here," she said. "The auctions were always held in an open square outdoors so people could see the slaves clearly. The buyers used to inspect the slaves' teeth, just like horses. They used to measure them, with rulers, just like they would a piece of furniture. Often a buyer would buy just the father, like Sarah's father, or just the mother, or just one of their children. Sometimes children and parents were separated for the rest of their lives after those auctions."

"That's horrible," I said quietly. I couldn't imagine the sadness that had been felt in the one-room cabin all those years ago. I felt a pang of guilt at having shown her the wallpaper, but it wasn't as if she didn't know those activities took place. And if the cabins were to be historically accurate they would have had such newspaper articles on the walls.

"It sure is."

She moved toward the door. "Did you paper the walls in the rest of the cabins, too?"

"Not yet, but I'm planning to. I started in this one."

"You know, there was another reason that slaves often covered their walls with newsprint," she informed me.

"What was the reason?"

"Many slaves believed that the evil spirits who wandered around in the night would not harm anyone in a particular place until they had read every last word that was printed on the walls. So the slaves papered their walls with newsprint—it kept the spirits from harming them because it was taking them so long to read everything in the cabin." She chuckled. "They outsmarted the spirits, that's for sure."

"What a great idea!"

"Well, I've got to get back to work. Starting to set up for Vivian's party, you know. See you later," she said, waving as she went down the steps.

I stared at the door after she left. I hadn't known about the reading spirits. Phyllis had taught me a lot since my arrival at Peppernell Manor.

I got cleaned up and went to pick up Lucy. I was tempted to drive slowly past the address Brad had given me for his new apartment, but I dared not. I had looked up a map of Charleston online and found the address. I was thankful that it was not near Lucy's school. I didn't want her to see him by chance before I was ready to tell her that he was in town.

I had been so busy the last few days that I hadn't peeked into the ballroom, where Phyllis was preparing for Vivian's open house. That evening after dinner Lucy and I walked into the ballroom and were stunned by the changes that had already been made.

The high ceiling had been strung with strands of tiny white fairy lights that looked just like stars from where we stood. There were dozens of flocked Christmas trees lining the walls of the room, two or three deep, standing on a carpet of fake snow, which was held in place by temporary brick borders that meandered along the sides and through the middle of the room. Some of the trees twinkled with more white lights, but some were left bare. Artificial cardinals sat on random tree branches throughout the large space. Here and there set among the trees were small tables, covered in cloths of white and blue to complement the color of the walls. All through the room small benches were tucked amid the trees, beckoning guests to sit and relax.

The whole effect was enchanting. Lucy couldn't even speak. She took my hand as we wandered around, gazing up at the ceiling and the tall trees. Finally she asked, "What happened?"

I smiled at her. "Phyllis has been fixing up this room for a special party. Isn't it beautiful?"

She nodded, too absorbed in looking around to answer me.

Phyllis appeared in the doorway and cleared her throat. We turned.

"Phyllis! This is absolutely gorgeous!" I told her. "You've out-done yourself. Do you do this every year?"

She smiled graciously. "Thank you. I decorate every year, but wanted a little something different this year that would highlight the ceiling and the new color on the walls. Do you think it works?"

She of course already knew the answer. "Does it work!? It's perfect! Has Vivian seen it yet?"

"Yes. She seems to like it, but she doesn't hand out praise to me very often."

"Well, she should."

"Thank you."

Lucy finally spoke again. "Can we go to the party?"

"Of course you're going to the party!" Phyllis answered.

Lucy was all smiles.

The next day I worked more on the wallpaper in the cabins. I had decided to paper all the cabins before starting on the next task, which would be to whitewash the outside walls. I had originally planned to alternate between the cabins and the basement, but I was so excited to finally begin work on the cabins, my pet project, that I decided to wait and work on the basement once the cabins were complete. Besides, it would be nice to be working indoors when the weather got colder.

As the days went by, I made swift progress with the cabins. I was glad, as the air had become dry and chilly. Though the winter in South Carolina would be nothing like the winter in Chicago, it was still cold working outside and I was anxious to get back indoors. I spent several days looking for the perfect furniture to place in the cabins. I didn't need much—just a rough-hewn table and a chair or two for each cabin. I had bought several two-by-fours and planned to fashion them into simple bed frames and lay two on the floor of each cabin, one on each side of the fireplace, representing the space each family had. I had also bought ticking material and planned to have it stuffed with material to mimic the look of a homemade mattress. The mattresses that the slaves used would have been stuffed with straw or dried grass or rags, but I needed to use a more durable substance. While I shopped for furniture I also kept my eyes open for vintage bedding that I could use. Phyllis had told me that slaves often didn't have much bedding—sometimes an entire family would have to share one blanket. I wanted just one sheet and one thin blanket for each bed.

I remembered seeing a table in the back of Vivian's store that would be perfect for one of the cabins. Perhaps I would be able to find a chair or two there, too. I headed over to her shop and when I pushed open the door I saw Heath talking to Vivian by the counter.

"What are you doing here?" I asked in surprise.

"Just came in to see Mom," he replied. "What are you doing here?"

"I'm looking for some simple antique furniture to use in the cabins," I explained. "Vivian, there was a small square table in the back the last time I was in here. Could I take a look around back there again?"

"Sure. I'd love to get rid of some of those tables back there and make room for new stuff."

Heath accompanied me to the back and supplied the muscle I needed to move some of the antique items around so that I could get a good look at the table. It was perfect. I also found a simple chair that I decided to pair with it. I told Vivian what I was taking so she could do the proper paperwork, then Heath helped me carry the table and chair out the back door of the shop. Before I left I had one more look around the back room; there were several other tables that might work in the cabins, but I wanted to look in some other shops first.

When I returned to the manor I set up the table and chair in the first slave cabin. They were perfect. Not beautiful, not even attractive. But they fit the space very well. I decided to go out looking for three more tables and several more chairs in the morning. I also needed some basic cooking utensils and tools that I could hang from the sides of the fireplaces.

I found exactly what I was looking for in another antique shop the following day. In fact, I found everything I needed in one store that was near Peppernell Manor. The shop owner even mentioned the possibility that the pieces I bought may actually have come from Peppernell Manor originally. It was an intriguing thought.

I set up the cabins and they looked just right. I had even found an old fiddle that I placed on a shelf in one of the cabins. I hoped it was just like the ones Phyllis's ancestors—Sarah's family—had used. I couldn't wait for Phyllis to see them completed. I went to the house looking for her. She wasn't in the kitchen and she wasn't on the first floor of the house. I went upstairs calling her name, but she wasn't on the second floor, either. I knocked on the door to her apartment; no answer. She wasn't in the basement. I went outdoors to look for her and finally found her coming around the back of the house with an armload of cut dahlias and viburnum.

"Hi, Phyllis. I've been looking everywhere for you! I'm finally done getting the furniture in all the cabins and I thought you'd like to have a look." I could hardly contain my excitement.

"All right," she replied calmly. "Just let me put these flowers in the sink and I'll be right with you."

I followed her into the kitchen and waited impatiently while she placed the flowers in the sink and ran water over their long stems. "Let me just arrange these quickly in a vase," she said.

When she had finally set the flowers on a pedestal in the front hall, she followed me out the door and over to the slave cabins. I pushed open the creaky door of the first cabin and stood stock-still, staring in horror at the scene before me.

CHAPTER 24

Shreds of wallpaper hung in long strips from the walls. In some places the paper had been torn off completely and lay in ribboned heaps on the floor. I let out a cry of dismay.

"What happened? I was just in here and everything looked perfect!"

Phyllis looked around in alarm, then turned and ran to the next cabin. Her face was grim when she emerged.

"No. Don't say it," I told her.

Together we looked inside the remaining two cabins. The walls had all suffered the same fate.

"I don't understand how this could have happened!" I cried. "I was only in the manor house for a short time!"

"Did you see or hear anything unusual?" Phyllis asked.

"No. It was quiet out here."

"Maybe we should have a look around," Phyllis suggested.

"Okay," I replied miserably. "But I doubt we're going to find anything. Or anyone."

I was right. We looked around the outsides of the cabins and in the surrounding wooded area, but there was no one to be seen. I groaned. "I'm going to have to repaper those walls. I don't have enough paper, so I'll have to wait until more can be made."

Phyllis looked at me sympathetically. "I'm sorry this happened, Carleigh. I know I've been the voice of doom about this project, but I think you've done a good job and done it respectfully. I hate to see this."

"Thanks, Phyllis."

"I think even Sarah will like it once she sees the care you've put into the job. I don't want her to see it like this, though," Phyllis said.

"I don't either."

"I'll keep her away. Don't worry," Phyllis assured me.

I wondered yet again about Phyllis's odd relationship with the long-dead Sarah.

"Do you mind if I speak frankly?" Phyllis asked.

"Please do."

"You remember what I told you about that dog of Heath's. You have to admit that bad things continue to happen around here since she came around. To be honest, I don't think they're going to stop until that dog goes away."

"Please, Phyllis—" I began.

"No," she interrupted, holding up her hand for silence. "Don't say anything. I know how you feel about my superstitions. But there's some truth to what I've said, isn't there?" She left the cabin and walked toward the manor.

I didn't answer. It was ridiculous that she still felt that way about Addie. Of course things had been difficult at Peppernell Manor since Addie's arrival, but it had nothing to do with her. I wished I could get Phyllis to understand that.

I walked forlornly back to the manor, where I placed a call to the shop where I had ordered the wallpaper for the cabins. The owner was shocked to learn what had happened, and assured me that she would put a rush on the replacement order. It would still take some time, though, so over the next several days I would work on the basement. I dreaded telling Graydon and Vivian and Ruby about the cabins. We spoke at dinner, and they were very concerned about who had vandalized the property. Graydon suggested immediately that I call the police.

But I wasn't ready to involve the police just yet. I was coming to grips with the probable identity of the culprit. I tried calling Heath to talk about it with him, but he was working late in his office and I could tell from his voice that he was feeling overwhelmed. I didn't want to add to his stress.

Certainly it had not been committed by anyone at Peppernell

Manor. Graydon and Vivian and Ruby would have to pay for the wallpaper to be replaced, so I was sure it wasn't any of them. It wasn't Phyllis, since she was out cutting flowers when I left the cabins in search of her. It wasn't Heath. It couldn't have been Evie; I was sure she would never have done such a thing. That left someone outside of Peppernell Manor.

That left Brad.

Why would he do something so stupid? Though I didn't want the police involved, I needed to find out why Brad was tormenting me. I planned to pay him a visit at his new apartment the following day and demand payment on the Peppernells' behalf for the replacement wallpaper. I didn't care that the police had warned me to stay away from him; I was going to talk to him.

But by the next day I had lost some of my bravado. I called him and asked him to meet me at a coffee shop near his apartment. He agreed and when we met, the conversation went exactly the way I had assumed it would.

"I have no idea what you're talking about, Carleigh," he informed me shortly.

"Brad, just stop it. I'm not here to argue about whether you did it. I know you did it. What I want is for you to pay for the replacement wallpaper."

"That's crazy! I'm not doing it!"

I was fed up and furious with him. "Brad, don't make me go to the police about this."

"I'm not making you do anything. I'm not paying for something I didn't do."

I pushed back my chair and turned to leave, but I wheeled around to face him again. "You can't possibly think this bodes well for you seeing Lucy anytime soon," I told him.

"Maybe I'll go to the police myself and have you arrested for harassment," he spat.

I left in a rage.

I went to Heath's office, hoping to find him there so he could take a walk with me; I needed to calm down. Luckily he was in.

"What's wrong?" he asked when he saw my harried face.

"I just had a row with Brad. He defaced the slave cabins and now he's denying it and refusing to pay for the wallpaper that has to be replaced," I answered furiously.

"Okay, let's take it slow," he said. "What happened?"

I related the story of the previous day's events.

"Why didn't you tell me this last night?"

"You sounded so busy and hassled that I didn't want to bother you with it," I admitted.

"Anything that happens to you, I want to know about it. Okay?"

"Yes."

"Now, let's get back to the vandalism. You think Brad did it?"

"Absolutely."

"Why?"

"Because he's mad at me. He's trying to get back at me for taking Lucy away from him while he's in legal hot water. He's still stalking me!"

"Okay," Heath said gently. "Have you talked to the police?"

"No. Not yet."

"Are you going to?"

"I guess I'll have to. Will you go with me?"

"You know I will."

We went that afternoon. The police said they would look into it. It was a thoroughly unsatisfying response, but it was unfair of me to expect anything else. Of course they couldn't go right out and arrest Brad without looking into the incident first.

"I hate to drag you into this," I told Heath as we were leaving the police station.

"I'd rather be dragged into it than see you facing it yourself," he replied, putting his arm around my shoulders. "Want to go to a movie tonight? Maybe it'll help you forget your troubles for a while."

"I can't go unless it's rated G. I don't want to go anywhere without Lucy until everything is settled with Brad."

When I had picked up Lucy and returned to Peppernell Manor, Vivian asked me to help Phyllis in the ballroom. The open house was only two days away, and Vivian was both giddy and frenzied by the preparations.

"Carleigh, would you mind taking a break from your work in the basement and helping Phyllis get the floor coverings in place? They're bulky and I want them just right. Phyllis can show you where they go. I would help but I have to run over to the florist to make sure they have everything in order." Without waiting for an answer, she swept out the front door and hurried to her car, now repaired from the damage she had done to it during the hurricane.

Lucy and I walked into the ballroom where Phyllis was tugging at a rolled-up white carpet.

"Do you need my help with that?" I asked her.

She grunted in reply. I took one end of the carpet and we started unrolling it between the brick edging that snaked through the ballroom. When we finished that roll, I helped her get another one from the corridor between the kitchen and her apartment. We unrolled the second one, then a third and a fourth before all the "snowy walkway" was in place. We worked for a while positioning the carpet exactly between the bricks so no hardwood floor would be visible beneath it, and it looked just right when we were done.

The room was beautiful. Lucy was playing hide-and-seek among the snow-flocked trees and the lights twinkled above our heads. Phyllis had discreetly set up wireless speakers in some of the trees to pipe Christmas music through the huge room.

"Where does all the food go?" I asked her.

"The food will be set up, buffet-style, in the dining room," she replied. "That way people can enjoy their hors d'oeuvres in the ballroom or in the drawing room or wherever they want to sit."

"You do this *every* year?" I asked again. It seemed to be an incredible amount of work for one open house.

She smiled. "It's actually fun. It breaks up some of the monotony around here. I love doing the décor for the party. And as I mentioned before, I don't remember the ballroom ever looking this good, so it's actually been easier for me this year than usual. In past years I've had to dress up the walls with garland and wreaths and all kinds of decorations so people didn't notice how bad the rooms looked."

"You're certainly very good at it."

"Thank you."

Lucy came twirling up to us. "When is the party?" she squealed. Phyllis laughed. "Very soon."

The next two days flew by in a flurry of activity and preparations. Phyllis and Vivian kept me and Evie busy, and Lucy trailed after me every minute. She didn't get a nap either day, which explained why she was miserable and cranky in the evenings. Graydon was smart enough to stay holed up in his office and Ruby stayed in the kitchen, preparing tray after tray of beautiful sweets. Apparently Vivian had decided to let Ruby cook something for the affair, after all.

The morning of the party dawned gusty and dark. Vivian fretted that the weather would keep people home, but Graydon told her in no uncertain terms that he was sick of hearing about the open house and he hoped no one would show up. She clucked at him and tried everything to keep him quiet; eventually she ordered him back up to his office along with a glass of whiskey to calm his nerves. Phyllis stayed in the kitchen issuing instructions to the assembled staff that had been hired to keep champagne glasses filled, butler around trays of finger foods, clear tables, and generally see to the guests' needs. Ruby, too, stayed in the kitchen, arranging silver trays of bite-size desserts and sending them out one after another in the capable hands of the staff.

She was dressed becomingly in a tea-length pink chiffon frock, with long sashes tied at the back of her waist in a big bow. She had an apron over her dress and looked out of place in the kitchen, but I wondered if she felt more comfortable there than in the ballroom or one of the other rooms with the guests.

Boone had surprised Evie by flying in for the occasion. He showed up in a dark gray suit with a Santa tie. Evie shrieked with delight when she saw him and he caught her and swung her around in his arms while Graydon and Vivian looked on happily. The whiskey had evidently done the trick and Graydon seemed back in his element, greeting guests as they arrived and directing them to the food and drink.

Evie looked marvelous in a dark blue dress with thin straps and a flare at the knees. Her very high heels brought her almost to Boone's chin.

I wore a 1950s-style dark green satin knee-length dress with a wide sash at the waist and puckered skirt. The V-neck accentuated a long strand of costume pearls I wore in a knot. My hair was up in a French twist and I felt dressed up and fancy. But Lucy stole the show in a tiny black-and-red plaid satin dress with white tights and sparkly black shoes.

I waited anxiously for Heath to arrive. When he finally got to the party, I was proud of just how good he looked in his blue suit and red tie. He held my hand and introduced me to many of the family friends who had arrived. I felt like a princess.

Lucy and I made the rounds with Heath and met lots of people. Lucy charmed everyone. Her sweet smile and adorable mannerisms immediately drew people to her. The guests all fawned over her dutifully and she was happy to be the center of attention. I thought more than once of how Cora-Camille and Harlan would have loved the party. I guessed Ruby was thinking the same thing—when she finally made her way out of the kitchen and greeted guests, she looked a little lost and forlorn.

Lucy and I helped ourselves to small plates of food and I took her to one of the benches in the ballroom to enjoy our meal. She was thrilled to be sitting under the snowy trees, pointing out the small birds perched on the branches as she ate. She swung her legs and talked incessantly about the birds and the decorations. She was having a grand time.

It wasn't long before Evie came by looking for us.

"Carleigh, can I borrow Lucy for a while? I've been telling some old family friends all about her and they haven't met her yet. I'll bring her right back."

I smiled at her and Lucy. "Want to go with Evie?"

"Yes!"

I shooed them away and thought back fondly to our arrival at Peppernell Manor, when Lucy was scared to even go near Evie. They had become great friends.

I sat for a while by myself, enjoying the soft Christmas music playing in the background and the murmur of guests' voices as they enjoyed the company and the delectable food and the festive holiday atmosphere. Heath came over and sat down next to me after several minutes.

"Where's Lucy?"

"Evie took her to introduce her to some old friends."

"Enjoying the party?"

"Very much. I can't believe that this happens annually. It's a huge affair."

"Mom thrives on it, as you may have noticed. Even Phyllis, who gets stuck doing most of the work, seems to love it."

"Phyllis told me as much. She said it lifts her out of the monotony of her normal duties around here."

"But I didn't come over here to talk about Phyllis. I came over to ask you something."

"What?"

And before I knew what was happening, Heath was on his knee in front of me, reaching into his jacket pocket. I could feel my eyes growing wide and my cheeks getting hot. I glanced around briefly and saw that people had stopped talking and were staring at us. Heath was holding a small black-velvet box in the palm of his hand and he opened it as he looked at me.

"Carleigh, the first time I met you we were at different places in our lives, but now that I've come to know you over these past several months, I have to say that you are the most beautiful and talented and wonderful and thoughtful person I have ever known. You are a tender and caring woman and mother, and I want to know if you'll be my wife."

Tears were streaming down my face and I laughed as I wiped them clumsily away. "Yes, of course I will," I answered, crying softly.

"You said you wanted a proper proposal. How was that?" he asked with a grin.

"Wonderful!" I told him, laughing.

I noticed again the people that had been watching us. They all began to clap and cheer as Heath took my arm and helped me to my feet. I looked at the ring. It was exquisite.

It was a large diamond, square cut and sparkling brilliantly in the twinkly lights, surrounded by tiny diamonds.

"I found that ring at my mother's store. She found it for me, actually. I told her I wanted something that represented your time here at the manor and she found one from the mid-1800s," Heath said.

"It's perfect," I said with a smile. How thoughtful of him to get a ring that would mean so much to me. People were starting to crowd around to congratulate us. It was all a little overwhelming. I kept peering through the crowd looking for Lucy. I wasn't sure how I would explain all of this to her, but I knew she would be happy. She loved Heath as much as I did.

It wasn't long before Evie brought Lucy back to my side. She hugged me and demanded to see the ring.

"Heath wouldn't show it to me before you saw it," she said, casting a pout in his direction.

"You knew?"

"Why do you think I came to take Lucy? Heath needed you all to himself for a few minutes. He enlisted my help and told me what he was up to. I am so happy for you both!" she squealed, and hugged me again.

Graydon and Vivian made their way to the front of the group surrounding us. Lucy stood on the bench next to me, talking to everyone.

"Congratulations to you both," Graydon said, hugging me and then Heath. "I knew he was going to fall for you, Carleigh," he said. "You're just the type of girl he needs."

Vivian nodded, agreeing. "You two are perfect for each other," she gushed in that Southern drawl. "I can't wait for the wedding!"

Ruby came up to us, too, and wrapped us both in a big embrace. "I wish Mother had been here to see this," she said hoarsely, her eyes glistening with unshed tears. "But she's watching. I know she is."

I felt a pang of sympathy for her and held her hand for a moment. "You'll help with the wedding plans, I hope, Ruby?"

She beamed. "Do you really want me to, I would love that!" She clapped her hands.

"Why is Ruby happy?" asked Lucy.

"Because she is going to help us make some very special plans," I explained. She seemed satisfied with that, so I didn't discuss the matter further.

Heath led me around by the hand, accepting the hugs and claps on the back from all the assembled guests. I got my fair share of hugs from women and men I'd never met as everyone shared in our happiness.

Eventually I told Heath I had to go upstairs to powder my nose. I intended to take Lucy with me to give her a short break from all the attention. I turned to her, holding out my hand. She wasn't there.

"Do you see Lucy?" I asked Heath.

He craned his neck and looked around. "No," he answered. "Let's go find her."

I hoped she wasn't getting tired and grumpy because she had been on her best behavior for so long. I went first in search of Evie, who said she hadn't seen Lucy. She took Boone by the arm and they went looking for her in the dining room. I saw Vivian and Graydon next, but they hadn't seen Lucy, either. I went upstairs, assuming she had gone up to our room for a little time alone. But she wasn't there.

I was getting a bit worried. I went back downstairs, where Heath was coming out of the kitchen trailed by Ruby and Phyllis. "She's not in there," he said. "I'm going to check the carriage house. Maybe the noise here got to her and she went over to see Addie."

"That's a good idea," I replied.

"What do you want me to do?" asked Ruby.

"Can you go check around the outside of the manor?"

"Yes." She hurried off. Graydon and Vivian came up to me in the front hall. "We haven't been able to find her."

"Heath is looking in the carriage house and Ruby is checking the outside of the manor." I turned to Phyllis. "Would you mind checking in your apartment?"

"Not at all." She left, but returned quickly. "She's not in there. Where else should I look?"

"Why don't you check in the basement? That's the only place we haven't checked inside the house."

Graydon and Vivian had left to check the withdrawing room and the sitting room behind the ballroom. Heath returned from the carriage house shaking his head.

"Heath, where can she be?" I was getting very worried.

"Maybe she's hiding in among the Christmas trees in the ballroom. She likes playing in there. Let's check."

I accompanied him into the ballroom, which had just a few minutes before been the site of indescribable happiness for me. Now the room seemed darker, more sinister, a room of worry and fear.

We started at opposite ends of the room, checking under and behind every tree. She wasn't there. A few guests cast wondering glances at us, whispering among themselves.

As Heath straightened up after looking under the very last tree, a guest came up to him and clapped him on the shoulder.

"Hey, Heath! Congratulations! I was surprised to see your ex-wife here! Did she know you were going to pop the question?"

I froze. Ex-wife? Odeile was here? Heath looked in my direction, confused.

A cold chill snaked up my back.

CHAPTER 25

"Let's go."

Heath grabbed my hand and we hurried to the front hall. Graydon and Vivian were there, along with Evie. Ruby wasn't back yet from checking outside the house.

"Did anyone else know Odeile was here?" Heath asked grimly.

"What?" Vivian's face registered genuine shock. "Who invited her?"

"No one. That's the problem. She crashed the party and I'm very worried. I don't know how she got in without any of us noticing her," Heath answered.

"What do we do next?" I asked frantically.

Vivian put her hand on my arm. "We'll find Lucy, Carleigh. She's probably hiding somewhere. I'm sure she's fine."

I appreciated Vivian's attempt to make me feel better, but it didn't help at all. Heath and I hurried out onto the veranda. Ruby still hadn't come back. I couldn't imagine where she had gone. We ran down the steps and went in separate directions around the house, shouting for Lucy. No answer.

By now I was frantic. I didn't know where to look. Odeile's presence at the party was not a coincidence—she was there for a malevolent purpose, and it somehow involved Lucy. My voice rose as I spoke to Heath.

"What do we do now? I'm going to call the police."

"Let Evie do that. We'll keep looking. We'll find her." He ran up the front steps into the manor, where Vivian and Evie were waiting in the front hall. I could hear their voices as if it was a dream. It didn't seem real.

"Did you find her?" came Evie's taut voice.

"No." Heath sounded grim.

"What should I do?"

"Call the police. Get them out here fast. Send an ambulance."

Ambulance. My heart, thudding in my rib cage, skipped a beat. I thought I was going to throw up. The dream-like quality of the conversation I had heard between Heath and Evie suddenly became very real. I bent over, my hands on my knees, trying to catch my breath.

Heath came running down the stairs. "Carleigh, are you all right?" he asked in alarm.

"No. I think I'm going to faint." I stood up and just for a moment everything went black in front of me. Voices faded away. Heath put his arm around me and helped steady me. He shouted for his mother.

"What can I do?" Vivian asked as she came hurrying out to the veranda.

"Mom, please get something for Carleigh to eat and drink. Quickly." She turned around and ran back into the house. Meanwhile Heath helped me to sit down on one of the front steps. Vivian returned just a moment later with a glass of sweet tea and a small sandwich. She held them out to me, but I pushed them away.

"I can't eat. I'm going to be sick."

"Carleigh," Heath said sternly, "eat that food. We need you strong and alert. You need to help us find Lucy."

The tone of his voice helped me to focus on what I needed to do. I took the plate from Vivian and ate the sandwich and drank the tea.

"Are you all right now?" Heath asked.

"I think so."

He helped me to stand up. I felt a little wobbly, but stronger. I looked up at him. "What should we do next?"

He turned to Vivian. "Mom, send Evie out here. She can help us. You should probably go back in with Dad and play hostess so people don't start to panic."

She nodded mutely and turned to go back inside. As she was going through the front door, Evie and Boone were coming out.

"Give us something to do," she told her brother.

"You two go look in the old barn," he instructed. "Maybe Lucy went in there to play."

I shook my head. "She'd never go in there by herself."

"It's worth a try."

"Okay. Where do you think we should look?"

Just then Phyllis appeared in the doorway.

"I just spoke to Sarah. She was in the basement. She said to get to the cabins right away."

This wasn't the time to debate Sarah's existence.

Heath stood up and grabbed my hand. We ran toward the cabins in the gathering twilight. I looked into the first cabin as Heath rushed down to the last one, yelling behind him, "I'll start at the other end!"

There was nothing amiss in the first cabin. The table and chair that I had set up were still in place, untouched. I headed back outside as Heath was exiting the fourth cabin. He shook his head. He ran to the third cabin in the row and peered inside.

"This one is empty," he shouted from the door.

I ran to the second cabin and burst inside, then stopped short in horror. The first thing I noticed in the semidarkness of the cabin in the woods was Lucy's small, limp body on the mattress I had fashioned on the floor. A primal noise erupted from my lips. Somehow my brain hadn't yet registered the sight of Odeile, seated on the chair I had just put in the cabin a few days previously, a gun in her hand trained steadily on me.

Heath arrived at the door of the cabin behind me and quickly took in the scene. "Odeile," he said quietly, "put that down. There's no need for this."

Her lips curled in a sickening smile. "Heath, darlin', I hear you're going to marry this dullard," she said, jerking the gun in my direction.

"I'm marrying Carleigh, if that's what you mean," he answered.

"And you're going to be the daddy of this awful creature."

"She has a daddy, Odeile. I'm going to be her stepfather."

The blood was rushing, pounding in my ears. I didn't know if my baby was dead or alive. I couldn't stand it. Odeile wouldn't hesitate to shoot me if I tried moving toward Lucy, I knew, but I had to do something, say something.

"Odeile, you and Heath can still be friends," I croaked.

"You shut up," she growled.

"Odeile—" Heath began.

"You shut up, too."

Then her tone changed suddenly. "Heath, why wasn't I good enough for you?" she whined.

Heath didn't answer.

"How could you want *her* instead of me?"

He stared at her in silence.

"You'd better answer me, Heath Peppernell. If you don't, I'll shoot her," she said, again twitching the gun toward me.

He swallowed. "Odeile, you know why we divorced. You didn't want children and I did. You were abusive."

"How could you want children? They're awful."

"I love Lucy just as if she were my own child," he explained. "She's a bright, sweet, kind little girl."

Odeile scoffed.

"Can I go to her, please?" I asked. Odeile sat and studied me for several endless moments.

"No!" she finally shouted.

"Odeile, the police are on their way. You have to put the gun down and let Carleigh go to Lucy," Heath told her gently.

"I said no!" she screamed.

I stood still, searching frantically for something that would distract Odeile so I could get to Lucy. But there was nothing.

Heath and Odeile and I stood staring at each other for what seemed like hours. Then she spoke again. She was talking to me.

"I shoulda run you over when I had the chance."

"That was you?" I asked.

"What are you two talking about?" Heath looked at both of us, his brow furrowed.

"She tried to hit me with her car one night on the main road," I replied.

"Odeile, what were you thinking?" he asked. "Why would you want to hurt Carleigh?"

"I just happened to be driving by when I saw her out walking with your sister and your parents and that miserable kid and it was my chance to keep you from falling for her!" she shouted. "So I went back and tried to hit her! But she hid like a frightened animal!" She turned to me.

"He should be married to *me!*" And in an instant, she had raised the gun and was pointing it at my head. Tears started to roll down my cheeks. Heath moved toward Odeile suddenly and a shot rang out. I didn't know what was happening.

"Carleigh, are you all right?" he yelled.

"Yes." I could only muster a whisper.

The room suddenly became slightly darker. I instinctively looked toward the door and was stunned to see Ruby standing there, a vision of pink chiffon with a confused look on her face.

"What's going on here?" she asked.

"Get out of here!" Odeile shrieked. But Ruby didn't move. She must have processed the scene before her and figured out what was happening. Odeile still held the gun, but it was pointed toward the floor. I couldn't believe she had missed me the first time. I was shaking, and Lucy hadn't moved. We could hear sirens close by.

"Odeile, the police will be here any second," Heath warned. His eyes flicked toward mine.

I don't know how I summoned the courage, but I took a step toward Lucy. Everything was happening in slow motion. As I moved, Ruby rushed into the cabin and put herself between me and Odeile.

A second shot rang out.

Ruby fell to the floor in a gauzy pink heap as I reached Lucy. I spun around to look at Ruby and watched in horror as the blood spurted from her stomach. Even Odeile seemed surprised by what she had done. She stared at the gun and took a step backward, tripping over the chair. Heath whipped off his suit jacket and tried pressing it into Ruby's stomach. Odeile, who had landed on her hands and knees, was scrabbling for the gun, which had skittered across the floor. Heath tried to beat her to the gun, but she grabbed it first.

Hands trembling, she raised the gun again.

Then for the third time, we heard a gunshot. I screamed and flung my body over Lucy's. Ruby lay motionless on the floor and Heath covered his head with his arms.

Three police officers stood in the doorway. When I looked up, one was lowering his gun and another was pushing into the cabin and heading toward Odeile, who was lying in a slowly spreading pool of blood. It covered the dark stains left behind when Sarah's father killed himself all those long years ago. The officer bent and held her wrist, feeling for a pulse. He looked at the other officers and shook his head.

"Over here!" I cried. Sobbing, I heaved myself off Lucy's small body, which still lay on the mattress. One officer ran over to her and another went to Ruby. He radioed for the ambulance to drive over the lawn to the border with the woods. He looked up at us.

"This woman is still alive, but we need to get her to the hospital immediately."

The other officer, the one with Lucy, was holding her tiny wrist in his big hand. He looked down at her and concentrated on finding her pulse. Finally he looked at me and nodded.

Lucy was alive. I had never in my life felt a relief like the feeling that flooded my body. Heath came over to me and wrapped me in his arms as I wept like a baby, so thankful that my child was alive.

It was only a minute before the EMTs were at the door with three stretchers. One medic knelt by Lucy and helped his partner slide a board under her. They carried her gingerly through the door and onto a stretcher that they wheeled toward a waiting ambulance. I followed closely behind them. As I stood at the cabin's door, though, I looked back at the scene behind me.

The medics with Ruby were performing CPR. Heath watched, silent and still, as they worked to revive his aunt. Part of me wanted to stay and make sure Ruby was going to be all right, but I knew I needed to be with Lucy. I ran to catch up with the medics wheeling my little girl to the ambulance.

We left Peppernell Manor, driving into the darkening evening with sirens blaring. Pretty soon I heard the sound of another siren somewhere behind us. That was a good sign—if Ruby had died, there would be no siren necessary. When we got to the hospital, the emergency room doctors took over immediately and I stayed as close to Lucy as they would allow.

It was a long time before they finally were able to stabilize her and determine exactly what had happened. She had been poisoned with a prescription medication. Odeile must have given her something to eat or drink with the medication in it and taken her outside onto the veranda. When Lucy was unconscious, it would have been easy for Odeile to carry her to the slave cabin.

When she awoke a long while later in a hospital room, Lucy was scared. She didn't seem to remember what had happened to her, and thankfully she had no recollection of being in the cabin. She apparently hadn't heard the screaming or the gunshots or the sirens.

I sat up in a chair all that long night while she drifted in and out of sleep. In the small hours of the morning, there was a knock at the door. Heath came in; he looked haggard and exhausted. I went to him and put my arms around his neck.

"How's Ruby?" I whispered.

"She's asking for you. The doctors say she's not going to survive. Mom and Dad and Evie are there. You'd better hurry. I'll stay with Lucy."

I ran the entire way to Ruby's room. Her eyes were fluttering open when I arrived, breathless. I took her hand in mine as Graydon and Vivian and Evie stood by, watching.

"You saved Lucy's life, Ruby. And mine. Thank you."

Her lips parted. She was trying to say something.

"No, Ruby. Don't talk."

"I killed Harlan."

Graydon and the others stepped quickly to her bedside. I spoke to her soothingly.

"No, Ruby. Someone else killed Harlan."

"It was me. There was no peace in our family. He was a bad person."

She was struggling to get the words out. Vivian held her hand to her mouth, looking at Graydon.

"She's hallucinating, Graydon."

"Let her talk, Viv."

"No. I'm not. I couldn't stand the fighting anymore."

"Harlan wasn't bad!" Vivian cried.

"He killed Mother. He told me so," Ruby whispered. We had to lean in close to hear her.

Right then I knew Ruby was telling the truth. A business associate hadn't killed Harlan; his aunt had killed him. She killed him because he killed her mother.

"You rest now, Ruby," I told her softly. "Thank you for telling us."

I left the room and returned to Lucy. Heath went back to see Ruby. I thought I would see her again, but I was wrong.

Heath came to Lucy's room a short time later. "She's gone," he whispered, tears beginning to well up in his eyes. He rubbed them impatiently and blinked several times, gathering himself. "Dad told me what Ruby said."

"About Harlan?"

"Yes."

I didn't want to tell Heath that I had known all along about Harlan and Cora-Camille, but I knew I had to. I couldn't allow our marriage to start off with such a secret.

"Heath, I have to tell you something."

"What is it?"

"Harlan was the one who tried to poison your grandmother, so she would die before being able to change her will to leave the management of Peppernell Manor to the state of South Carolina. At the same time, he was trying to get her to sign on with the investors that he brought to the manor, and she refused.

"When the poison didn't seem to be working fast enough, he dressed up as your grandfather and tried to talk to her in the middle of the night one night. She had a heart attack. I knew that Harlan had killed your grandmother.

"Please forgive me for not telling you. I felt it wasn't my place to tell anyone, since I'm not part of the family. I felt it was up to Evie to tell people what Harlan had done, since she was aware of the facts. And when he died, there seemed to be no reason to tell anyone."

There. I'd told him. And I felt an overwhelming relief at being able to share what Evie and I had heard on her phone the day Harlan was shot.

Heath was quiet for a moment, then he took one of my hands in his. "Of course I forgive you. You were in a very awkward spot. I wish Evie had told someone, though I don't know what I would have done with the information, either."

He looked over at Lucy. "I'm glad she's okay. Have you told Brad that she's here?"

"Not yet. I'll call him in the morning."

And that's what I did. He was upset and angry, blaming me for Lucy's disappearance from the party.

"I told you, Brad, she was with me every minute except for the few minutes when Evie had her. I just let go of her hand for a second. I will live with it the rest of my life. It could have happened to anyone. Even you."

"I want to see her."

I told him her room number. Even with the charges pending against him, this was a situation in which I couldn't deny him seeing her. He had to see with his own eyes that she was okay and I understood that feeling.

I learned later that the police had gone through Odeile's purse. Apparently she, like me, had a penchant for before-and-after pictures. They had found such photos on her cell phone of the ruined wallpaper in the slave cabins. So Odeile had been the culprit. I had been so sure it was Brad. I apologized to him and he accepted my apology graciously.

Lucy was in the hospital for several days, and I stayed by her side the entire time. I let Brad visit as often as he wanted, and my parents even came from Florida to see her.

Not long after she got out of the hospital I got back to work restoring Peppernell Manor. My work took me through the spring, but I finally finished the manor house and the barn and the privy. Everyone was thrilled with my work, and the family loved to entertain in it and show off their new—old—house. I earned a solid reputation in Charleston, and my restoration work was featured in a national architecture magazine.

Most importantly, Sarah loved the renovated manor house and slave cabins. Phyllis came to talk to me one day as I was working upstairs in Evie's bedroom.

"I just wanted to tell you that I spoke to Sarah again. She said you got the cabins just right. That's just how they looked when she lived there."

I smiled. "Thank you, Phyllis. I'm really happy to hear that. Did Sarah have anything else to say?"

"She loves the fiddle."

"I'm thrilled!"

"Thank you for doing the cabins justice," she said shyly.

"I wouldn't have restored them if I couldn't do it right," I told her.

Just then Addie came bounding into the room. Heath had taken to leaving her at the manor house during the day so she would have company and stop chewing all the furniture in the carriage house while he was at work.

"Things around here have been so peaceful lately, and nothing bad has happened since the day of the open house," I noted pointedly. "Do you still think Addie is bad luck?"

Phyllis smiled and dodged the question. "I'm getting used to her being around," she said, as she reached down and fluffed the dog's ears.

Shortly after I finished the restoration of Peppernell Manor, I moved my business permanently from Chicago to South Carolina and never looked back. My assistants, though they had done a great job in my absence, were only too happy to hand the reins back to me. When I opened my business in Charleston, I asked Phyllis to come to work for me as an interior designer. She kept her job at Peppernell Manor, but agreed to work with me part-time.

Vivian finally agreed that there had been enough sadness, enough grief and violence, over the future management of Peppernell Manor. She let go all of her talk of investors and tourists. I'm sure the topic will be revisited someday, but for now, life at the manor has become quieter.

Ruby was missed at Peppernell Manor. Though she had made some poor choices during the last months of her life, her family forgave her, too. It was strange to think that not so long ago, I had been angry with Ruby for taking Lucy without my permission. Now she was gone, giving her own life to save mine and Lucy's.

Going through Ruby's things shortly after her death, Evie found a gallon of black paint in the back of Ruby's closet.

So she had been the one.

We could only guess at the reason. Though we'll never know for sure, we suspect she did it to slow down the restoration and scare off the investors.

The day Heath and I and Lucy became a family on the patio of the carriage house, the sky, pink from the setting sun, floated above us softly. It was a warm late-summer evening with the scents of roses and Confederate jasmine and honeysuckle perfuming the air. It was low-key and intimate, with just Lucy, my parents, Heath's family, and Phyllis present. And Addie, of course, who sat quietly next to Phyllis as she surreptitiously fed her treats throughout the ceremony.

I never imagined when I first set eyes on the carriage house that it would one day be my home. And in the twilight of that South Carolina evening, we finally had the Lowcountry boil that I had been promised when I first arrived at Peppernell Manor. It was delicious.

Turn the page for a special excerpt of Amy M. Reade's

SECRETS OF HALLSTEAD HOUSE

*"You are not wanted here. Go away from Hallstead Island
or you will be very sorry you stayed."*

Macy Stoddard had hoped to ease the grief of losing her parents in
a fiery car crash by accepting a job as a private nurse to the wealthy
and widowed Alexandria Hallstead. But her first sight of Hallstead
House is of a dark and forbidding home. She quickly finds its
winding halls and shadowy rooms filled with secrets and suspicions.
Alex seems happy to have Macy's help, but others on the island,
including Alex's sinister servants and hostile relatives, are far less
welcoming. Watching eyes, veiled threats . . . slowly, surely, the
menacing spirit of Hallstead Island closes in around Macy. And she
can only wonder if her story will become just one of the many
secrets of Hallstead House . . .

A Lyrical Press e-book original on sale now!

CHAPTER 1

My journey was almost over.

It was raining, and I looked out through the drizzle across the blue-gray water of the Saint Lawrence River. Only a few boats were out on such a raw and rainy day. From the bench where I sat on the Cape Cartier public dock, I could see several islands. Each was covered with trees—dark green pine trees and leafy maples, oaks, birches, and weeping willows. In the chilly late September air, the leaves were already tinged with the colors of fall: yellows, reds, oranges, browns. I could glimpse homes on the islands, but I didn't see any people. It was beautiful here—so different from the city I had just left behind.

Even though twenty years have come and gone since that day, I can still remember the calm that settled around me as I waited for my ride to Hallstead House in the middle of the Thousand Islands. My nerves were still ragged, but the river had an immediate and peaceful effect on me. I was only twenty then, but I had been through so much. Though I had been traveling for just a few hours, my journey to this place had begun six long weeks earlier.

As I listened to the raindrops plunk into the river, the sound of the motor from an approaching boat cut into my reverie. It was an older boat of gleaming mahogany with a large white awning covering most of it, protecting the cabin and the pilot from the rain. It puttered up to the dock slowly and in a few moments had pulled alongside, close to where I sat. The pilot moved to the stern and climbed out quickly, securing the boat to the dock with a thick rope. He turned to me with a questioning look and said, "Macy Stoddard?"

"Yes."

He shook my hand curtly. "I'm Pete McHale. I work for Alexandria Hallstead. She sent me here to pick you up. That all the luggage you brought?"

"Yes, that's it."

He shot me a disapproving look and said, "I hope you brought some warm stuff to wear. It starts getting cold up here pretty early in the fall. It's colder here than it is in the big city, you know." He smirked.

Determined to stay positive, I ignored his look of reproach and replied that I had plenty of warm clothes. Once he'd stowed my two large suitcases in the boat under the awning, he helped me on board, where I chose a seat in the front so I could see where we were going and stay dry. I had been in a boat once as a child when a furious storm blew up, and I had hated boats ever since. Still, though I was unhappy and nervous to be riding in one, there was absolutely no other way to get to my island destination. Pete untied the boat and we slowly pulled away from the dock. As he scanned the river and began turning the boat to the north, I glanced at his profile. He looked like he was in his mid-thirties—medium height, with light-brown, windblown hair, and green eyes with creases in the corners that made it look like he squinted a lot. He wore faded jeans and a Windbreaker.

When he had steered the boat out of the small, sheltered bay at Cape Cartier and into the more open channel, he glanced at me and said, "We'll be at Summerplace in about ten minutes."

"Summerplace?"

"That's the name of the house on Hallstead Island."

"Oh. I thought it was called Hallstead House."

"Its official name is Hallstead House. The people who live on the island just call it Summerplace."

We sat in silence for several moments, and finally I asked, "Why is it called Summerplace?"

Pete sighed. Evidently he didn't relish playing the role of tour guide. "It's called Summerplace because it used to be a summer retreat for the Hallstead family. Now Miss Hallstead stays there for as much of the year as she can. In early to mid-October she moves the household over to Pine Island and spends the winter there."

To keep my mind off my abject fear of being on the water, I turned my attention to the islands we were passing. Each one had a home on it, and all of the homes were beautiful. Some looked empty, since their occupants had probably left after the summer ended, but some still had boats tied to docks or housed in quaint boathouses. The homes themselves, most of which were huge and had large, welcoming porches, were surrounded by the ever-present trees. Several had bright awnings over the windows.

In the face of Pete's apparent ambivalence, I had determined not to ask any more questions. But as I sat looking around me I forgot my self-imposed rule. "Are there really a thousand islands in this area?" I blurted out.

"There are actually over eighteen hundred islands in the Thousand Islands," he replied. To my surprise, he seemed to warm to this subject and continued. "In order to be included in the count, an island has to be above water three hundred and sixty-five days a year and support at least two living trees."

I continued to draw him out, asking, "What do you do for Mrs. Hallstead?"

His attitude changed again, becoming colder. "It's *Miss* Hallstead. She never took her husband's name. But to answer your question, I'm one of the handymen. I'm also the boat captain—I maintain and pilot this and one other boat. I don't do a lot of chauffeuring. The people who live on Hallstead Island don't get out much. I just ferry the visitors."

"Who else lives on the island besides Miss Hallstead?"

"Just another handyman and a housekeeper. They're an older married couple. Leland and Valentina Byrd. They have quarters next to the main residence.

"How did you get the job as Miss Hallstead's private nurse?" Pete asked.

"My agency got a request for a private nurse for an elderly woman who had broken a hip. They knew I was looking for a change, so they offered it to me."

"Oh. Aren't you a little young for a job like that?"

"I'm almost twenty-one," I said a little indignantly. "I've been working for over a year at a hospital."

"Oh. I beg your pardon."

I turned to observe my new surroundings. Each island that we passed seemed to have its own unique personality. Some seemed dominated by magnificent homes; others were more notable for their stunning natural beauty. I prattled on with my usual tact. "Who can afford to live in these places?"

"A lot of these islands used to be owned by big businessmen. Nowadays they're mostly owned by regular people, but some of the bigger ones are still owned by the families of the original owners."

"How long have the Hallsteads been coming here?"

"Three generations now. The Hallsteads are an old oil family. They own HSH Oil Company—the 'HSH' stands for Henry S. Hallstead, the company founder and Miss Hallstead's grandfather. He bought the island originally."

"Do the Hallsteads still run the oil company?" It was none of my business and I regretted the question immediately. Pete shot me a look confirming my thoughts, but he answered my question nonetheless.

"Yes, they do. They run the day-to-day operations."

"How do you know all this?"

"I've been around for quite a while," he said dryly.

"Does Miss Hallstead get many visitors?"

Pete smirked. "Hardly. The only two people who ever stay at the house with her are her adviser and her nephew. They each have rooms in the house."

"Do you live on the island?"

"You ask a lot of questions."

"I'm just curious." *And nervous.*

"I can see that. I usually stay on the island. I have rooms over the boathouse. My family lives on Heather Island, which is not too far from Hallstead Island. I stay there every so often. Hallstead Island can get a little gloomy."

"Gloomy? What's gloomy about it?"

Pete didn't answer. He steered the boat slightly to the right and pointed to an island looming up ahead. "That's Hallstead Island. The boathouse is just around the other side, right off the channel. I'll drive you around back so you can see the island before we dock."

As the boat slowly approached, I got my first glimpse of the place that would be my new home. It was stunning. Where the island rose out of the river, a stone wall was visible above the surface of the water. The wall was about five feet high and appeared to stretch around the entire island. It had been built of gray stones of varying thickness, stacked on top of one another, and it had the effect of making the island look almost fortress-like. On the wall were long striations of colors ranging from white to dark gray to mossy green. I asked Pete what they were and he informed me that they marked past high-water levels of the river.

Rising from the stone wall were gently sloping expanses of rock, some covered with moss, some bare of any vegetation, looking dark and slick from the rain. Still other areas of the rocky surface contained large crevices choked with shaggy shrubs and wild grasses. As we continued around the considerable perimeter of the island, I saw several neighboring islands. One or two of them seemed rather large, like Hallstead Island, and one of them was tiny, with no more than a cottage and a few trees rising from the surface of the water. The boat moved slowly, barely creating a wake, and we rounded the northern end of the island. A leafy red maple tree leaned far out over the water. It was an unusual tree and looked as if a ceaseless wind had caused it to grow sideways. As we passed under, it was so near the boat that I could have reached up to touch the dancing leaves on its gently curving branches.

Trying to forget my churning nerves, I turned my attention toward the center of the island. The trees there grew in a dense stand. Some were leafy, but mostly they were evergreens, tall and dark and sturdy looking, moving in unison as the wind gently blew through their long, graceful branches. They grew thickly, reminding me of a peaceful, primeval forest. I closed my eyes and listened to the soft, low song of the wind in the trees and the tapping of the raindrops on the boat's canopy. For a moment I was even able to shut out the quiet hum of the boat's motor.

"It's beautiful," I breathed, almost afraid that talking aloud would break the spell of silence and beauty around me.

"It is," Pete agreed quietly. I glanced over at him and saw that he, too, was gazing appreciatively at the island.

"Where's the house?" I asked.

Pete looked surprised. "Don't you see it?" He pointed into the dark cluster of trees, nodding toward the middle of the island. "Summerplace—Hallstead House—is right in the middle of those trees."

I looked more closely, and this time I spied a dark-green structure rising from the forest floor. I couldn't see it very well, but as I scanned the woods I saw several dark-green turrets, each with a rich chocolate-brown roof. I would have to wait until I was closer to see the rest of Summerplace.

"The house certainly blends in well with its surroundings. I can hardly see it."

Pete nodded, saying, "Miss Hallstead likes it that way." His comment about Summerplace being gloomy came to mind, and I had to admit that the home did conjure up an image of darkness and gloom, at least from what little I could see of it.

But I wasn't ready to make any judgments yet. After all, this was to be my new job and my new home, at least for now. I forced myself to be cheerful, and asked Pete, "The boathouse is around the back of the island?"

"Yeah—it'll just take a minute." He steered the boat slowly around the side of the island facing away from the channel. The back side was just like the front: a low stone wall, rocks, grasses, wild shrubs, and lots of trees. In another moment we pulled up to the boathouse, a large, square, two-story structure painted the same shade of green as the main residence. It had a dark-brown roof, and above the roofline at each corner rose a small turret with several tall windows marching around it. A long balcony stretched around the structure's entire second story. A large cupola in the center of the peaked boathouse roof held a verdigris weathervane in the shape of a ship. In front, three large boat bays stood open, and I could see two boats moored inside.

"I love it!" I cried spontaneously.

"It's a pretty fair reproduction of Summerplace, only on a much smaller scale," Pete noted proudly. "Of course, it's not exactly like Summerplace because the front is all taken up by boat bays, but you get the idea. We keep this boat in there, plus a smaller one, plus my own boat. My rooms are upstairs, and the rest of the second story is used as storage and for maintenance equipment for the house and boats."

I nodded, absorbed in taking in the details of the boathouse and watching Pete maneuver our boat into its bay and up against the dock. He turned off the engine, jumped up onto the dock, and secured the boat with thick, heavy ropes. He hopped into the boat again to get my suitcases, and then, carrying both, he led the way out of the boathouse. I was very grateful to get onto land again.

It had started to rain a little harder, and I followed Pete away from the boathouse toward Summerplace. We made our way from a slippery, rocky surface to a well-worn path that entered the trees through a graceful arch of branches. Our shoes made almost no sound on the carpet of wet leaves and pine needles, and the trees created their own darkness, especially on this dreary day. A chill blew through me with the wind.

Neither of us spoke in the hush of the trees until Pete turned back to me and said, "Here's Summerplace."

We had reached an area where the trees were thinning and, almost out of nowhere, Summerplace appeared before me. It was dark and breathtaking. Just like its miniature double, the boathouse, Summerplace was painted a deep shade of forest green that perfectly matched the trees surrounding it. It was quite large. It had two stories, and a turret rose from each corner of the home, four in all, like those on the boathouse, but on a grander scale. Each turret was at least one full story higher than the rest of the house and wreathed in tall windows. The rich brown roof was peaked in the center, and it held an enormous cupola topped by a weathervane like the one on the boathouse, shaped like a ship and covered with the green patina of age. Around the ground floor was a wide porch covered by dark brown awnings, and around the second floor, again like that on the boathouse, was a wide balcony. Neither the porch nor the balcony held any furniture.

Pete was watching me as I got my first real look at Summerplace. "What do you think?" he finally asked.

"I don't know yet," I answered truthfully. "It could be beautiful, but it's a little forbidding."

Pete nodded. "I tried to get Miss Hallstead to choose a different color than the dark green, but this is the way she wanted it."

He led the way up the wide steps to the front porch. "It doesn't welcome me," I noted, half to myself. Pete had reached the front door, and he put my suitcases down and turned to face me.

"I don't think the front porch is the only thing you're going to find unwelcoming about this place. Don't expect all of the people here to be happy about your arrival," he said gravely.

Pete's words unnerved me, and I felt my fear rushing back. I was unsure about my new job and my new home, and I shook my head as if doing so would help me shake off my rising doubts. I forced a note of confidence into my voice that I didn't feel. "Let's go in," I told him. After all, it couldn't be any worse than what I had left behind.

If I had known then of the events that were already taking shape in the gloom of Hallstead House, I might not have had the courage to go inside.

Photo by John A. Reade, Jr.

Amy M. Reade is also the author of *Secrets of Hallstead House*. She grew up in northern New York, just south of the Canadian border, and spent her weekends and summers on the St. Lawrence River. She graduated from Cornell University and then went on to law school at Indiana University in Bloomington. She practiced law in New York City before moving to southern New Jersey, where, in addition to writing, she is a wife, a full-time mom, and a volunteer in school, church, and community groups. She lives just a stone's throw from the Atlantic Ocean with her husband and three children as well as a dog and two cats. She loves cooking and all things Hawaii and is currently at work on her next novel. Visit her on the web at www.amymreade.com or at www.amreade.wordpress.com.